M. Timothy Nolting and his wife, Deb, reside on a small acreage adjacent to the Village of Bushnell, Nebraska. An aspiring writer since his high school days, Tim was born and raised in Northeastern Kansas as a fourth-generation member of a farm/ranch family. Migrating from Kansas to Colorado and finally to the high plains of Nebraska, Tim enjoyed a professional career that allowed him to travel the U.S. and abroad. However, he claims that his most favored place is where he is now, with family nearby.

Tim is recognized regionally for his writing and presenting cowboy/western poetry, and for short personal and historical essays, which have been published weekly in several local newspapers and periodicals. Tim's long held interest in the history of the American West and observations of human nature conspired to create this novel, ...*By the Way They Treat Their Horses.* Tim is currently writing an autobiographical narrative as well as an historical non-fiction work of the range cattle industry beginning in the late 1860s, across the Nebraska Panhandle and adjacent regions of Colorado and Wyoming.

This work is dedicated to my parents, Manfred and Francys, and although they are no longer with us, I know they are looking over my shoulder every day. Also, to my wife Deb, my partner and muse, who has encouraged me to 'keep going' on the 15-year journey that brought this story to completion. And with immense appreciation to 'The Panhandlers', especially Craig Larson, the bedrock of our writers' group.

M. Timothy Nolting

...BY THE WAY THEY TREAT THEIR HORSES

AUSTIN MACAULEY PUBLISHERS™

LONDON * CAMBRIDGE * NEW YORK * SHARJAH

Ordering Information
Quantity sales: Special discounts are available on quantity purchases by corporations, associations, and others. For details, contact the publisher at the address below.

Publisher's Cataloging-in-Publication data
Nolting, M. Timothy
…By the Way They Treat Their Horses

ISBN 9781685626563 (Paperback)
ISBN 9781685626570 (ePub e-book)

Library of Congress Control Number: 2023908675

www.austinmacauley.com/us

First Published 2023
Austin Macauley Publishers LLC
40 Wall Street, 33rd Floor, Suite 3302
New York, NY 10005
USA

mail-usa@austinmacauley.com
+1 (646) 5125767

First and foremost, I am deeply grateful to my wife, Deb, who has steadfastly encouraged my pursuit in bringing this story to completion.

Many thanks to our friend and author, Linda M. Hasselstrom, who provided encouragement and advice in the early stages of the manuscript during a weekend writers' retreat at her Windbreak House in South Dakota.

Thanks to Lyn and Bruce Messersmith, fellow poets and writers who were among the first to read the finished manuscript, provided helpful critique, and encouraged pursuit of publication.

And finally, to Austin Macauley Publishers who have given me this opportunity.

Table of Contents

Foreword

In 1869, after their defeat at Summit Springs, the Southern Cheyenne were removed from the Rocky Mountain Plains and moved to their designated lands in Indian Territory. Maria Sanchez's father was Mexican, and had traded frequently with the Cheyenne, bringing trade goods from Mexico and eventually settling permanently with the tribe where he took a Cheyenne bride.

Born in 1873, Maria had no grandparents, a devastating loss in the Cheyenne culture where family units of grandparents, their children and their children's children were dependent on one another for survival. Maria's Cheyenne grandparents were killed by Chivington's troops at Sand Creek in 1864.

Maria's father, whom she had never known, was mostly absent from the reservation, with frequent trips back to Mexico. After the summer of 1876, when Maria was three years old, and Custer had been defeated in the Battle of Greasy Grass at the hands of Cheyenne and Sioux warriors, Senor Sanchez never returned to his family on the reservation, and Maria's mother had eventually married into another Cheyenne family, named Little Wolf.

Physically and emotionally abused by his stepfather, young Eli Brandt was treated more like a slave than a son, and his mother, Elke, did little to interfere on Eli's behalf. At sixteen years of age, like the grandfather he never knew, Eli Brandt ran away from home. The young man was tall, nearly six feet, at a time when most men measured five-and-a-half at most. He was muscular but slender, dark eyes set deep, black hair, and a complexion that appeared to have been darkened by the sun.

In his early teens, Eli had watched the herds of longhorn cattle being driven north from Abilene, Kansas past the homestead on the banks of the Blue River and on to the Union Pacific railhead in Nebraska. Horseback cowboys with wide-brimmed sombreros, leather chaps and high-heeled boots stirred him with excitement and a longing for adventure. Over time, the trails moved

11

farther west avoiding Abilene by way of Ellsworth, Kansas then north to Kearney, Nebraska. It was at Abilene where Eli begged a job with a Texas outfit and, over the next several years, progressed from cook's helper to horse wrangler and finally to the enviable rank of cowboy. The independence, freedom, and sometimes wild lifestyle appealed to his sense of adventure, and the hardships of weather, flighty cattle, and hard men honed a fierceness of temperament.

In 1885, Eli rode with one of the later cattle drives from Texas to Ogallala, Nebraska. He spent winters in Texas or across the Rio Grande in Mexico. Spring and fall was spent on the trail or working on one of the many ranches that were being established across the western plains.

In the late winter of 1888, Eli got word of the planned opening for settlement of the unassigned lands in Oklahoma territory. So, on 22 April 1889, along with thousands of other hopeful landowners, Eli found himself waiting for the boom of the cannon to begin the first Oklahoma Land Rush. A fast horse and skillful riding carried him toward the leading edge of the mass of riders and buggies and wagons, but when he reached the claim that he had wanted, someone had already planted their flag, and he was warned off at gunpoint. Obliged to comply with the warning, Eli staked his claim on a neighboring section.

With an eye on the possibility of more land within the territory in the future, Eli took a mixed-blood wife, Maria Sanchez-Little Wolf. Marriages were quickly and easily arranged among reservation families who hoped for a better life for their daughters with white settlers.

In 1889, Maria Sanchez-Little Wolf was sixteen, and her adoptive family believed her future would be better with a white homesteader than any life she would have on the reservation. Eli Brandt was eleven years her senior.

Over the following two decades with Eli Brandt, Maria Sanchez-Little Wolf would travel a violent and tumultuous road of hardship, abuse, heartbreak, and survival.

Chapter 1

Eli left the homestead just as the eastern pre-dawn horizon became a soft ribbon of pink, a touch of color in nature's beauty to which Eli was oblivious, as he cruelly dug his spurs into the soft flesh of the stallion's flanks and headed west at a reckless gallop.

Eli's day had begun not unlike many others before. The anger and cruelty that seethed inside him lay just beneath the surface and erupted quickly and often. He had wakened from a restless sleep, fully aroused. Maria had attempted to deflect his mindless rut by drawing her knees close to her pregnant belly and had wrapped her nightshirt tightly around the calves of her legs. She knew, from previous futile attempts, that she would not be able to keep Eli from overpowering her, but neither would she submit without a struggle. It was a battle that she knew she could not win but a fight that she must stand to and not surrender to meekly.

Eli yanked her clasped hands from her knees with one coarse, calloused hand and rapped her across the bridge of her nose with the closed fist of his other.

"By God, woman, you will not refuse me!" Eli growled. "You're my own damned wife, and I'll take my pleasure where and when I want it!"

"It's too close to my time," Maria cried as a bright red trickle of blood ran across the curve of her lip. "Don't! Don't! Please, don't do this to me!" she begged.

"Shut your damned mouth!" Eli barked as he raised his fist above her face.

Hot tears welled up in Maria's eyes but she refused to let them spill as she turned her face away from Eli's threatening fist and willed her body to relax beneath him.

When he had satisfied himself, Eli rolled to the edge of the bed. Maria flinched involuntarily when she felt his rough hand on her naked belly.

"Damned well better be a boy!" Eli threatened.

Moving away from his unwelcome touch, Maria slid from the bed and stood awkwardly as she tugged at her nightgown until it fell to her swollen feet and covered her nakedness. As she waddled barefoot across the dirt floor, Eli demanded the preparation of a pot of coffee, breakfast, and a lunch to be packed in his saddlebags.

"And be damned quick about it too!" he demanded. "I'll be out to saddle up, and I'll take my coffee when I get back in."

Pouring an ironstone bowl half full of water from a pitcher on the small, handmade kitchen table, Maria rinsed the blood from her face, washed her hands, and dried them on a flour-sack dish towel. She then began the morning's chores of coffee and breakfast. Eli dressed, pulled on his boots, and grabbed his well-worn hat and wool-lined canvas coat as he shoved the soddy door open with his shoulder.

"Coffee will be on the table when I'm back, or else!" Eli warned as he slammed the door behind him and headed to the barn.

Eli considered himself a horseman, and boasted loudly and often of his ability to break a horse and to teach the dumb sons-a-bitches just who was boss. Brute force, the sting of a whip or rope, and cross hobbling were just a few of his tricks of the trade.

This morning, he had decided to saddle the big stallion he had recently purchased to stand at stud for the bulk of the broodmares that he kept.

The stallion was the newest addition to the horseflesh that Eli owned. He did know good horses when he saw them, and the stallion was indeed one of the finer specimens of the Quarter Horse breed. The stud was deep-chested, stocky, and muscular with plenty of stamina. He was a blood bay with four white socks and a diamond-shaped blaze. Eli called the stud his Jack-of-diamonds, and planned to profit heavily from the foals the stallion would sire. But the stallion was high-spirited and unbroken, a condition that, to Eli, was unacceptable.

When Eli brought the stallion to the homestead, he ponied him behind the well broke and aging broodmare that was the foundation of his breeding stock. It was obvious from the start of the full day's journey that the stallion had never before been ponied. At the end of the long lead rope, the stud reared and struck at the unfamiliar tether that was restraining the freedom to which he was accustomed. Eli kept the lead tied hard and fast to the saddle horn and the determined struggles of the stallion often nearly up-ended the old mare. On those occasions, Eli dismounted in a rage and with an extra coil of stiff, new rope, furiously whipped the stallion across the neck, withers, and chest. In defiance and fear, the panicked stallion struck out. Eli deftly avoided the dangerously close blows of the stallion's front hooves while expertly landing the punishing blows of the coiled rope. When Eli and the stud finally reached the home corrals, the stallion stood unsteadily on trembling legs that were streaked with the blood and sweat that ran freely from his beaten chest and neck.

Eli led the stallion into a small pen with no feed or water, tied the stallion's left foreleg up to his chest with a loop around the hoof, and tied it uncomfortably tight around his neck. The stallion, able to move in only an unsteady, three-legged hobble, was then left in the tiny, lodge-pole prison for two full days.

At the end of the second day, exhausted from his struggles, weak from hunger and parched from thirst, the stallion finally surrendered in a shuddering heap of sweat-soaked hide. With the stallion's spirit broken, it was then that Eli began the cruel task of breaking the stud to saddle. The stallion learned to respond out of fear—fear of the rope, fear of the whip, fear of the spur, and hatred for the man who wielded these tools of punishment.

This morning, the stallion stood nervously in the confinement of his stall. Eli kept him in the barn most of the time and seldom let him run free in the pastures. Eli told neighbor folks who inquired that he kept the stallion stalled because "that stud is just too valuable to let run loose. He might get wire cut, or worse yet, stole." Truth was, Eli found it nearly impossible to catch the stallion once it was turned loose and so, with the stallion locked in his stall, Eli could easily slip a halter over his head and lead him to the crossties for saddling.

The day had begun with a battle of wills between Eli and Maria, and Eli had won a bit too easily, and so he was in a mood to continue the battle. He knew the stallion would give him the fight he was looking for and provide more than ample opportunity to vent his anger. Both man and beast were caught in a cycle of anger, fear, abuse and retaliation, a vicious cycle that would not end until either horse or man was dead.

Eli forced the bit through the tightly clenched teeth of the stallion's mouth and jerked the bridle over his ears. A saddle pad was thrown across his back and when the stallion danced sideways to avoid the flapping blanket, Eli slapped him across the nose with the stiff ends of the heavy leather reins. The saddle was slammed into place and the sharp blow of a knee to the gut assured a quick and tight cinching.

Eli led the wild-eyed and skittering horse to the hitching rail in front of the soddy, tied the reins securely around the rail, and stomped to the door.

Maria grabbed the coffee pot and began pouring the dark, steaming liquid into a blue enameled tin cup just as Eli grabbed the rope handle of the soddy door and jerked it open.

"I'll have my breakfast now!" Eli barked as he sat at the table and wrapped his hand around the hot tin cup. The coffee was too hot to drink from the cup, so Eli poured it onto a saucer and, lifting the saucer to his lips with both hands, noisily sipped the cooling liquid. The habit reminded Maria of a camp dog lapping from a puddle of rainwater.

Maria spooned scrambled eggs, sausage, and fried potatoes onto Eli's plate, then quickly retrieved two slices of bread from out of the warmer above the stovetop and dropped them next to Eli's plate. Eli jerked his fist, which held the fork, toward Maria's distended belly, then gave her a twisted, mouth-full-of-eggs smirk when she nervously jumped away.

As Eli ate, Maria prepared a lunch of buttered bread, hard-boiled eggs, and fried sausage. Then, she wrapped it all in a clean cotton towel and stuffed it carefully into Eli's saddlebags. The scrape of a fork on the ironstone plate, overly loud slurping of coffee, the noise of pots and pans, and the clunk and clatter of the morning's kitchen chores were the only sounds made. Morning conversation had ceased long ago and the cooking fire that Maria had built in the old stove could never warm the cold space that had separated husband and wife.

Maria knew not to ask Eli where he would be going or when he might return. She felt certain that her birthing time was very close and hoped that Eli might be home early. Then she found herself hoping that he would not be coming home at all.

"Coffee!" Eli demanded, as he jabbed his cup out for Maria to refill.

Maria jumped at his command, retrieved the pot from the stove, and hurried toward Eli's outstretched hand. As she poured the coffee into Eli's cup, the steaming liquid sloshed across the bottom of the cup, up and over the lid and onto Eli's hand.

"Dammit, woman!" Eli howled as he jumped up from the table and kicked his teetering chair backward across the room. "You clumsy, ignorant she-dog!" Eli yelled as he hurled the tin cup, striking Maria on the back of her head. Maria had quickly turned away as the cup flew from Eli's hand toward her face, so she was spared another cut or bruise on her face. The cup clattered to the floor, and Eli snatched his saddlebags from the table, kicked the door open, and left.

The tethered stallion reared back against the reins when the door exploded open, and Eli used the saddlebags as a bludgeon against the side of the horse's head. Amidst a stream of curses and the frightened blowing and bucking of the stallion, Eli hauled himself into the saddle, quickly found the stirrups, and cut deep slashes into the stallion's flanks as he spurred him into submission and lunged blindly across the open prairie.

Maria sank to her knees on the dirt floor, buried her face in the palms of her calloused hands, and wept.

Chapter 2

Maria's clenched teeth left deep indentations on the leather strap as she drew another sharp breath against the spasm of pain. Despite a cold February breeze that chilled the soddy, sweat ran freely across the sharp features of her face, over the drum-tight skin of her belly, and between the firm mounds of her swollen breasts. Tiny rivulets followed the contours of her body and pooled on the soaked sheets under the arch of her back. Today, as usual, her husband Eli was nowhere near the soddy. His work on the homestead was just enough to meet the minimum requirements for proving up the claim. The promised frame house had yet to become a reality. The past year in the small, dark and constantly dirty soddy was not what she had expected. Eli's contrived courtship had promised a frame house with glass windows, wood floors, a door that would keep out the dust and cold, and a brand new, cast iron 'Majestic' cookstove. However, none of the promises had materialized, and she had begun to realize that they would not. As difficult as life had been on the reservation, it had been far better than the nuptial slavery that was her current misfortune.

Eli's criticism was constant and sharp despite Maria's unending efforts to please him. His words stung almost as painfully as the back of his hand. Through his bitterness and abuse, she had begun to believe that all of their bad luck was her fault alone. It was her fault that the soil was poor, her fault that the rains had not come, her fault that the crops had barely fed the stock and left nothing for sale or trade, her fault that too much had been spent on seed, equipment, and fencing.

In the early days of her pregnancy, Maria had asked about plans for the house. Eli's response had cut the thread of hope she had harbored.

"If I can find some dumb son-of-a-bitch to buy this place after I've proved it up and got the deed," Eli growled, "we'll be movin' on. There's gotta be a fertile piece of ground somewhere in these damned Oklahoma hills. Until then," he continued to rant, "I'm damn sure not puttin' a single penny into no god-damned, high falutin' house."

Maria had not asked again.

And so, Eli spent his days riding the hills looking for a decent piece of land and some dumb son-of-a-bitch. Evenings were spent in the cramped quarters of the soddy where Maria prepared the meals, kept up with the household chores, and endlessly mended the worn and tattered clothing. The coming child was her private joy, and she smiled within herself at thoughts of the arrival of her firstborn. At times, she caressed the growing fullness of her belly, and the smile reached her thin lips, and the corners of her mouth turned slightly upward while her dark eyes sparkled with anticipation.

If Eli happened to catch a glimpse of her good pleasure, he would wag his head and grumble in tones just loud enough for her to hear, "It sure is one hell of a time to be having another damned mouth to feed."

Or, if he was feeling especially vindictive, he would berate and threaten with, "When time comes for you to whelp that pup, you damn sure better be doin' it like a white woman and not some god-damned squaw!"

Maria was trapped. Returning to her people would be disgrace, and though she thought often of leaving, she had no place to go. In order to make life somewhat bearable, she retreated into herself. She seldom spoke to Eli, avoided him whenever possible, yet also tried to appease him in order to stave off the frequent abuse. It was the threats that had made her determined to deliver her baby like a white woman, flat on her back in the iron bed.

Her water had broken in a gush as she stood on tiptoe to hang the last of the morning's wash. She had known her time was close and was neither surprised nor scared at the onset of labor. After the last shirt from the wicker basket had been hung to dry, she returned to the soddy to finish the morning's chores and get things in order for the birthing. She added fuel to the cookstove and placed an iron kettle filled with water over the flame. The night chill still hung brisk in the room and stoking the fire would bring a welcome warmth. Taking a cotton towel off the rim of the ironstone bowl that sat near the stove, she checked to see if the dough she had mixed earlier was ready for a final kneading before she filled the loaf pans for baking. The dough was not quite ready, so she began to fold the sparse pile of laundered undergarments that lay across the bed. She held her simple cotton slip in both hands and buried her nose in the crush of fabric between her hands. She had always loved the smell of sun-dried garments and the fragrance of sage that the cloth gathered while it hung on the clothesline. As she filled her nostrils with the fresh, clean scent, a sharp and sudden pain seared through her body. It felt as though she had been struck a blow across her lower back, and as the pain grew, it spread forward through her belly and downward.

Maria knew that it was time. After finishing the folding of her clothes and adding several more large pieces of wood to the fire, she changed from her everyday dress into the fresh cotton bed shirt that she had not yet folded and put away. Climbing into the iron-framed bed, she prepared herself for the birthing. When she knew that the time was right, she raised herself slightly, grabbed her knees in her small, calloused hands, and began to push. That had been nearly four hours ago.

Maria had known the pain would be intense, almost unbearable at times, but that it would subside between the increasingly frequent contractions. Her mother and grandmother had instructed her in the birthing process and had often taken her along when attending the birthing of others in her village. She wished her mother was with her now, but she was alone and scared. The pain had become constant and excruciating.

Something was wrong.

When her labor had begun, she could feel the baby moving, feet and arms pushing against the inside of her womb. But the longer the labor continued, the less frequent the movement became. She had become used to the near-constant stirring over the past several days as nature prepared the baby for the coming birth. At the beginning of labor, the baby would move between each contraction, but now she realized that she had felt nothing for several minutes.

Maria willed herself to relax. Breathing deeply and slowly, she focused on the bulge in the muslin sheet that hung above the bed. She kept a sheet fastened to the ceiling of the soddy to keep the dirt and dust from the earthen roof from sifting down onto the bed. Sheets were also fastened above the crude wooden table and the cookstove.

Often, Maria would imagine them to be billowing rain clouds hanging overhead. Actual rain clouds had been scarce for the past year, and she longed for rain to settle the constant dust. Focusing on the sheet hanging overhead, she was reminded of the old German lady, Mrs. Volkmann, who had taught her the trick of keeping dirt from sifting down into the food she was preparing. Mrs. Volkmann and her husband Klaus had staked a claim on the adjoining section, but they had stayed less than a year before abandoning their claim. Maria had been sad to see them leave. Mrs. Volkmann had been the only woman in the territory who had treated her kindly. *If only Mrs. Volkmann were here now*, Maria thought, *she would surely be a much-needed midwife.*

As Maria's thoughts distracted her from the pain and her breathing became calmer and more controlled, she pressed her fingers and the heels of her hands into the tightness of her belly. Recalling the instructions of her grandmother, she knowingly pushed and prodded as she felt for the contours of the child inside. First, she felt the head, fairly high up on the left side of her womb, with a shoulder slightly below. On the lower right side, she felt the heel of a tiny foot. From the position of the baby, she knew its bottom was being pressed into the birth canal.

Although she had never done this before, Maria knew what she had to do. By manipulating the fetus with her hands on the outside, she had to turn the baby inside and position it properly above the birth canal. And she knew it must be done quickly. It had been quite some time since she had felt her baby move. It had to be turned and delivered soon.

Raising her hips from off the bed, Maria pushed and massaged the child inside her. Remembering the many times she had helped her mother and grandmother, she deftly pushed the head downward as she slowly massaged the legs and buttocks to move them upward. Gently yet surely, she was able to reposition the child for delivery. She knew the birthing must now be done quickly. The hours of labor had left her tired and weakened, and the child inside her would not survive much longer.

Despite Eli's stinging admonitions to the contrary, Maria knew this child would be born of an Indian woman. The white man's ways had proved, once again, to be wholly inadequate. She swung her legs over the side of the bed, pushed herself up from off the sweat-soaked sheets, and stood barefoot on the dirt floor.

Cradling her belly in her right hand and supporting herself against the sod walls with her left, she waddled to the corner of the soddy, lifted the bed shirt above her waist and, pressing her back against the corner, squatted in preparation for delivery. Delivery like an Indian, a god-damned squaw.

The birthing now went quickly. With Maria's first push, a tiny head was delivered. With the second and third push, shoulders and torso appeared. On her fourth and final push, at last, she held a motionless baby boy in her bloodied and trembling hands. She quickly wrapped him in a rough woolen blanket, then turned the pale and lifeless form onto its stomach and draped him over her outstretched hand. With her other hand, she gently patted his back while carefully bouncing the baby in a jerking, up and down rhythm. Not too soon, the newborn sneezed, spraying the fluid from his nose and mouth. Then with a heave of his tiny chest, the boy child drew in his first breath of Oklahoma air, air mixed with the dust that settled to the floor while dancing on the beams of fading daylight.

Maria wiped the fluid from the baby's face, cut and tied the cord, cradled the infant against her breast, and nursed him.

Holding her bundled son in her arms, Maria allowed herself a broad smile as she gazed at the dark-haired child.

With a sudden start, she realized that now there was work to be done. The bed had to be stripped, the birthing corner cleaned, and supper started before Eli returned home. The fire in the cookstove had gone out and would have to be rekindled so that supper could be fixed. A warm fire would take the sharp chill out of the darkening soddy.

But there was no fire that would take the deep chill of fear from out of her heart.

How will Eli treat his firstborn son? she asked herself. *Will I be able to keep him safe from a father whose dark heart seems filled with cold and cruel anger*? Her fearful thoughts were severed by the sharp cries of the newborn that she held in her arms.

Maria shivered against the cold.

Despite her exhaustion from the long and difficult birthing, Maria swiftly and efficiently began preparing the soddy, and her son, for Eli's arrival.

As she cradled the child in the crook of her left arm, her right hand scattered bits of kindling and struck a match that quickly spread its yellow flame over the pieces of broken twigs and dried grass. It took her but little time to have a strong cookfire burning again in the cold iron stove.

In the corner of the soddy, she began the task of preparing the afterbirth that she would later bury, when she heard the nicker of Eli's horse at the hitching rail just outside the door.

As Eli jerked open the door, Maria stepped back into the shadows of the soddy corner and clutched her newborn close to her breast. Eli stood as a dark silhouette in the doorway with the fading light of day behind him and glared at the drying placenta that lay near Maria's feet. He quickly glanced at the disheveled bed, then fixed his burning eyes on Maria as he strode brusquely across the darkening room, his powerful fist raised menacingly above his shoulder.

"You good for nothing, black-hearted, heathen squaw!" Eli bellered as the first blow landed just below the ribs in the softness of her belly. Maria held her son tightly as the air rushed from her lungs and the enraged face of Eli wavered before her eyes.

Later in the evening, after Eli had finished his solitary supper, Maria sat on the edge of the bed nervously nursing the child that her instinct now told her she must protect at all costs.

"What you plan on callin' that scrawny half-breed son-of-a-bitch?" Eli sneered as fire leapt from the head of a wooden match and he lit a pipe of pungent tobacco.

"Jacob Cain," whispered Maria between split and swollen lips while dark eyes stared flatly above the black and blue cheekbones of her sharp features.

Six months later, Maria was pregnant again. For the better part of four weeks after Jacob was born, she had been able to avoid Eli by keeping her firstborn constantly near her or in her arms, and she slept on the floor beside the wooden crate that was Jacob's cradle. That Eli had tolerated her absence from his bed was a welcome respite for Maria from his brutal, carnal demands. But months-long abstinence proved to be the limit of Eli's suppressed appetite when he had forced her to his bed and took his pleasure.

Jacob was a rambunctious toddler, scurrying around the soddy when Maria gave birth to a baby girl. As the dark-eyed child grew, she carried her mother's features, slender of build with a narrow face, high, prominent cheekbones and raven-colored hair. Maria named her first girl-child Eve, but from early on, the girl was called Evie. Evie would always be Eli's favorite and, despite her stubborn independence, he would never raise his voice or his hand against her.

In April of 1892, the month that Eve was born, the Cheyenne and Arapaho lands in the Oklahoma Territory were opened to white settlers. Eli sold his section in the Unassigned Lands to the Sooners, who had staked the claim he had hoped for, and staked a new claim on the newly opened reservation lands. Maria, as a Cheyenne tribal member, was eligible for an additional adjoining claim. The combined 320-acre homestead was located on the northern side, in the horseshoe bend of the Cimarron River.

Chapter 3

At six years old, Jacob Cain had already learned to always keep a little distance between himself and his papa. He did not yet know or understand the cause for Eli's sudden flares of violence and rage, but he had learned that it was best to avoid being seen or heard. When Eli was away, Maria would dote over her firstborn. She entertained him with sticks and crude blocks that she fashioned from irregular pieces of wood found near the chopping block where Eli split firewood and where she would often behead a fat hen for a fried chicken supper.

Both Jacob and Maria reveled in the times they spent together. When Eli was away, there was laughter and foolishness, singing and light-heartedness. When Eli was home, Maria was constantly shushing Jacob as she scurried about the soddy like a chickadee flitting restlessly among the sparse branches of a prairie cedar. On this day, Eli was gone, as was quite often the case, and Maria was building corrals for Jacob from long splinters of cedar. Inside the miniature corrals stood a cloth horse that Maria had made by twisting and tying pieces of cloth until the cluster of knots and twists somewhat resembled a horse. Jacob held the makeshift toy in his small hand and pranced the pony around the cedar corral giggling with joy as Maria clapped her hands and shouted, "Run, pony, run!"

Evie would reluctantly join the playtime after considerable coaxing from Maria. Most often, she preferred to be off by herself, quickly tiring of whatever games that Maria introduced for the children's amusement. Evie was her papa's little princess, jumping to her feet and running to greet him whenever she heard Eli's arrival. He would sweep her up in his arms, heft her up across his shoulders or cradle her in one arm while tickling her under the chin with his free hand.

But Jacob had learned that when the nicker of his papa's horse was heard coming toward the yard, Mama's laughter stopped abruptly, toys were hurriedly stuffed behind the wood box, while rag ponies and laughter were replaced with gruffness and rough handling. Eli defended his rough treatment of Jacob by declaring that it would "someday make a man of him instead of turning him into a runny-nosed runt of a Mama's boy." But Jacob treasured the time spent with his mother and dreaded the darkness of the times spent with his father. And although he had learned these early-life lessons well, it was to be a lifetime before he understood how the two separate worlds shaped him in ways not unlike the twisted and knotted pony his mother had made for him.

Maria heard the horses before either Jacob or Evie were aware of the men shouting outside the door.

"Brandt! Eli Brandt! You home?" hollered the cowboy, who appeared to be the leader of three men that reined in their horses in front of the pine door.

"Brandt! Come on out here. We need to talk!" the cowboy barked urgently.

The horses skittered impatiently in the yard, seemingly as agitated as the cowboys on their backs, and raised a swirling cloud of red Oklahoma dust as Maria slowly opened the door and stepped into the hot mid-day sun. Jacob followed, standing close beside Maria. Evie peeked around the edge of the partially closed door, then pushed it shut and returned to her solitary play.

"Mister Brandt's not here," Maria replied firmly as she raised her hand to her brow shielding her eyes from the dust and sun in order to see more clearly who it was that so urgently needed to see Eli.

Each of the three men quickly raised his right hand to the brim of his sweat-stained hat and tugged a silent but polite "Howdy, Ma'am" with thumb and finger.

"Sorry, Ma'am," replied the one who appeared to be the leader of the three, still holding the edge of his hat brim. "We'd like to have a word with your husband. When do you reckon he'll be around?"

"Mister Brandt rode into town this morning," Maria answered as Jacob stepped shyly forward and reached up for Maria's hand.

"He should be home come evening. If you've come far, you're welcome to wait down at the barn," Maria continued as she squared her shoulders and drew herself up to stand just a bit taller and more solidly, an unconscious and natural posturing of a mother protecting her young.

"Not far," the cowboy replied as he leaned forward in the saddle and placed both hands, one atop the other, on the well-worn saddle horn.

"We'll come back in the mornin', after breakfast. Tell your ol' man that Charlie Davies from the Anchor-D will be by to have a word."

"I will," Maria answered flatly.

Davies touched his hat brim and smiled down at Jacob, who instantly ducked behind the folds of Maria's dress. "Thank you, Ma'am," he said, dropping his hand and gathering up the reins.

Charlie Davies carried himself with a casual ease that belied his acute awareness of his surroundings. Always vigilant and observant, Davies could react instantly to unexpected situations involving horses, cattle, and men. His uncanny insight had frequently prevented what might have been disastrous wrecks. Charlie Davies was not a big man, but his confident manner seemed to magnify his slender build and shorter stature. In his early forties, Charlie had acquired a slight graying of the sideburns that extended along the lines of his jaw and joined the ends of his salt and pepper mustache. His tanned face and deep-lined crow's feet reflected the long days in the saddle, the constant glare of sun, and windblown Oklahoma dust. But despite his rugged exterior, there was a glint of softness in the deep blue of his eyes and a quick, disarming smile.

The three men turned their horses and rode an easy lope down the path that led past the barn and a set of corrals that held a half-dozen mixed-breed cows. The three men slowed as they reached the corral and looked long at the cattle penned there, then spurring their horses, galloped east across the prairie.

Maria and Jacob watched the cowboys as they rode toward the ridge that bordered their claim, ever-shrinking silhouettes that fluttered in the shimmering waves of heat that rose from baked ground. Maria knew that the brief visit from the three men had not been a social call and sensed that Eli would not consider their returning tomorrow morning as good news.

If he knows they're coming back, Maria thought, *I'd bet he'll take off before sunup.*

Maria looked down at Jacob, who still held her hand tightly, and taking his other hand in hers, she knelt down in front of him. "Let's not tell your papa those cowboys were here," Maria said playfully as she smiled and winked.

Maria and Jacob watched the horizon until the three riders had disappeared. Still holding Jacob's hand, Maria led the boy back inside, pulled the plank door closed, and leaned against the rough doorjamb. She held Jacob's hand tightly in the fist that she had unconsciously formed around his small hand and stared absently across the room.

"Mama," Jacob winced as he tugged against the grip that held him. "Ouch!"

"I'm sorry, Jacob," Maria crooned as she released her grip and knelt down beside him. "Now," Maria said with a bright smile, "we're going to have a secret. Just me and you. You too Evie; come on over here, sweetheart. Can you keep a secret?" Jacob nodded his head and answered her question with a smile. Evie hesitantly nodded her head and wrinkled her nose and forehead into a fearsome-looking frown.

"We're going to pretend that those three cowboys never came to our house looking for your papa. It'll be our secret and we must never tell anyone." Maria had lowered her voice to a soft whisper but kept a playful tone so as not to frighten Jacob and Evie.

"Can you do that?"

"Yes, Ma'am," Jacob replied in soft tones that matched Maria's whisper.

"Um, huh," Evie answered.

Maria knew that Eli had often come home in the dark of night, herding two or three cattle ahead of him. After holding them in the corral for a couple of days, he would turn them out to pasture with the rest of the herd. Then, every three or four months, he would gather up the fifteen or twenty head he had accumulated and trail them north to market. She had asked Eli, once, where he had gotten a particularly nice pair of sleek, fat Hereford calves that he had instructed her to bucket feed.

"You don't worry your tiny pea-brain over my business, woman, you hear?" Eli had snapped. "It ain't none of your god-damned business, that's for damned sure. Just feed the little sons-a-bitches like I told you to and keep your damned mouth shut. Understand?"

Maria had cowed under his verbal battering and knew that she dare not ask further or ever again. She knew that pursuing a complete answer would end only in another severe beating. However, Maria suspected that most of the cattle in Eli's herd were stolen, and the visit by the three cowboys from the Anchor-D had heightened those suspicions. Maria seldom openly defied Eli or fought back. Her inferior strength, though more than adequate to match the needs of her demanding pioneer existence, was no match for the powerful arms and hammer-like fists of Eli.

But just maybe, Maria thought, *maybe someone else could deal out the beating that Eli deserved.*

The notion had suddenly lodged in Maria's head as she watched Mister Davies and the other two cowboys closely study the calves that Eli had come home with and penned a couple of nights ago. She would just have to wait and see what the morning would bring. And she would pray that Jacob and Evie would remember their secret.

The three men had ridden in silence since leaving the Brandt place. As they had passed the small, haphazardly built corral, they closely checked the cattle that Eli had penned there.

"Them's our cows, Charlie. By damn them's ours fer certain," said the dark-haired cowboy in an almost too-loud whisper.

"Shush!" Charlie snapped as he sharply spurred his horse.

In a flurry of dust, Charlie's horse dug his hooves into the powdery red soil and had soon distanced himself from the other riders. The two men riding with Charlie followed suit and quickly spurred their ponies to a gallop. When the three riders finally came abreast of one another, they slowed to an easy, long-gaited, ground-covering trot.

Charlie Davies had ridden for the Anchor-D for fifteen years and most of those years were as a cow boss in the Territory. Like countless others, Charlie had drifted west after the war and soon found work chasing wild longhorn cattle across the plains of West Texas. Proving himself a good hand and being easy-going with the crews he worked with, Charlie gained a reputation as a hard-working and fair-minded man. It was no surprise to the boys he worked with when Charlie was hired as cow boss for the Anchor-D and sent from the headquarters to the range in the Territory. During his fifteen years with the outfit, Charlie had seen a passel of cowboys come and go. Most were farm boys who had grown tired of walking barefoot behind a plow horse. Some were drifters with only a first name, no past, and no future, who were trying to remain unknown on the obscure plains of Oklahoma Territory.

The two men who rode with Charlie had both come up from the headquarters ranch in Texas. Bo, the older of the two, was likely in his late twenties. His thick dark hair, deep brown eyes, sun bronzed face, and the heavy stubble of his unshaven face gave him a hard look. Bo lived up to the look. He was brash, impetuous, and short-tempered but a good hand with the horses and loyal to the brand. Charlie found it best to keep Bo with him whenever possible

28

in order to minimize the trouble he often stirred up among the rest of the boys. Bo fancied himself a "bad hombre" and Charlie often wondered why he didn't just pay Bo his wages due and send him on his way.

Nate, the other rider, was a boy of seventeen, at most, who regarded Charlie as perhaps only one notch lower than God. Nate had drifted west in the late '80s and literally stumbled across the Anchor-D and Charlie Davies. With no food, no water, and leading an old broken-down horse so lame that Charlie had to put it down with a .45 slug to the brain, the kid had staggered into Charlie's camp on a hot and muggy night in late June. Nate's blonde hair had been bleached nearly white for lack of a hat, and his fair-skinned face was blistered from the sun. That had been nearly three years earlier and though Charlie would never admit to it, Nate had become the closest thing to a son that he would ever have. Charlie had taken the boy under his wing and now, whatever Charlie asked, Nate was ready and willing to do. Under Charlie's tutelage Nate had become a fair hand and had already proved himself worthy of being called a good hand.

"Say, Charlie," Bo abruptly asked, breaking the silence of the past hour, "wasn't that kid the half-breed we seen dancin' his little war dance at Butlers store a while back?"

"Yep," Charlie replied flatly, "same boy."

"So's, old man Brandt's nothing but a cow-thievin' squawman!"

"Suppose so."

"Then why'n tarnation didn't we just open up that corral gate and run our cows outta there?"

"'Cause I want Brandt to know I'm on to his game. We'll take care of it tomorrow," Charlie said sharply, trying to end the conversation.

"Well …I sure wouldn't mind takin' care of his squaw woman," said Bo, with a lecherous drawl as he shifted in the saddle. "Bet she'd give a feller a good ride on an old buffalo robe."

Charlie reined in his horse and reached across to grab the reins of Bo's horse. "I don't hold with any man mistreatin' any woman, white or injun'," Charlie warned, "and as long as you're on my payroll, you'll treat Mrs. Brandt respectfully, or you'll be answering to me, you hear?"

"Yes Sir!" Bo snapped with a mock salute.

Charlie held the reins of Bo's horse until the young man's eyes broke away from the stare-down that the two men had held. Bo's 'bad-man bravado' had been mostly foolish talk, but he knew that Mr. Davies' reprimand was no bluff. Bo knew full well that no man crossed Charlie Davies.

Charlie, Nate, and Bo rode on in silence until they reached the bunkhouse. A late-day sun cast long and lanky shadows that rippled over the rocky ground. Charlie dismounted and stood gazing at the rush of color that streaked the western sky as the setting sun brushed the clouds with shades of bright yellow-gold, warm reds, and soft blues.

"I wonder..." Charlie mused as he thought of Maria Brandt and her son standing in front of the crude soddy just a short two-hour ride beyond the horizon.

Maria had supper ready when Eli came riding hell-bent up the lane. From a full gallop to a sliding, dust scattering stop, the heavily lathered stallion stood heaving for air under the restrictive saddle cinch. Eli dismounted, flung the reins over the corral gate, loosened the cinch and jerked the saddle from the stallion's back. With his characteristically rough handling, he jerked the bridle over the stallion's sensitive ears and let the heavy bit rattle sharply against the horse's teeth.

Freed from his tethers, the stallion reared slightly as Eli slapped him across the chest then turned and trotted toward the water trough where he drank long and deep. With thirst quenched and burning lungs soothed, he sauntered to the center of the dusty corral, pawed the ground with his right front hoof, dropped to his knees, then rolled briskly in the warm, dry dust.

Eli had scooped a bucket of oats, hung the bridle, thrown the saddle on the rack, and was halfway to the soddy when the stallion stopped rolling, sprang to his feet, and shook the dust from his drying coat. Maria heard the long, shrill nicker of the stallion in the same instant that she heard Eli announce his arrival.

"You best have supper on the table, woman! I'm damned hungry and ready to eat!"

Maria wordlessly went about finishing the supper preparations, scurrying between the cupboards, the cookstove, and the table. Eli pulled his chair from under the table, swung a leg over the back and slammed his fists down on the tabletop as he sat. Maria jumped as ironstone plates, knives, forks, and spoons rattled, but continued to serve the bowls of meat, potatoes, and vegetables that she had prepared.

"Where's that little runt of a boy?" Eli queried as he glanced around the room. "Come here, boy!" Eli barked, "Bring your papa his pipe and tobacco."

Jacob peered out from behind the curtain that separated his small bed from the rest of the room and took a small, tentative step forward.

"Come on, boy!" Eli cajoled as if coaxing a reluctant dog from under a porch.

Jacob hurried across the room, retrieved Eli's pipe and tobacco, then shuffled sideways down the long edge of the table. When Jacob was within reach, Eli snatched the boy's tiny wrist and jerked him roughly into a suffocating bear hug. Jacob whimpered and struggled against the arms that crushed the breath from his lungs and chafed his smooth-skinned face with the rough, three-day growth of whisker stubble.

"Stop it, Papa!" Jacob begged as he pushed against Eli's chest with the powerless arms that were pinned between them.

Maria rushed from the stove to the table with the bowl of gravy she had just poured from a cast-iron skillet. She quickly set the bowl on the table, then pushing the long fingers of her slender hand between Jacob's chest and Eli's gripping arm, she enfolded the child's shoulder and gently drew him away from Eli's grip.

"He ain't hurt!" Eli snapped as Maria turned away with Jacob in her gentle arms.

To emphasize his point, Eli gave Maria a severe backhanded slap across the back of her thigh. Maria flinched with the stinging pain as she carried Jacob to the chair beside the cookstove.

"There," Eli sneered, "that's something that hurts! The boy's gotta toughen up if he's ever gonna clear a path for himself. Your coddling is makin' a damned sissy outta him!"

"You might be able to do as you please with me," Maria countered, "but you'd best not hurt my boy!"

"Listen at you," Eli mocked. "Who the hell you think you are to tell me what I can or can't do! If the boy needs learnin', I'll do the teachin' and you'll be damned smart to not interfere!"

Maria silently wrung her hands in the folds of her apron, took Jacob by the hand, and led him to his place at the supper table. Evie sat next to Eli and, as they settled in, Eli took Evie's hand in his, bowed his head and began, "Heavenly Father, bless this food…"

Chapter 4

Maria sat suddenly upright in bed, wide awake in a flash of fear from a dream that had played itself out in her sleeping consciousness during the pre-dawn morning. As she sat on the bed, knees drawn to her breast, she realized that although she felt the cold fingers of fear grip her heart, she had no recollection of the dream itself. In the quiet darkness of the soddy, she could hear the steady breathing of Jacob and Evie as they slept and was aware of the weight of Eli next to her. His tall and muscular frame created a sort of valley in the mattress that seemed to draw her in, like a whirlpool she had experienced as a child while swimming in the White River. She had learned to sleep while clutching the edge of the lumpy mattress in order to keep herself from rolling against Eli.

Maria sat quietly, eyes open but unseeing, in the thick darkness. Taking long, deep breaths, she calmed the fear that lingered, slowly fluttering within her like the pulsing wings of a dying butterfly. She knew the forgotten dream had been frightening, even terrifying, but fear was her constant companion and she had learned to control the frequent panic that it caused and suppressed the anger that built within her. She hated Eli for the mastery he held over her but felt powerless to break the invisible chains that kept her shackled to the fearful submission and brutal abuse.

As wakefulness seeped into the jumbled thoughts of sleep, Maria remembered Mister Davies' visit of yesterday. Offering up a quick and silent prayer of thanksgiving for a secret kept, she slid quietly from the bed and out the door to the lop-sided, tarpaper-covered privy behind the soddy.

When Maria returned to the soddy, Eli and Jacob were still sleeping. Evie sat on her bed, rubbing the sleep from her eyes. The old Seth Thomas mantle clock, which had belonged to Eli's mother, chimed the hour of 5 o'clock, and Maria silently wondered how long after breakfast it would be before Mister Davies returned. She would have Eli's breakfast ready in little more than an hour and Eli was always quick about being gone very shortly after he had eaten.

How long, Maria wondered, *will I have to try to keep Eli here before Mister Davies arrives? Will Jacob and Evie remember our little game of secrets?*

As quietly as possible, Maria began her routine of morning chores. A splash of coal oil on the cookstove kindling, the snap of a match and yellow flames instantly began to lick the cold iron. As the fire crackled, Maria took the folded apron from off the table, shook it open with a deft twist of her wrist then tied it around her waist. From the slab of cured bacon that hung beside the crude fireplace, she cut thick strips and laid them side by side in the heavy cast iron skillet that sat on the stovetop. Leaving the soddy again, Maria stepped outside into the cool, pre-dawn air, looked skyward toward the assurance of the ever-constant Big Bear, and then walked quickly toward the barn. Once inside the barn, the smells of horseflesh, oiled leather and sweetgrass hay distracted her from her chores and caused her to momentarily stop, close her eyes and absorb the brief peace and restfulness she felt each time she went to the barn in the morning darkness. She was reminded of home, the familiar smells, and the memories of her youthful happiness. Too soon, the urgency of her task jerked her to action, and hens squawked their displeasure as Maria snatched warm eggs from beneath their downy breasts and placed them carefully in the gathered folds of her apron. As the indignant hens settled back into their nests, Maria made her way back to the soddy.

Bacon already sizzled in the skillet as she laid the fresh eggs on the table, took the oak water pail from its peg on the rafter above the stove, and once again slipped quietly outside. The early morning sky had already begun to lighten at the edge of the eastern horizon. Stars had begun to fade in the faint light of approaching dawn, and the bright morning star flashed its mirrored signal of the rising sun. Maria hung the bucket on the spout of the pump and vigorously pumped the heavy iron handle until the clear, cool water splashed its crystal dance on the bucket's wooden staves. Returning to the soddy with the bucket full of fresh water, Maria heard Eli's deep, rattling morning cough as he hacked and spat on his quickstep trip down the path to the outhouse.

Back at the stove, Maria turned the bacon, started a pot of coffee and cracked a half-dozen eggs into an ironstone bowl. Scrambled eggs, bacon, sliced bread, fried potatoes, and steaming coffee were on the table when Eli walked through the door. Jacob still slept soundly and Eli, finding nothing else to criticize Maria for, began to rant about the virtues of early rising.

33

"You gonna let that lazy, no count boy of yours sleep all damned morning?" Eli grumbled as he heaped his plate with more than his share of potatoes and eggs. "Why the hell ain't he up like the rest of us? If he ain't at the table come mealtime, he'll damn well do without. It's like they say, 'The early bird' …If he won't get up for breakfast, he can just go hungry by damn."

"Let the boy sleep," Maria answered with unusual firmness. "There's no reason he has to be up."

"Don't backtalk me, woman!" Eli snapped as he flexed his arm and feigned a backhanded slap.

Maria involuntarily flinched at the threat but remained stiffly seated at the table. *I wish I had the courage,* Maria thought, *to either fight back or leave.*

Eli had deliberately and boldly emptied every serving dish before he pushed himself away from the table. With a forced belch, he tipped himself back on the hind legs of his chair and patted the swell of his belly with gluttonous satisfaction.

"There'll be no breakfast for that lazy boy of..." Eli began but was interrupted by the rhythmic clatter of hoofbeats as several horses rapidly approached.

Eli sprang to his feet, knocking the tilted chair backward with a clatter and took three long strides to the Winchester that hung above the door.

The horses came to a stop, and as Eli took the rifle in his hands, he heard the call from outside the door.

"Hello, the house!" said the urgent voice. "Eli Brandt," the voice continued, "this is Charlie Davies from the Anchor-D; we need to talk!"

Eli held the rifle with one hand and grabbed the dust-caked and broken-down Stetson he wore with the other. Pulling his hat down snugly, Eli took the rope handle of the door in his hand, pushed it open, and stepped out to meet the three men who sat horseback in front of the soddy.

"What makes you think we need to talk?" Eli inquired casually. "Especially this damned early in the mornin'. I ain't hardly finished breakfast."

"Must be a late riser," Davies said quietly to no one in particular.

"We stopped by yesterday," Davies continued, a bit louder and more business-like.

"I told your missus we'd be by this mornin' after breakfast. I figured this ought to be about the right time."

Eli's eyes flashed with a sudden dark, intense anger as he turned back toward the door where Maria stood, holding onto the edge of the door with both of her hands as she peered out from the doorway. Eli's fierce glare and Maria's quick disappearance back into the soddy told Davies that Mrs. Brandt had not passed the message on to her husband from their earlier visit. For an instant, he wondered why, then suddenly realized he had made a grave mistake. Not that there would be any consequences for him, but he had a strong hunch that Mrs. Brandt might not fare so well.

Eli tightened his grip on the rifle in his hands as his body stiffened against the anger building inside. From beneath the collarless white cotton shirt Eli wore, Davies could see his neck reddening as the veins beneath his jaw pulsed with rising rage. Silence hung like a heavy morning fog as the two men locked eyes in a wordless standoff. Davies leaned forward with his forearm resting casually on the saddle horn while Eli stood like chiseled marble, knuckles white in their vise-like grip.

"State your business, Davies," Eli spat as he forced each word from between tightly clenched teeth. "Then you and those no-count saddle bums you got with you can get your god-damned, worthless asses of my place!"

Davies stiffened visibly in response to Eli's insults. Like a rattler coiled in the brush, as a coyote hunts nearby, Davies was ready to strike if necessary but more than willing to let trouble pass by if at all possible. Charlie held the reins tightly in his left hand while his gun hand was poised above the Colt on his belt. Bo, in the hot-tempered impetuousness of youth, had no inclination of restraint.

"You old son-of-a-bitch!" Bo hissed as he jerked his Colt from its holster.

From the corner of his eye, Charlie saw Bo draw his gun and level the barrel at Eli. Jerking his horse's reins hard to the right and jabbing his spurs into soft flanks, Charlie forced his horse into the shoulder of Bo's mount, blocking Bo's line of fire and throwing him off balance. Bo's arm swung wide and his reckless shot ricocheted off a pile of rocks at the entrance of the root cellar, a good thirty-foot distance from the soddy. Eli also saw Bo draw his Colt and simultaneously jacked a shell into the chamber of the 30-30 and swung the barrel toward Bo. Eli's shot, low and blocked by Charlie, slammed into the top of Charlie's boot, through the flesh of his calf and the leather of the saddle's fender. Charlie's horse squealed and reared as the bullet pierced horseflesh and tore at the soft tissue inside.

"Jesus Christ!" Charlie yelled as his horse went down. "Hold your fire! Hold your fire!"

Nate, unaccustomed to gunplay, jerked leather and lunged his horse away from the melee, raising his arm to cover his face in an instinctive reaction of self-defense. Eli caught Nate's reaction at the edge of his vision and interpreting the movement as aggression, swung his Winchester toward the boy, chambered another shell and fired. The bullet struck Nate just below the collarbone on his right shoulder. Blood and flesh exploded out of Nate's back as the bullet tore through his body. The bullet's impact drove Nate backward and out of his saddle. Eli chambered a third shell and took aim at the boy on the ground.

Bo's horse had taken to squealing and pitching like an unbroken colt and Bo had both hands full of leather to stay in the saddle. Charlie saw the spray of blood from Nate's shoulder as he pulled himself out from under his fallen horse. Jerking his pistol from its holster and holding the weapon with his outstretched arm, he took a half-dozen hurried but painful steps toward Eli and held the muzzle of his Colt inches from Eli's face.

"I said hold your damn fire!" Charlie thundered as he thumbed the hammer back.

Eli lowered the rifle and slowly released the hammer onto the unfired round. Bo's horse had begun to settle down as it nervously pranced under Bo's expert handling. Bo searched the ground for his dropped weapon. Nate's horse had made a panicked flight to the barn as the flapping fenders of an empty saddle fueled its fear. Charlie's horse had regained its feet, but the bloody bubbles from its nostrils sealed its pending fate. Nate curled himself into a tight, fetal ball with knees drawn close to his chest as he choked back the need to vomit and fought off the searing pain of ripped flesh.

Inside the soddy, Jacob had wakened with a scream when the quiet prairie rustlings of early morning were ripped to shreds of chaos with the first explosion of gunpowder and lead. Maria had quickly gathered him into her arms as she sat on the edge of his bed. Drawing Jacob to her with a protective arm, she cupped her hand over his ear and pressed his head onto her breast to muffle the rising crescendo of gunfire. Evie wrapped both of her arms around Maria's arm and buried her head in the folds of Maria's dress.

As echoes of the last shot fired faded into the surrounding hills, Maria heard raspy cries of pain outside. She did not know who was suffering or who might be dead but was certain that someone needed tending to.

"It's okay, little ones," Maria said in soft, soothing tones, "It's all over now but I need to help whoever might be hurt. You stay right here. Okay?"

Jacob, eyes wide with fright, nodded his head in reply, and Evie reluctantly loosened her grip on Maria's arm.

Maria heard voices outside the door but was unable to determine the words being spoken as she filled a small wash pan with water and grabbed a clean dishcloth from the cupboard. As she reached to open the door, the settling quiet was once again shattered by a single, sharp gunshot. Maria recoiled and dropped the dishpan that splattered cold water down the front of her dress and over her feet. Evie jumped and let out a sharp scream as she buried her head under the mound of blankets that surrounded her. Opening the door, Maria saw Mr. Davies standing next to Eli with his pistol held inches from Eli's left eye. Bo was standing over Charlie's horse that lay in a crumpled heap beneath Bo's still smoking Colt. Bo had unsaddled Charlie's horse and had mercifully ended its suffering.

Nate lay writhing in the dust as blood continued to pour from his open wound. With a dishpan in hand, Maria walked briskly toward the well to pump more water. Eli quickly figured out what Maria was about to do and, despite being subdued by the threat of Charlie's pistol, his seething rage turned to her.

"By God, woman, you lift a finger for one of these bastards, and I promise you'll be damned sorry! I'll fix you up good, Woman!" Eli continued to rant as Maria began pumping fresh water into the dishpan. "I ain't bluffin', you black-hearted dog!" Eli threatened as Maria knelt beside Nate.

"And I ain't bluffin' neither," Charlie Davies interrupted in a calm yet threatening voice.

"You know why we've come here, Brandt, and I ain't got the time nor the inclination to be polite about it. If you expect to stay healthy, I reckon you'd best be movin' on out of this country. And I'll make you a promise too. If that boy over there dies, I'll make certain sure that you follow close behind." Charlie took the rifle from Eli's hands, holstered his pistol, and emptied the shells from the rifle onto the ground.

"I'll be damned if I let you run me off my own place!" Eli warned, "I'll see you in hell first!"

"Likely so," Davies replied flatly as he went to Nate and helped him up. Bo had gone to the barn and retrieved Nate's horse, and Charlie helped the young man into the saddle. Climbing up behind him, Charlie reached around and gathered up the reins, tipped his hat to Maria, and nudged the horse forward.

"You can either bury my horse or let it rot," Charlie said as he rode past Eli.

"He can rot in hell with you!" Eli growled.

Bo picked up Charlie's saddle and tack, swung astride his horse, and quietly followed Charlie and Nate as they rode away. "You'll pay for this," Bo hissed as he rode past Eli. "Somehow, I'll make sure you pay."

As they left, Charlie Davies turned in the saddle and looked back at the pitiful scene of the morning's fiasco. He watched as Maria hurried inside and Eli stooped to pick up the rifle that Davies had thrown in the dust. Picking up the rifle, Eli stood and turned to follow Maria into the soddy. Once inside, Eli pulled the door closed and raised the rifle so that the butt was held high in his right hand and the barrel, gripped in his left, was pointed down. Maria turned to see him approach her with heavy, earth-pounding strides. Jacob, startled once more by the slam and rattle of the door, sat huddled on his bed against the wall, his face pale with the fear of knowing what he was about to see. Evie sat silently, drawing her knees to her chest, her body trembling as she stared into the dark corner of the room at the foot of the bed.

"You traitorous bitch!" Eli's words dripped with the venom of his dark rage as he swung the rifle butt, which struck Maria, full force, across the side of her head. The blow lifted Maria off her feet and threw her backward against the wall. As her limp body slumped to the floor. Eli turned and glared at Jacob, who shook uncontrollably, tears streaming down his face, his mouth open in a silent scream.

Eli took a single menacing step toward Jacob, raised the butt of the rifle, and jabbed it toward Jacob's face. Jacob cowed in the corner of his bed, drawing the blankets around him.

"You best be scared, boy!" Eli sneered. "You ever do me like your mama done and, by God, I'll fix you good!"

Eli stormed from the soddy and headed to the barn where he roughly saddled the wild-eyed stallion, mounted in a rage, and laid cruel steel to horseflesh. When Jacob heard the fading hoofbeats of Eli's horse, he climbed down from the bed and ran to Maria. Sitting on the floor beside her, he held her bloody face in his small hands and watched as her eyelids fluttered, then slowly began to open.

"Mama! Mama!" Jacob sobbed over and over again, "Oh, Mama!"

Chapter 5

Maria stood at the well after having pumped the oak bucket full of fresh water for bathing. Resting her hands on her hips, she leaned backward at the waist to relieve the ache and tiredness in her back. As she stretched, she carefully scanned the surrounding hills and the distant horizon for signs of an approaching rider. Eli had not yet returned after having left her in a semi-conscious heap on the dirt floor of the soddy. That was three days ago and although she was constantly alert in anticipation of his return, she was grateful for the peace that came in his absence.

Maria had spent nearly two days in bed while Jacob and Evie helped to nurse her bruised and torn face. Her left eye was still closed tight against the swollen knot of purple and black skin. The jagged tear of flesh from her cheekbone down to her jaw was smeared with salve, and the raw flesh that puckered from the long wound showed the certainty of permanent scarring. Maria had told Jacob to wake her whenever she might fall asleep. And so, he had kept a valiantly fought vigil of wakefulness until he could no longer hold his ever-heavier eyelids open and had finally fallen asleep in the late afternoon of the second day. The thunderous pounding in Maria's head and the frequent vomiting had mercilessly continued until just this morning, the third day.

Getting up with the rising of the sun, Maria prepared a breakfast of poached eggs and hot oatmeal for herself, Jacob, and Evie. After their meal, Maria and Jacob harnessed the team and hitched them to the heavy rope that Maria had tied around the hind legs of Charlie Davies's dead horse. Together they hauled the carcass to a dry ravine several miles from the soddy. Jacob rode in the bed of the wagon while Evie sat on the wagon seat with Maria. Maria had guided the horses to the edge of the ravine and removed the trace chains from the dead horse's hooves. Together, Maria and Jacob struggled to roll the stiffened carcass into the ravine and then proceeded to scrape away the earth from the sides of the ravine and over the horse until the carcass was completely covered.

The repulsive chore had taken the better part of the day for the two of them to complete. Evie had fallen asleep in the back of the wagon, and Maria was looking forward to a much-needed sponge bath to remove the dust and grime and the smell of death. Maria carried Evie to her bed, and Jacob had already climbed onto his bed and fallen soundly asleep.

As Maria stooped to pick up the bucket of water, she glanced a quick flash of movement at the crest of a small hill nearly a mile distant. Stiffening her body and raising her hand to her brow, she shielded her eyes from the glare of the late afternoon sun. She was soon able to distinguish the form of a single rider approaching at a steady trot. As she watched, she looked for recognizable characteristics of the horse and rider and quickly determined that it was not Eli. Stooping once more to retrieve the bucket of water, Maria gripped the bucket's worn rope handle and hurried to the door of the soddy. Once inside, she slid the latch in place and waited. She did not wait long before she heard horse and rider approach.

"Brandt! Eli Brandt!" came the harsh shout of an angry voice that sounded to come from some distance away. "Make yourself ready, Brandt, and step on outside!" Maria unlatched the door, slowly pushed it open, and stepped cautiously out.

"Mister Brandt's not here!" Maria shouted as she looked quickly around to determine from where the voice had come.

"This is Charlie Davies," came the voice from behind the corner of the barn. "I come for your husband, Ma'am."

"I know," Maria said flatly.

Davies stepped from behind the barn and lowered the rifle that he had held at the ready. Carefully surveying the surrounding area, he walked slowly toward Maria with a noticeable favoring of his left leg.

"Where is your husband, Ma'am?" Charlie asked in the quiet politeness he always used when addressing a lady.

"He's not been here since you all rode off a few days ago," Maria replied as Davies abruptly stopped his approach and stood staring at Maria's battered and swollen face.

Blinking away his stare, Charlie felt his gut twist and tighten at the sight of Maria's face and the thought of how it had likely happened. Charlie Davies was a hard and rugged man and had never backed away from a fight, both giving and taking his share of cuts, bruises, and bullet holes. But, the thought of someone beating a woman turned his stomach and prompted deep rumblings of anger and loathing toward any man who would commit such brutal violence. Charlie shifted uncomfortably as he reached for the crown of his hat and pulled the dusty Stetson off his head. Turning slightly to avoid looking directly at Maria, he gazed toward the horizon, shielding his eyes with the hat he held in his hand.

"Mr. Brandt do that to you?"

Maria said nothing, and Charlie silently cussed himself for his rudeness.

"Sorry, Ma'am," Charlie said as he placed his hat back on his head and snugged it down.

"That young cowboy you all tended to," Charlie continued with his quiet drawl, "well Ma'am, he died yesterday. I come here intendin' to even up the score like I promised, but I reckon that ain't happenin' today. If you're stickin' round, you tell your ol' man I'll be turnin' this whole blamed mess over to the Territorial Marshal, Marshal E. D. Nix. I'm headed back to Texas."

Maria stood unmoving and silent as Mister Davies turned and headed back toward the barn. She heard his horse quietly whicker as he approached. As she watched him limp slowly away, Charlie stopped and turned toward her once more.

"The boy okay?"

"Yes. He's fine. Thank you."

Charlie's gaze dropped to the toe of his boot as he rubbed the back of his neck with his gloved hand. "Ever been to Texas?" Charlie asked, peering up from under the brim of his hat.

"No, but maybe someday," Maria answered.

Charlie tugged at his hat brim and nodded as he turned back toward his horse. Maria raised her hand in acknowledgment, but Charlie didn't see Maria's shy wave, nor did he see the slight smile that crossed her lips.

Chapter 6

Maria sat on the ground in the late afternoon shadows that lay long and black like quilt blocks attached to the base of sod walls. An early fall breeze carried the scent of distant rain across the prairie. The fresh, clean smell mixed with pungent sage, and the subtle aroma of cedar was a soothing balm for Maria. With eyes closed, she leaned back against the cooling dirt walls and drew long, deep breaths to fill her lungs with the healing fragrance of Mother Earth and wondered if the air smelled as sweet in Texas.

Jacob, in uncharacteristic exuberance, darted back and forth across the yard, around the soddy, and over the earthen mound above the root cellar. With the carefree abandon of childhood play, he squealed with delight as squawking hens scattered before him in a flurry of dust and feathers. Jacob swung his rope high overhead while closing the gap between himself and the hapless chicken he pursued.

"Ky, Yi, Yi," Jacob shouted as he let his loop fly, then stopped short in stoop-shouldered disappointment as the coil fell short of its mark and the panicked hen fluttered to freedom.

For a small boy afraid to laugh or run and shout, a day can seem like a week or a week an eternity. Jacob did not know how long his papa had been gone. He only knew that a great, pressing weight had been lifted. In the lightness of being released, he felt as if he could fly, fly like the hawks that sailed above the prairie on outstretched wings. He had learned, long ago, that when his papa wasn't around, Mama was more playful. When Papa wasn't around, laughter was more frequent, and Mama's eyes would sparkle when she smiled at him. There had been a lot of laughter and sparkling eyes today, and Jacob secretly wished for every day to be the same.

But Evie missed her papa and endlessly whined to Maria, "When's Papa coming home?"

"Papa will be back soon, Honey," Maria promised, not knowing if it were the truth or not.

Maria knew that Eli's absence would likely not continue. Although Eli had often been away overnight, this longer absence was unusual, and she was feeling anxious with the uncertainty of when Eli would return. A part of her hoped that he would never come back to the homestead and yet she knew, with dreadful certainty, that he would. She wondered why he had stayed away these past five days. Had he known that Nate's wound was fatal? Was he hiding out somewhere in the hills, keeping an eye on the place? Had he seen Mister Davies? Or had he just up and left for good, leaving her and Jacob and Evie behind? The thought of Eli being gone for good both pleased her and frightened her. Maria thought of what a relief it would be to no longer have to tolerate the painful beatings that she suffered whenever she was within reach of Eli's rage. She thought of the freedom she might enjoy, freedom from the abuse of Eli's crude, carnal demands that had resulted in two painful miscarriages in the four years since Evie had been born. And yet, as she daydreamed of the freedom she might find, the all too familiar feelings of doubt and fear began to darken the bright glimmerings of hope that she held.

Where would I go? Maria silently asked herself. *What would I do? How could I take care of Jacob, Evie, and myself? Would anyone really want to take on an Indian woman and her half-breed children?*

Both pride and shame kept her from returning to her family for help or rescue. She knew in her heart that she could not stay, and yet she had no place to go. And so, the battle within was settled with the tragic but stoic resolve to stay and endure.

The shadows that stretched from the base of the soddy walls had grown longer as the sun sat low on the rolling prairie hills. A gentle north-easterly breeze caused Maria to shiver as goosebumps raised the hair on her arms and reminded her that October brought a crisp edge to the chill of evening shadows. Leaning against the wall of the soddy, she watched Jacob's distorted shadow stretch from the earthen corner of the soddy across the dusty yard. The long and lanky shadow crouched in ambush with a spindly arm cocked overhead. Suddenly, with a quick jerk, the shadow launched a coil of rope that miraculously settled around the neck of a fat Banty hen that had been dusting herself in one of the final remaining fingers of sunlight. Startled by the flying rope, the hen scrambled to her feet and began a frantic retreat just as Jacob jerked the slack. With its neck broken, the old hen flopped helplessly at the end of the rope while Jacob whooped and hollered, "Stretch 'im out, boys and lay on the iron!"

Maria laughed out loud at Jacob's delight in roping the chicken. As she rushed to the flopping chicken held tightly in Jacob's well-placed loop, she clapped her hands in applause. "Well, my little cowboy, guess we'll be having fried chicken for supper!" Maria exclaimed, lifting the hen over her head as if it were the prize from a great victory. Jacob strutted beside her as they marched ceremoniously to the chopping block.

The aroma of chicken, deep-fried in bubbling butter, filled the soddy as it sizzled and steamed in the cast iron dutch oven that sat atop the cookstove. Jacob helped Evie carefully lay plates and flatware on the table as Maria tended to the cooking. As she lifted the lid of the dutch oven to check the progress of the frying chicken, the door burst open with the rattle of rough sawn planks and worn hinges. Maria, startled by the unexpected suddenness of the banging door, shrieked in panic as the cast iron lid clattered sharply on the stovetop, rolled off the edge, and landed with a thud on the dirt floor. Instinctively she rushed toward the children. Jacob stood statue-like at the end of the table with a fork held suspended over the place where he had intended to lay it down.

Evie shrieked with joy. "Papa!" she cried and ran to Eli who scooped her up with his hands and held her to his chest as she wrapped her arms around his neck.

"How's my little princess?" Eli crooned, then set her on the floor and gently patted her backside, sending her back into the room.

Eli stood, unmoving yet menacingly in the doorway as he glared at Maria with a cold and hate-filled stare. A thick layer of dust covered Eli's face and exaggerated the evil look of red-rimmed eyes irritated by sun, wind, and dust. Pulling his hat off his head, Eli slapped it sharply against the legs of his overalls. Dust billowed from the hat's crown and tumbled down the folds of denim to the hard-packed dirt floor.

"Fetch my tobacco, boy!" Eli demanded as he hung the misshapen Stetson on the peg beside the door.

Jacob let the fork he held in his hand clatter to the table as he rushed to the drawer that held Eli's supply of tobacco. Scurrying back across the room to Eli, Jacob stopped just out of reach and held the pouch of tobacco at arm's length.

Eli snatched the pouch from Jacob's outstretched fingers then grabbed his wrist. Hunkering down on his heels, he pulled Jacob toward him and roughly tousled his short-cropped hair. "Good boy!" Eli intoned as if he were praising a dog for retrieving a downed prairie chicken.

Jacob squirmed away from Eli's rough grip and sidled up next to Maria, finding comfort in her soft cotton apron against his cheek.

"God-damned Mama's boy!" Eli grumbled as he stood and pulled his pipe from his jacket pocket and crossed the room toward Maria.

Maria backed away as Eli approached but relaxed when he stopped and pulled his chair away from the table. Swinging one leg over the back, like mounting a horse, Eli sat and began to fill his pipe.

"Fix me up a pot of coffee!" Eli ordered. "Is supper ready yet?"

"It's ready," Maria answered, amazed at the way Eli acted as though he had just come in from an afternoon in the field instead of a five-day absence.

"Damn well better be!" Eli growled as he struck a match and took several quick puffs to light his pipe. Thick smoke encircled his head as he shook out the match flame. "I'm hungry 'nuff to eat a horse!"

Visions of Charlie Davies's dead horse lying just outside the door flashed through Maria's head. A giddy smile welled up inside her, amused by the thought of serving horsemeat to Eli for supper. Maria took another plate from the cupboard, a knife, fork, and spoon from the cabinet drawer, and handed them to Jacob.

"Set these at your papa's place," Maria instructed Jacob as she pointed toward the table with her chin.

Jacob carefully placed each piece in front of his papa. Eli leaned back on his chair with hands clasped behind his head and took a long leisurely pull on his pipe.

"It's a damn shame," Eli began as he took the pipe from his mouth, "that I have to be so rough. If you'd just do what I tell you to do and be a hell of a lot more respectful, it wouldn't be so hard for you."

Maria said nothing as she began to take the chicken from the pan. *I guess maybe it's my fault that he gets so mad,* Maria thought.

"That Davies fellow from the Anchor-D came by yesterday," Maria began as if ignoring Eli's words. "Said that boy you shot, died."

"That's his own damn fault," Eli replied. "Shouldn't have been trespassin' on my place, makin' threats on me!"

"Davies said he's turned the matter over to the territorial Marshal."

"Humph!" Eli snorted. "He likely won't be 'round these parts for months to come. But, 'peers like to me, you've done fixed things up so's we'll have to be leavin' here. If you'd of been the wife you're supposed to be…" Eli let the accusation hang in the air like the heavy stench of stale tobacco that filled the room. "I'd be doin' myself a favor if I left you here to rot into the ground with the rest of the buffalo dung." Eli leaned forward, with his elbows resting on the edge of the table; he took the pipe from between his teeth and, pointing the stem accusingly at Maria, continued his thinly disguised threat. "You ever cross me again, woman, it'll be your last."

"What the hell!" Eli bellowed as he slammed his fist on the table. "Ain't no good reason for stickin' 'round these parts anyhow. Ought to give this whole shit pile of a territory back to the god-damned injuns!"

Maria spoke not a word but went about the task of finishing the preparations of the evening meal. What had begun as a celebration of Jacob's successful chicken roping had become as solemn as a wake. Laughter had slunk into dingy corners the moment Eli had darkened the doorway. Jacob had retreated to the far side of the room, where he sat cross-legged on the floor, repeatedly tossing his rawhide loop over the dipper handle that stood above the rim of the water bucket. He watched as his mama transformed from a brightly colored songbird whose cheerful tune had filled the space between dawn and dusk with merry laughter into a broken-winged prairie hen that kept a constant, wary-eyed watch for expected danger.

Jacob felt an unexplained tightness inside at the place where he knew his heart lay. The tightness tugged at his chest and crept upward to his shoulders and neck. It gripped his throat like the choking off of a scream and sent hot tears rolling down his cheeks. It was the first time that he had recognized the overwhelming sadness and deep anger that he held inside. He did not fully understand the dark transformation that his mama so often went through, but he did know that his papa caused it. However, along with the sadness and anger, he did not yet understand the spark of reverent fear that he had for his papa who held so much power over the lives of others.

Chapter 7

Charlie Davies pulled the latigo through the cinch ring, snugged it up with both hands, looped the end through the saddle ring, and finished off the resulting knot with a solid thump, using the heel of his hand to secure the expertly laced strip of leather. Lifting the stirrup off the horn, he let the fender fall, then resting his arm across the cantle, stopped to watch a small flock of southbound geese. Charlie marveled at their seemingly effortless flight, an admiration that he had always had for the graceful Canadians. The early morning sky was a high clouded and steel gray, appropriate for the beginning of a cool October day. The willows by the creek had already taken on the yellow of fall, and scrub oak splashed scattered shades of red across the Oklahoma hills. The small flock of migrating geese reminded him that it was high time he was headed south himself. He had planned to leave for Texas over three weeks ago, but final arrangements had taken longer than expected. Nate had been in the ground nearly a month now and Charlie often found himself missing the boy's company.

The past month Charlie had spent with making sure that the holdings of the Anchor-D in Oklahoma Territory were up to snuff and ready to be handed off to the new foreman. The two-year-olds had been shipped, yearlings were in the north pastures, and bred cows had been separated and stocked in pastures to the south. He had made sure that all windmills were oiled and tanks were holding, fences in good repair, corrals in top shape, and the more than 600 head of Longhorn-Hereford cross cattle were winter-ready.

The Territorial Marshal had not been through D County lately and so Charlie had written a deposition and left it with the postmaster in Taloga. Charlie had heard of Deputy Marshal Heck Thomas's posse bringing in Bill Doolin's body and hoped that Marshal Nix would dispatch him to the panhandle.

Charlie's biggest job had been to keep a rein on Bo's temper. Since Nate's killing, Bo had talked of little else but revenge and Charlie had coaxed, cajoled, and threatened in order to keep Bo from carrying out his vengeful plans. He had hoped that the Marshal would have been around long before now, taken care of the Brandt problem, and left Bo with nothing to do but let the law handle it. But now, Charlie was long overdue at headquarters in Texas, and the best solution was for Bo to go along. Once he and Bo were gone from Oklahoma, chances were that Bo would forget about revenge for Nate's killing and settle into the routine of wintering in a west Texas cow camp.

"Bo, Hey Bo," Charlie said, watching the flock of geese pass overhead, "Got a question for you."

"What?" Bo replied as he swung his saddle up onto his horse's back.

"See that flock of geese up yonder?" Charlie said as he pointed skyward.

"Yep, what about it?"

"Know why the right side of that vee is shorter than the left?"

Bo gazed at the passing formation of flapping black spots and pondered Charlie's question as he lifted his hat and scratched his head as if the rigorous scalp massage might bring about the right answer. Shaking his head as he pulled his hat back on, Bo replied, "Nope, Charlie. Don't know. Why?"

"'Cause it's got fewer geese in it!" Charlie said with mock superiority.

"Damn you, Davies!" Bo grumbled as he scooped up a dry horse apple and threw it at Charlie with intentionally poor aim. Charlie ducked and burst into a fit of laughter as it sailed past. Charlie tried but was having a hard time to keep from laughing as Bo glared indignantly at being the butt of his joke.

"We best be getting' a move on," Charlie said, trying to be a bit more serious. "Them geese will be crossing the Red long before we do."

Bo finished saddling his horse and was tying his heavy coat behind the cantle as Charlie grabbed the lead rope of the packhorse and swung astride his pony.

"Say, Charlie," Bo said as he tucked the toe of his left boot in the stirrup and swung his leg across the saddle, "I'm gonna ride into town. See if them boots I ordered come in yet. If not, I'll have ol' man Butler forward 'em on. I'll catch up with you at the crossin' on Rawhide Creek."

"Meet you there," Charlie agreed. "Rawhide Creek."

"You know, Charlie," Bo mused, "maybe I'll just keep on goin' north, way north, see if there's any gold left up in that Klondike country. Hear tell folks is picking up nuggets just layin' there on the ground. Maybe I could ring in the twentieth century as a millionaire 'stead of a dollar a day cowpoke."

"Suit yourself, Bo, but I ain't waitin' on you," Charlie said sternly. "If you ain't there when I am, I'm keepin' on south. I'll stop an' camp just before dark."

"Ah hell, Charlie, I'll be at the crossin'. Texas winters are plenty cold enough for me. I ain't hankerin' to freezin' to death in Alaska. See ya at the crossin'."

Charlie nudged his horse to a walk and headed south. Bo slapped his hat across his horse's withers and spurred him to a quick, dust-raising gallop toward town. Bo continued east until he was out of sight from the bunkhouse and the trail that Charlie was taking. Then, turning north and veering back to the west, Bo headed directly toward the Brandt place.

****

"Dammit, boy! I said you'll ride in the wagon with your mama," Eli roared. "I'll herd your pony with the rest of the horses. Maria! What the hell are you doin'? We ain't takin' all that shit. Put it down. Put it down now! Get some chickens in the crate and throw 'em on the wagon. Box up the cookin' things, fill the water barrels an' get my mama's clock an' the family Bible. Don't just stand there slack-jawed an' stupid, woman! I'm ridin' out to gather up the horses. We'll leave soon as I'm back an' if you ain't ready, by God, I'll leave ya here."

Eli had made the announcement that they were leaving the Territory and heading up Kansas way just that morning, as he had lit his pipe after wolfing down a substantial breakfast. Maria had been taken by surprise and felt both betrayed and trapped by Eli's sudden demands. However, for Eli, there was no other option but to leave, like an animal that abandons a soiled nest.

Eli's life had been filled with soiled nests, and the easiest solution had always been to leave the old behind and start anew. But men like Eli Brandt don't ever truly find new beginnings. Perhaps their backs are too rigid, their minds too set and their necks too stiff to ever really start fresh. The old ways, the old habits, and the old demons that are just as much a part of life as breathing out and breathing in, are always there to pull the Eli Brandts back into the muck. And all they leave behind are scars.

50

Now, once again, Eli had found himself in a situation far too complicated to sort out or resolve, and so it was time to go. Eli had told Maria that he knew people in Northeastern Kansas, and there was still land available along a stretch of river called The Blue, a part of the country where his parents had settled years ago. His hope was that it was far enough away from the Territory to make pursuit impractical, that is if the Territorial Marshal decided to pursue the matter at all. After all, Eli reasoned, no one had any proof of cattle rustling and as for the shooting, it was Davies's men who had fired first, self-defense for certain.

Maria stood in the doorway with a look of anger and bewilderment. In her hands, she held a wooden box containing scraps of memories accumulated over seven long years. There were Oklahoma rose stones gathered during solitary walks among the hills of red dirt and crude hand-made toys that she had fashioned for Jacob and Evie's amusement and play. There were feathers, bones, and other objects that had caught her fancy and ended up in what she thought of as her box of smiles, the box that Eli had just demanded that she "put down now!" She turned and walked stiffly back inside the soddy and set the box on top of the old cast-iron cookstove, another item that would not be loaded on the wagon. Standing in front of the stove, she leaned heavily on the edges of the wooden box, her calloused hands gripping the top of each side. Taking a deep breath, she drew herself up until her spine was straight and her shoulders back, then let her breath out in a single, long, slow-release. Before resuming her hurried packing and loading, she reached in the box and took out a scuffed silver concho that she had found, not long ago, in the dust in front of the soddy. The concho had been made from a large Mexican coin and was used as a decoration on a saddle. In addition to the engraved scallops around the coin's edge, the engraver had etched the initials C. D.

Maria turned the concho between her thumb and fingers, thoughtfully rubbing her thumb across the engraving, then tossed it back into the box. Picking the box up with forceful determination, she turned around and headed through the door and toward the wagon. Her box of smiles was going to Kansas.

Chapter 8

Eli had left to gather up the horses, and Jacob was walking toward the wagon with both hands gripped tightly around the feet of a flapping, squawking chicken. Maria opened the hatch of the chicken coop so Jacob could stuff the reluctant hen inside. After losing more than a few feathers, the hen angrily clucked her displeasure while Maria slid the hatch closed. Jacob shook a few clinging pin feathers from off his fingers, then wiped his runny nose on the sleeve of his too small flannel shirt and rubbed his teary eyes with the heels of his hands.

"Why won't Papa let me ride my pony to Kansas?" Jacob pleaded. "I could help with the horses too."

"Your papa's got his own mind of how things are to be done," Maria tried to explain. "You'll just have to do as he says, and maybe you can ride along later. We'll see."

Jacob shrugged his shoulders as he struggled to hold back the tears that pooled in his eyes and bit his lower lip to stop its quivering. "I just wanna help," Jacob sobbed.

"You can help me," Maria suggested. "I need someone strong, like you, to be with me in the wagon. I'll teach you to drive the team, and you can take the reins when I get tired. And Evie will need someone to keep her company too. It's a long way to Kansas. Okay?"

"I reckon," Jacob conceded as Maria ruffled his hair with her hand then gently squeezed his shoulder.

"It'll be okay, Son."

"Okay," Jacob said, with hands stuffed in his pockets and head down, watching himself scratch at the dirt with his toe.

"Okay then," Maria said cheerfully. "Now, come on, cowboy. Let's get this wagon loaded, so we're ready to go when your papa gets back with the horses. Let's catch a few more chickens, then you go get the old milk cow haltered and lead her to the wagon. I'll pack our grub, get our cooking pots together, and fold up the bedding."

"Yes, Ma'am," Jacob replied with a quick smile.

"Evie!" Maria called, "Where are you?"

"Here, Mama," Evie answered as she came running around the corner of the shed. "Here I am."

"Will you help me in the kitchen?" Maria asked.

"Sure, Mama."

Maria and Evie went toward the soddy while Jacob headed to the barn for the cow.

"What about more chickens," Jacob shouted over his shoulder.

"We'll get those later," Maria called back.

The wagon was loaded, the team hitched, and the old milk cow was tethered to the back of the wagon box when Eli and his small herd of horses topped the rise beyond the soddy. Maria stood in the doorway where she had been remembering the years that she had spent there.

The old sod-built cabin was crumbling with age and disrepair as the seasons had taken their toll. Layers of old newspapers, gathered from infrequent trips to town, covered the inside walls where Maria had carefully smoothed new over old as she attempted to keep the walls looking fresh and clean. The muslin sheets, billowing like ship sails from the roof beams, were long past due for a washing and hung dusty and smoke-stained above the hard-packed dirt floor.

Six years, Maria thought. *Six years and still no permanent ceiling, no plastered walls, and no wood-planked floors.*

The heavy cast-iron cookstove stood cold and solitary in the corner. The oven door hung askew on the broken hinge that Maria had tried to fix with a rusty piece of barbed wire. She wondered if there would be a new stove in Kansas or if that eight-year-old promise would also remain broken. The rough-hewn table and chairs, cupboards, and other meager furnishings stood stark and gray in the mid-morning light that sifted through the open door and single glass-paned window. The meager belongings that could not be fit into the wagon were scattered around the room. Some lay abandoned on the table while dusty cupboard shelves held cracked cups, broken bowls, and chipped amber-colored Mason jars.

Jacob came and stood beside his mother in the doorway, looking in at the cluttered emptiness that was surrounded by dirt. There was dirt seeping through the yellowed newspapers on every wall, dirt sifting down through dusty sheets and onto plates and pillows and down the backs of those who sat below. Staring into the gaping darkness, Jacob thought of the dead horse that he and Maria had buried in the ravine, surrounded by dirt.

Jacob reached up and took hold of his mother's hand. Maria gently squeezed his hand and looked down at his upturned face, and he saw the tears that streaked down her cheeks, and in his youthful heart, he knew that in this place was sadness.

Maria reached for the rope handle of the plank door and as she slowly pushed it closed, glanced one last time at the things she had left behind that cluttered the surface of the thick pine mantle above the soot-blackened fireplace. Maria turned away as one side of her mouth curled up in a half-smile, and she winked at Jacob.

"Let's go, Jacob!" Maria said with sudden excitement, gripping Jacob's hand and pulling him toward the wagon.

"I've heard stories told that up in Kansas there are flowers that grow taller than a man, with stalks as thick as your arm and flowers as big as a plate and as bright yellow as the sun!"

"Really!" Jacob exclaimed in wide-eyed disbelief.

"Yes, really!" Maria said in a whisper as if it were a secret.

"Quit your damned jabbering!" Eli commanded, riding up behind Maria and Jacob.

The two of them ducked instinctively, unaware that Eli was behind them, then turned and scurried toward the wagon.

"Get your lazy carcass up on the wagon and get a move on," Eli continued, giving his orders for departure as the lathered stallion pranced nervously under a too-tight rein.

A dozen horses skittered rambunctiously around the barn and empty corrals. Half of the small herd was pregnant mares, the other half, one and two-year-old colts and fillies, all offspring of Eli's Jack-of-Diamonds. It was from the sale of the young horses that Eli planned to stake his new beginnings in Kansas.

Eli rode a tight circle around the horses, crowding them together, then letting them get lined out as he pushed them north. An older mare took the lead and the others followed behind, settling into their natural order of dominance. When Eli was satisfied that the horses were all following the lead mare, he turned the stallion around and galloped back to the wagon. Reining up beside the wagon's high mounted spring seat, he reached down and lifted Evie off the seat and onto the saddle in front of him.

"There you go, little lady, you can ride along with Papa for a while," Eli said sweetly. Then turning his attention to Maria, he growled, "Get a move on, woman! You gonna just sit there all day lookin' stupid?"

"Gi up!" Maria called out sharply as she slapped the lines across the backs of the team and the wagon lurched forward. With another crack of the lines, the team stepped out in a brisk canter and quickly passed the band of horses trailing alongside the rutted two-track road.

The horses and wagon stirred up a swirl of red dust that rose up behind them and was picked up by a towering dust devil that spiraled into the cloudless autumn sky like a small red tornado. Jacob held onto his hat with one hand and squinted skyward to watch a pair of hawks ride the thermals above the swirling dust. Maria tugged lightly on the lines, and the team slowed to an easy trot ahead of Eli, Evie, and the horses.

"They're sending us off with a blessing," Maria said, nudging Jacob on the shoulder as she lifted her eyes toward the sky.

"The hawks carry our prayers to the spirit world," Maria said softly. "Tell them your prayers, Jacob."

Jacob watched as the hawks spiraled higher and higher and were soon out of his sight, and he wondered if there was someone in the spirit world who was really listening.

"Quit fillin' the boy's head with that damned injun' bull-shit!" Eli snapped as he unexpectedly rode up beside them. "Boy," Eli admonished, "don't you pay no mind to that hocus pocus spirit talk. Ain't no damn birds carryin' prayers no place. You'd best be rememberin' that!"

Eli snapped the reins across the stallion's withers and galloped back toward the horses. Jacob turned around in the wagon seat to see if he could spot his pony among the herd and make sure he was keeping up. From his vantage point on the wagon and the crest of a hill they were crossing, Jacob could see the homestead nestled among the hills in the distance. There was smoke rolling out of the opened door of the soddy and flames leapt from the barn.

"Papa, Papa," Jacob shouted, pointing to the rising smoke, "our house is on fire!"

Maria jerked herself around on the wagon seat in time to see a lone rider disappear into a long, narrow draw between the rock hills behind the barn. Heavy gray smoke billowed from the soddy's door and broken window, and bright flames licked at the cracks between the pine boards of the barn. While they watched, a burst of flame shot from the weather-worn boards of the barn and engulfed the entire building in bright orange fire.

Jacob sat stock-still on the wagon seat, his mouth hung open in confused amazement.

"I'll be damned!" Eli exclaimed as he stood in the stirrups, Evie gripping the horn with both hands. "That son-of-a-bitch Davies!"

But suddenly, Eli was laughing. At first, just a closed mouth, short chuckle, and then an all-out belly-laugh as Eli threw back his head and slapped the side of his leg. When his laughter subsided, Eli turned toward a bewildered-looking Maria who just shook her head and frowned.

"What?" Maria asked, not understanding Eli's outburst of laughter.

"Oh my," Eli said as he wiped the tears from his eyes with a gloved hand, "Davies thinks he's burning me out, stupid son-of-a-bitch. I've already sold the damned place. Money's in my pocket! Ain't no skin off me. Quit gawkin', woman, and get a move on!" Eli growled.

Maria gripped the lines in her hands. "Gi-up!" she commanded. As the team settled into a steady walk, Maria felt the unmistakable flutter of new life. She had feared that it might be and had hoped that it wasn't, but she knew the feeling from twice before. Gripping both sets of lines in one hand, Maria pressed the other against her belly. A thin smile creased her pressed lips as a single tear tumbled down her cheek. Reaching across the wagon seat, she put her hand on Jacob's knee and with a bright twinkling of her dark eyes gave him a warm and reassuring smile.

New life and new land, Maria thought. *Perhaps things will be better in Kansas.*

With a deep breath of determination and resolve, Maria took the lines with both hands and slapped them smartly across the backs of the horses. As the wagon dropped out of view of the burning homesite, Maria pictured Eli's clock, flames lapping at its scorched face as it sat in its revered place on the thick pine mantle.

Chapter 9

Eli pushed the small band of horses north at a pace much faster than Maria was able to maintain with the team and wagon. She wondered if Eli was more anxious to reach Kansas or leave Oklahoma, but it was obvious from the start that they likely would not be traveling together. Eli had left Evie with the wagon and pushed the horses farther and farther ahead.

Jacob watched intently as his papa drove the herd forward, slapping his coiled rope sharply against the heavy leather chaps that he wore. The snap of rawhide rope on leather chaps caused a shuddering of fear to ripple through the herd as they stretched their muscled necks forward and thrust velvet muzzles into the false freedom that lay ahead. Jacob watched as his pony strained to keep up with the long strides of the other horses and winced in sympathy when a dun-colored mare snapped a hunk of flesh from his pony's rump.

Jacob still hurt from the disappointment of being forbidden to ride his pony and help his papa move the horses. Now, watching his pony struggle to maintain a place in the herd caused him even greater hurt. Under the push of Eli's urgent pace, he and the horses had gradually traveled beyond the crest of the rolling horizon that lay ahead and soon disappeared in the shimmer of rising waves of midday heat.

"Mama," Jacob asked, "Do you think Papa will let me ride with him tomorrow?"

"We'll be traveling for a long time, Jacob," Maria replied. "Maybe not tomorrow, but surely in a couple of days, your papa will let you saddle Little Bit and ride along. Just be patient and try not to aggravate your papa, okay?"

Maria turned to see a single tear cut a path down Jacob's dusty cheek before he could wipe it away with the sleeve of his shirt. She reached across the wagon seat and touched Jacob's cheek with the back of her hand. She saw the hurt in Jacob's eyes and wanted to tell him that she understood. She wanted to tell him that she knew of the pain that gripped his heart and choked out the joys that should be a part of young boy's growing up. She wanted to tell him that, someday, everything would be all right, but in her heart, she feared that it would not be so. Despite all that she wanted to tell him, Maria said nothing as she forced a smile from her thin lips and let her own tears cut clean paths down dusty cheeks.

The tracks left by Eli and his band of horses were easy for Maria to follow. Although Eli had not told her where they would camp, she was certain they were heading toward Cedar Springs on the old Western Trail. Eli had trailed far ahead of the wagon and it had been dark for nearly an hour when Maria and Jacob pulled into camp. Eli sat silhouetted by the campfire as he lay back against the swell of his saddle.

Maria heard the contented nicker of horses as they grazed unseen beyond the curtain of darkness that surrounded the fire. Inside the circle of flickering light, Eli rose from beside the fire and tossed the burning stick he held into the welcoming flames. Evie jumped from her perch on the wagon and rushed forward to meet Eli. He knelt on one knee as she ran to him and wrapped her arms around his neck. For a brief moment, Maria had a hopeful feeling that the peaceful setting just might hold a warm welcome.

Eli stood and walked briskly toward the wagon, "Where the hell have you been, woman!" Eli fumed as he grabbed the lines of the offside horse and jerked them from Maria's hands.

"Get your lazy ass down off that wagon and get to fixin' supper. When I make camp at night, I damn well expect you to be there and supper ready made. Jake, you ain't done a damned thing all day long. Now get out there and gather up some firewood for the night."

"We can't keep up if you're going to push the horses like that." Maria countered.

"Don't sass me, woman!" Eli barked as he took the ends of the lines and slapped Maria sharply across her legs.

Jacob jumped from the wagon seat to the ground and quickly disappeared into the safety of darkness. Maria winced as the sharp pain on her legs intensified and spread like the sting of cactus nettles.

"A team and wagon cannot keep up the pace you set," Maria insisted through clenched teeth.

The sudden bite of leather across Maria's cheek brought instant tears. Gathering the folds of her dress in her cramped and tired hands, Maria stood in the wagon, crossed to the other side, and resolutely stepped from wheel spoke to the ground. The glistening of tears intensified the glaring fire that burned in her dark eyes, a fire of bitterness and contempt that burned hotter than the angry welt that rose, red and raw, on her cheek. Walking stiffly to the back of the wagon, Maria arched her back to relieve the cramping from the constant jostling of a long day on the wagon seat. As Eli settled himself next to the campfire, Maria struggled with the bulk of the heavy wooden camp box that she had unlashed from the back of the wagon. As she dragged the box from the wagon toward the fire, Eli leaned back against his saddle, touched a long dry twig to flames, and leisurely lit his pipe.

"Jacob," Eli hollered into the darkness, "bring me more wood for the fire and get the damned harness off them horses while your Ma's fixin' supper."

Jacob appeared at the edge of the darkness, his lanky arms wrapped tightly around an unwieldy bundle of firewood. He walked to the fire where Maria busily unpacked the camp box and dropped the armload of gathered wood at Eli's feet.

"Papa," Jacob spoke softly as he stared into the orange flames, "can I ride with you tomorrow? Can I please?"

"By damn, boy! Just do what you're told. Unharness them horses and get them brushed down and grained. You'll ride with me when I say and your damned whining ain't gonna make that happen any time sooner. Now get back out there and bring in more wood for the fire. That piddly-assed little pile you brought in ain't near enough for the night. Get to it, boy. Now!"

Jacob's shoulders slumped as he turned and shuffled slowly toward the wagon, kicking the toe of his boot into the ground as he went. Maria knelt beside the camp box and began unpacking the cast iron tripod and the pots and pans she'd need to prepare the evening's meal. Evie huddled in the shadows beside Eli, pulling her knees to her chest and resting her chin there.

"What harm is there in letting the boy ride with you?" Maria quietly asked. "He's old enough to be of some help to you and you know how he loves to ride."

"God-dammit, woman! Can't a man have any peace? The boy will do as I damn well say and learn just who the hell it is that's in charge 'round here. I thought you'd have figured that out for yourself by now. Ain't you learned a damned thing? What I say goes and that's the whole of it. Jesus Christ, woman, ain't you ever gonna learn when to keep your damned mouth shut?"

Jacob unharnessed the horses and draped the heavy tangles of leather and buckles neatly over the tongue of the wagon. After brushing the dust and drying sweat from the horses' withers and backs, he hobbled the pair then quietly slipped into the darkness beyond the camp.

Jacob was remembering the day his Grandfather Little Wolf had brought him the beautiful white pinto with black and brown patches. He remembered how his mama had wrapped her arms around Grandfather Little Wolf's neck and laughed out loud as he whirled her in a circle. When he set her back down on the ground, he motioned for Jacob to come to him and, taking him by the hand, led him to the back of the buggy where the pony was tied. The pony had worn a brightly colored blanket across his back and a single eagle feather in his mane.

"He belongs to you, Jacob," Grandfather Little Wolf said as he ran his hand down the paint's strong back. "You care for him like you should, and he will take care of you. He's just a little bit of a horse," Grandfather Little Wolf had said, "but he's just your size for now."

Jacob remembered how Grandfather and Grandmother Little Wolf had been quick to leave soon after his papa came home.

"When my boy's ready for a horse, I'll get him a real god-damned horse," Eli had told Grandfather Little Wolf, "not some half-sized good for nothin' damned injun' pony!"

Grandmother Little Wolf and Maria were crying when they left and Grandfather Little Wolf was tight-lipped as he climbed into the buggy. Eli had let him keep the pony, but it was always a battle to get permission to ride whenever Eli was around.

With a low whistle, Jacob called in his pony and quickly located him as he heard the soft whicker of recognition. With head held high and ears turned forward, the pony trotted in from out of the darkness.

"How are ya, boy?" Jacob crooned softly as he rubbed the pony's cheeks and neck and scratched him playfully behind the ears. "You doin' okay?"

Jacob rubbed his hands over the pony's back, rump, and legs to check for any signs of injury. He felt the small flap of skin on the pony's rump where the old mare had nipped him earlier that morning. Little Bit flinched as Jacob's hand snagged the torn flesh but held steady and trusting while Jacob continued to stroke his neck and untangle his twisted mane.

A light westerly breeze brought a welcomed cooling to the end of an unseasonably warm, early autumn day. A rising moon cast its soft twilight glow over the rolling sea of prairie grass. Horses grazed undisturbed with only an occasional stomping of hooves or swishing of tails to dissuade persistent flies. Little Bit tucked his muzzle into Jacob's armpit and, with a toss of his head, pushed Jacob backward and sat him down with a thump in the tall prairie grass.

"Hey, Little Bit! Cut it out!" Jacob scolded with mock severity as he pulled himself up off the ground.

Taking a handful of mane, Jacob swung himself easily up and across his pony's back and, tucking his heels tightly just behind his pony's forelegs, the two raced away from the burdens of camp and deeper into the thrill of darkness where thought of gathering firewood quickly vanished. Jacob felt the power in his pony's stride as muscle rippled beneath his thighs in cadence to the rhythmic pounding of unshod hooves on soft prairie sod. The cooling touch of night rushed past his face, caressing his cheeks and drawing wind-blown tears from the corners of his eyes. Coarse clumps of the pony's mane spilled in a tangle from between the fingers of Jacob's clenched fists, an intermingling of hide and flesh, horse and boy, careless freedom and reckless wildness. Into the night they rode, chasing the darkness that stretched before them and closed behind as they rode through. This was freedom, here, where the unbound spirits of horse and human flew fearlessly ahead, where hearts pounded with the thrill of simply being alive. This was freedom. This was where Jacob longed to always be. In this place, there were no split lips or bloody noses, no sting of leather straps or painful ridicule that left his heart weak and fluttering in the hollow of his chest.

Jacob wondered if his mama had such a place to go and thought that one day he would try to find the words that would explain to her the happiness, the joy, and the freedom that he felt when it was just him and his horse, when the world and all the ugliness in it melted away in the darkness.

Jacob heard the booming curses of his papa and the sharp snap of flesh on flesh as he slid off the sweat-lathered back of his pony. The other horses tossed their heads in annoyed curiosity or spooked and shied away, trotting off a short distance as Jacob walked through the herd and toward the campfire.

"…and just where the hell is that god-damned, good-for-nothin' spoiled little boy of yours?" Jacob heard the thunder of his papa's voice and watched as Eli jerked his mama toward him with one hand and slapped her across the mouth with the back of his other.

"Don't, Papa! Don't!" Jacob cried out as he ran from the darkness toward the fire. "Here I am!"

Eli flung Maria to the ground and wheeled around to face Jacob. Grabbing a stout stick from the dwindling pile of firewood, Eli snatched Jacob's hand in his giant fist and brandished the stick above his head as if he were about to kill a rattlesnake. The first blow cracked against Jacob's arm as he raised it to deflect the impact. Crying out from the sharp pain, Jacob doubled over, drawing his arm into his belly. The second blow landed across Jacob's shoulders and drove him to his knees.

"Get up off the ground, you whimpering sissy," Eli sneered. "You been out ridin' that damned horse, haven't ya? Now get out there and fetch the god-damned firewood like you're supposed to be doin'!"

"Woman!" Eli barked as he turned again toward Maria. "Throw the little shit's supper in the god-damned fire. He'll damn well go hungry until he learns to obey. By God, he'll learn to obey me, or he can starve to death."

"Your choice, boy," Eli continued as he jabbed Jacob in the ribs with the end of the stick. "Your choice. Either learn to obey, or I'll bury your bones somewhere out there. Somewhere out there," Eli threatened and waved the stick, like a scepter, out toward the darkness beyond the fire.

****

Jacob jerked violently from his fitful sleep as the dawn-splitting crack of rifle fire echoed across the prairie. He heard the panicked whinnying of horses and the earth pounding, rolling thunder of hoofbeats as the cavvy scattered in all directions away from camp. Frantically searching the surrounding hills and open prairie for the cause of the horses' sudden panic, Jacob first saw his mama running across the campsite. Was it wolves? A mountain lion? He heard the shrill scream that seemed to come not only from Maria's gaping mouth but also from the hills around them. The scream seemed to come at him from all sides, attacking him with its high-pitched terror. He looked out across the waves of grass and watched his papa jerk the lever of his Winchester and chamber another shell while raising the rifle to his shoulder.

It was then that Jacob saw the patch of black and white, thrashing violently in the tall grass and realized where the other screams had come from. The Winchester cracked again, and Jacob heard the words that Maria's shrieking voice had wrapped itself around.

"You son-of-a-bitch," she screamed, "I hope you rot in hell!"

Maria stopped short, her trembling hands covering her mouth, her eyes wide with fear when Eli turned and pointed the rifle at her breast.

"Shut your god-damned mouth, woman!"

Jacob sank to his knees, numb with pain and seething hate. He wanted to scream, but the emptiness inside him had no voice. He wanted to fight, to lash out with pounding fists, but his body had no strength. He closed his eyes against the sight of his pony thrashing on the ground, but the picture continued to burn vividly inside his head.

Jacob curled himself into the darkness behind his tightly closed eyes. He wrapped his arms around his knees, his head drawn in against his chest. He heard the grass rustle as his papa's boots sliced a path beside him, and he smelled the strong, sweet wisp of burnt gunpowder as Eli passed by.

As Eli passed the quivering, huddled heap that was his son, he pushed the muzzle of his rifle against Jacob's shoulder and spat out his venomous warning.

"By damn, boy, maybe that'll learn ya to do as I damn well say."

Chapter 10

Maria stood at the kitchen window watching the mid-June heat waves dance on the horizon and distort the sharp edges of the rising Kansas sun. The early morning light gave a soft glow of false youth to the harsh lines of weather and worry that marked her face. Silky strands of gray coursed through the blackness of her hair that hung full and loose across her shoulders and down her back. In her quiet musings, she slowly raised her hand to her face and, with her finger, traced the ridge of the white scar that ran from her high, sharp cheekbone down to the firm line of her jaw.

Kansas was neither much better nor any worse than Oklahoma had been, Maria thought as she retraced the long scar with her thumb. Certainly, the ground was better richer. Dark black soil and abundant rain produced lush pastures for horses and cattle and plenty of hay for winter feed. Eli's horses had not brought the prices he had hoped for and though they did amount to a sizable stake, he had still needed to take a mortgage on the place. A wood-framed, two-story house with barns and corrals was certainly a luxury but getting ahead seemed beyond possibilities and getting by did not come easily.

But Eli could not be satisfied and his constant displeasure had continued to be directed toward Maria and Jacob in outbursts of ever-increasing frequency, in violent and uncontrolled rage. Maria lived in constant fear of Eli's bruising attacks and yet held an unexplainable hope that perhaps someday it would all stop. Love had never been a part of her relationship with Eli, but still, she felt a perverse bond to him and ultimately, somehow responsible for his actions. They seldom spoke to one another in everyday conversation and maintained separateness in most domestic chores. Since Maria's second daughter Flora had been born eight years ago, after they had arrived in Kansas, Maria had somewhat managed to avoid Eli's crude advances by keeping Flora with her both day and night except for those times when his rage turned to lust, and she was unable to escape his overpowering strength. Eli would physically drag her to the barn or catch her, unawares, in the house when Flora, Evie, and Jacob were outside. He would bar the door to prevent any unexpected intrusion and have his way. But Maria's deepest regret came from being unable to prevent the abuse that Jacob endured.

Today was a Saturday and Jacob had been a bit slower than usual in getting out to hay the horses as he lay in bed contemplating a day to be spent outside the schoolhouse. The horses were feeling a bit rambunctious as they crowded into the corral, nipping and nudging each other for position at the feed bunk that Jacob had not yet filled. As Eli swung the corral gate closed, one of the overly exuberant horses bumped Eli from behind and slammed him into the gatepost.

"God-dammit, boy! What the hell are you doin'?" Eli growled. "You get the damned hay in the bunk before the damn horses get let in."

Eli crossed the corral and grabbed the pitchfork that Jacob held. Tightening his grip and flexing the muscles in his arm, Jacob's grip held firm on the handle and Eli was not able to jerk it free. A look of astonishment flashed across Eli's face and for a short, sudden moment, he and Jacob faced each other, pitchfork between them, in a brief stalemate. In that moment, Jacob realized that his strength had matched that of Eli's.

Eli suddenly realized that he would not be able to quickly jerk the pitchfork from Jacob's grasp and so he loosed his grip and shoved the pitchfork handle forward into Jacob's face. With Eli's sudden push and the tension of Jacob's resistance to Eli's grip, the pitchfork handle snapped back and cracked against Jacob's brow. The split skin spurted blood immediately as Jacob released his grip, dropped the pitchfork, staggered backward, and pressed his hand against his brow to hold back the sting and the gush of blood.

"You stupid son-of-a-bitch," Eli sneered. "You was born stupid and get more stupid every day! Now, finish haying these horses and go bleed somewhere else."

Eli picked up the pitchfork and snapped it forcefully back into Jacob's hand then headed into the barn. Jacob finished his chores and went to the house.

"Mornin', Sissy!" Jacob called playfully to Flora as he came through the kitchen door and carelessly tossed his hat onto the washstand.

"Mornin', Jake," Flora chirped, her dark eyes sparkling above her bright smile. Evie held the stack of dishes high on her chest with both hands gripped

66

tightly on the edges as she walked to the table and began to set each plate in its proper place.

"Breakfast is ready," Maria announced, turning her distracted gaze from out the window to greet Jacob. "Where's your pa?"

Jacob half turned to address his mother as he poured a pitcher of water into the blue enamel wash pan. "In the barn," Jacob replied flatly. "He's on his way in."

Maria watched as Jacob touched the washcloth to the rivulet of blood that streamed from the jagged and swelling cut above his eye. Rushing to him, Maria wordlessly took the cloth from Jacob. Holding Jacob's chin in her left hand, Maria pressed the bloodstained washcloth tightly against the bleeding gash above Jacob's eye. The damp coolness of the cloth soothed the sting while the steady pressure began to restrict the profuse flow of blood.

"Might need to take a stitch or two to hold that closed," Maria said matter-of-factly as she continued to apply pressure to the wound.

"It don't need no stitchin', Ma," Jacob protested. "It'll heal up fine without that. I'll just hold a rag to it till it stops bleedin'."

Jacob picked his hat up off the sink stand and hung it on the nearby peg.

"What was it provoked your Pa this time?" Maria asked.

"I don't know," Jacob answered with a shrugging of his shoulders. "Don't hardly take anything for him to build up to a mad anymore. I think he was born mad and just gets madder every day," Jacob replied in a tone that mimicked the cutting sarcasm of Eli's voice.

As Maria held the cloth to Jacob's forehead, she realized, for the first time, that they were standing eye-to-eye. At sixteen years, Jacob had already attained the stature of a grown man. Broad shoulders supported muscular arms and large rough hands, with a powerful, crushing grip developed through hard and constant work. His dark hair and black onyx eyes, sharp, rugged features, and the strong line of his jaw had replaced the boyish features of her memory. Jacob was no longer a little boy.

Although Jacob's stature and features reflected his Cheyenne heritage, the world he had grown up in was a white world, and he had adapted to its demands. In Kansas, Grandfather and Grandmother Little Wolf and the Indian lands of Oklahoma territory had been far away. Jacob had not seen his grandparents since the day they had given him the little black and white pony. Maria no longer told the stories of her ancestors or sang the songs that Jacob had heard as a small boy. In Kansas, Jacob had been compelled to attend the one-room school in nearby Vilets. It was there that the taunting of "half-breed," "stinkin' injun," and other vile epitaphs had taught him to wield the power learned from his pa, and schoolyard beatings left others bloodied and bruised and Jacob the victor. But still, under Eli's iron-fisted control, Jacob endured the physical punishment and the degrading onslaught of Eli's hell-fire and damnation insults and curses.

Maria rinsed the blood-soaked rag in the wash pan while Evie continued to quietly set the table for breakfast. Evie was used to seeing both her brother and her mama with cuts and bruises, and bloody water in the washbasin was not unusual. But Evie and Flora had never felt the sting of harness leather, willow switches, or calloused hands. To Evie, Papa was fiddle music and merry singing. For Flora, it was snuggly hugs and pony rides astraddle Papa's bouncing leg. This was a side of Eli that neither Jacob nor Maria had ever seen before Evie's birth. And now there was Flora, Eli's baby girl who was coddled and cuddled.

Both Maria and Jacob harbored a deep resentment of the special treatment that Evie and Flora received, though both of them were thankful that the girls were spared the abuse. However, Maria was always watchful and had never let circumstances develop such that Evie or Flora would ever be out of her sight and alone with Eli for any extended period of time.

Maria took biscuits from the warmer above the cookstove as Evie placed the last knife, fork, and spoon in the precise location next to Eli's plate, then hurried from the table to stand at the kitchen window.

"Here comes Papa!" Evie exclaimed, peering through the window to the outside to watch Eli approach the house. The dark, braided pigtails that hung down her back bounced against her shoulders as she hurried to the door and opened it.

"Mornin', Papa," Evie said playfully as she held the folds of her bright calico dress in each hand and curtsied like a princess welcoming the king. Evie had learned that she could sometimes dispel the tension between Eli and Jacob with her playfulness, and she often tried.

"And good mornin' to you, fair lady," Eli replied, lifting his hat from his head and waving it in a low sweeping arch as he bowed deeply at the waist.

Flora rushed forward, threw her arms around Eli's neck, and kissed him on the cheek with an exaggerated smack. With her arms wrapped tightly around his neck, Flora giggled happily as she was raised off the floor when Eli stood. Holding her at the waist in his large hands, Eli stretched her out before him, then set her gently on the floor.

"Now, my lady," Eli continued with the charade, "go find the cook and tell her the master is home and hungry enough to eat a horse!"

"Oh, Papa," Flora cooed, "Mama's already got breakfast ready and it's biscuits and gravy, not horse!"

Flora grasped Eli's thumb in her small hand and led him toward the washbasin. Jacob quickly emptied the crimson water into the slop bucket beneath the washstand and backed away as Eli and Evie approached.

"Looks like you come up against another hard lesson, eh boy?" Eli remarked as Jacob retreated. Eli's mocking stare was met by a glint of defiance in Jacob's dark eyes.

"You showing a little backbone there, boy?" Eli jeered.

Jacob dropped his gaze to the floor but his anger continued to burn in the flexed muscles of his biceps, the grind of teeth in his clenched jaw, and the white knuckles of the iron-hard fist that dug fingernail furrows in the palms of his hands.

Someday, you'll see just how well I've learned my lesson. The thought was so clear in Jacob's head that he instinctively flinched, fearing that he had spoken out loud. But Eli passed quietly by without rapping him across the mouth with the back of his hand, so it must have been a silent thought.

Someday, Jacob continued to himself, *someday I'll make him back down. Someday I'll fight back, and he'll be the one wiping blood off his face. Someday will be the last day.*

Jacob recalled the look of surprise, or was it a flash of fear, in Eli's eyes when he was unable to jerk the pitchfork from his grip. Already Jacob was stronger than any of the boys at school, even those older than him. Each of them had yielded to Jacob's strength at one time or another. Jacob's fists were as explosive as his anger and blind rage, guided the punishing blows that ended schoolyard fights as quickly as they had begun. It was soon learned that no one challenged Jacob Brandt. No one, that is, except Eli Brandt.

Flora held her grip on Eli's thumb as she led him to the wash stand while Eli playfully pretended to struggle, trying to break free from Flora's tight hold.

"Now, Papa, you wash up for breakfast," Evie ordered, her dark eyes dancing as she thrust her hands upon her waist and cocked her head to one side.

"Yes, Ma'am!" Eli replied, cracking his heels together and jerking to rigid attention.

Jacob shook his head in silent disgust, turned, and walked toward the table. Watching the playfulness between Eli and his sisters churned the emotions in his gut. Disgust, jealousy, hate, and hurt boiled inside and seemed to press the breath from his chest. He wanted to shout away his anger. He wanted to slam his clenched fists into something or someone.

Maria set the bowl of thick white gravy on the table and briefly laid her hand on Jacob's shoulder as he pulled his chair from beneath the table and sat down. With her lips pressed tightly together and the subtle shake of her head, Maria signaled her acknowledgment of Jacob's turmoil and also a warning to not provoke Eli any further. It was obvious to her that Eli was in a mood for trouble and that whatever had gone on between him and Jacob during morning chores was not over yet.

"Let's eat," Maria said as Eli and Evie approached the table.

Eli took his place at the head of the table. Maria sat to his right with Flora beside her, and Jacob sat on Eli's left with Evie beside him.

According to Eli, mealtime was for silence except for prayers before eating. Talking at the table was forbidden, and the strict rule was enforced with the foot-long strap of harness leather that Eli kept on his lap at mealtime. Its use was rarely required, since memory of the sting of leather across lips and cheeks lingered for a long while, and testing Eli's patience was seldom worth the risk.

As soon as Eli had finished the abrupt "Amen," following his pious and rote delivery of the morning's blessing, he settled back in his chair and announced, "We're moving to Arkansas."

Maria gasped and drew her hand to her throat, "Arkansas! Whatever for? We've barely gotten settled here. Evie's got her friends from school, and Flora is doing very well and likes her teacher and classmates."

"I said we're moving to Arkansas," Eli repeated, slapping a spoonful of gravy over his biscuits. "I didn't ask for any damned discussion about it. You'll go where I say and I said we're going to Arkansas."

"But why? What's wrong with here?" Maria pleaded. "Why Arkansas?"

"Dammit, woman!" Eli shouted, throwing his fork onto his plate with a clatter and thrusting his knife toward Maria's chest. "Will you ever learn not to sass me? We're going to Arkansas because there's money to be made in

Arkansas. They're building a railroad up from Helena across the state and up to Missouri. From there, they say they'll take it down to Little Rock. Hear they're paying foremen nearly two dollars a day. Laborers are getting a dollar and a quarter. I can hire on as foreman, and Jacob can work on a track crew. Hell, woman, the two of us can earn a thousand dollars in a year's time; two years an' we'll have money in the bank."

"We can't squeeze that much out of this place, with crops and stock, in three, four years runnin', not with havin' to feed these three," Eli continued, waving his arm over the table with a broad sweep that included Flora, Evie, and Jacob.

"Jacob doesn't belong on any railroad crew. He's only sixteen years old. And what about this place?" Maria asked. "What do we do with it?"

"Already rented it out," Eli snapped, then picked up his fork and cut off a mouthful of biscuit and gravy. "They'll pay cash rent and tend to our livestock to boot."

"Rented it!" Maria cried. "To who? When? I ...you had no..."

"None of your damn business," Eli sneered. "Don't go worryin' your little pea-brain over what you've got no say in."

"So, we'll be coming back?"

"Maybe so, maybe not."

"But when are we supposed to leave?" Maria said, stunned and hardly able to speak.

"We got ten days to clear out."

"Ten days!" Maria said, her shoulders dropping in resigned disbelief, "I can't..."

"Ten days, woman!" Eli barked.

"Why don't just you go? Me and the kids will stay. We can manage here and be here when the work ends in Arkansas."

"By God, woman, you'll go where I say and that's the end of it!"

"I ain't goin'!" Jacob declared.

Eli's hand dropped to his lap and before Jacob could move, the leather strap had smacked across Jacob's mouth. Jacob turned in his chair, away from Eli's reach and covered the back and side of his head with his hand and arm. Tears welled in his eyes as he fought back the pain of the sting that pulsed across his lips and cheek.

"You'll go where I say you're going," Eli growled between clenched teeth.

Jacob pushed himself away from the table, got up from his chair, and headed toward the kitchen door, took his hat from the peg on the wall, pushed it onto his head, and opened the door.

"I ain't goin'!" Jacob repeated as he stepped outside and slammed the door behind him.

"You'll go!" Eli shouted over his shoulder while biscuit crumbs spewed from his mouth and white gravy slid down his chin. "By damn, boy, you'll go!"

Jacob took the three stairs outside the kitchen door and down to the ground in a single long stride and ran to the barn. Tears still tumbled down his cheeks from the lingering sting of Eli's leather strap. Inside the barn, Jacob retreated to the farthest empty stall, where he hunkered down in the corner, knees drawn to his chest with his arms and his face buried there.

"Ain't goin' to no damned Arkansas," Jacob sobbed.

When the kitchen door slammed shut, Eli responded by pounding his clenched fists on the table's edge. Plates and cups and tableware rattled as he shoved himself away from the table's edge and sprang to his feet.

"By God, woman!" Eli roared in red-faced rage, pointing an accusing finger at Maria. "It's you. It's your damned sass that makes that boy so disobedient. You'll see, by God; you'll see and so will he."

Maria, Evie, and Flora sat still and silent and stared at the plates in front of them. Eli turned brusquely around and stormed toward the door, grabbed his hat, and crumpling it in his fist, slammed the battered Stetson against his leg, "He'll see!"

Eli slammed the door behind him, stomped down the stairs, and headed toward the barn.

"Boy!" Eli shouted as he swung the barn door open. "Come here, boy!" Eli demanded, as he rolled up his shirtsleeves.

Jacob remained silent and pressed himself into the shadow of the stall's corner.

"Where the hell are you, boy?" Eli raged, heavy footsteps thudding on the packed dirt floor. He stopped halfway down the alleyway and lifted a singletree from off a spike that had been driven into the heavy support beam. The iron hooks at the ends of the singletree rattled in their rings as Eli gripped the heavy three-foot-long hickory beam in both hands.

"Boy!" Eli growled as he stepped into the stall.

As Eli raised the club above his head, Jacob cowered into the corner, turning his face away from Eli's hate-filled gaze. The first blow landed across Jacob's shoulder and forced a high-pitched yelp of pain from Jacob's mouth. The second blow smashed into Jacob's lower back and exposed hip, and he involuntarily stiffened, throwing himself backward and out from the protection of the stall's corner. Eli swung the club like a baseball bat, and Jacob threw up his arm to stop the next blow and heard the crack of bone when it struck his forearm. Jacob could not stifle the scream that exploded from his throat as he cradled his broken arm with the other. He did not see the next blow coming and made no move to protect himself. A bright flash of light, like jagged lightning, zigzagged across Jacob's vision when the singletree smashed into the side of his head. Blood gushed from the ragged edges of his torn ear and from the gash that ran above his ear to the base of his skull. And suddenly, there was only darkness and relief from the pain in his unconsciousness.

Jacob lay unmoving in the stall.

Eli tossed the singletree into the dusty straw that covered the dirt floor where Jacob lay and turned to leave.

"Looks to me like you'll be goin' to Arkansas," Eli sneered.

Fueled by his explosive rage, Eli marched from the barn to the house.

"God-damned mama's boy," Eli growled, each word accentuated with a grunt as his heavy boots stomped the dirt path with every step.

Rage and lust collided in Eli's rampage when he stormed into the kitchen, where Maria stood beside the cookstove. Evie and Flora were still seated at the table, eyes wide with apprehension.

"Get out!" Eli shouted, his eyes darting back and forth from Evie to Flora.

"Get out!" he demanded, waving his arm toward the front door.

The girls jumped from their chairs and scurried across the room, Evie pushing Flora ahead of her.

When the door closed behind them, Eli turned to Maria, "By Jove woman, one day you'll learn!"

Eli closed the distance between them in two long strides and grabbed Maria by her wrist. She tried to pull away but Eli's grip was too strong. He jerked her to his side and wrapped his arm around her waist, pulling her toward her bedroom.

"No!" Maria shrieked.

Eli released his grip on her wrist and slapped her sharply across the mouth and, despite her strong resistance, dragged her to her room and kicked the door shut behind them.

Chapter 11

For the first week of their travels to Arkansas, Jacob rode in the bed of the wagon, cracked ribs bound tight with strips of bed sheets and his broken arm held close against his belly to shield it from the bumps and jolts along the way. Maria had set the bones as best she could, using broken slats from an old chicken coop as a splint. His right eye was still swollen shut but the bright purple bruising had begun to fade to a mix of yellow and green. And although the split skin across his brow from the pitchfork handle had not needed to be stitched, the long, ragged gash along the side of his head had exposed the skull, and the wound had to be closed. Maria had done the stitching with a fine sewing needle and silk thread while Jacob was still unconscious.

Maria drove the team and wagon while Flora and Evie alternated between walking alongside and riding next to Maria on the wagon seat. Eli rode the stallion, pushing a small band of mares ahead, avoiding the drudging pace of the wagon and the annoying chatter of Flora and Evie.

At the end of the first week, ranging far ahead, Eli had chosen a spot for the evening camp east of Lawrence, Kansas. The next day would take them across the Kansas and Missouri border, where they would head due south to Arkansas. At the campsite, Eli waited for Maria to arrive with the wagon, gather firewood, and prepare the evening meal while he rested in the soft sheepskin lining of his upturned saddle, curved pipe stem clenched between his teeth, smoke curling up and around the brim of his hat. It was more than an hour later when Maria arrived at the camp.

"Bout god-dammed time you caught up," Eli barked. "Whip them horses up to a good trot and keep up with me. Molly coddlin' that boy of yours is gonna cost me a week wages, maybe more."

Maria unhitched the horses and Evie helped drag the harness from off their backs and drape them over the wagon tongue. Flora and Evie gathered firewood while Maria kindled the fire for cooking and Jacob carefully lowered himself out of the back of the wagon and settled in under the shelter of the wagon box, keeping his distance from Eli.

"If you're in such a big hurry," Maria prodded, "go on ahead. I'm sure we can find Arkansas without you."

"There you go with that damned sass of yours," Eli growled, taking the pipe from his mouth and pointing the stem accusingly toward Maria's face. "You mind your mouth, woman. 'Sides, ain't nobody to watch out for you and the girls if I ride on ahead."

"We'll manage," Maria said matter-of-factly.

"Humph," Eli grunted, clamping the pipe stem between his teeth and drawing in a long breath of smoke. "The boy's no damned good, and you," Eli let the smoke drift from his mouth, "you're 'bout as worthless as teats on a boar hog."

"You would know," Maria said quietly, the words lost to hearing in the rattle of pots and pans when the cook box slipped from her grip.

"You clumsy bitch!" Eli spat the words as he leaped to his feet and lunged toward Maria.

Maria stepped back, held her hand up, and turned her face away, anticipating the coming blow. She didn't see Jacob pull himself out from beneath the wagon, pick up a large iron skillet in his good hand and stand behind her.

Eli stopped short, his raised fist hovered overhead, then slowly dropped to his side as Jacob stepped forward.

"Boy," Eli said through clenched teeth, his eyes narrowed in an unspoken threat as he raised the pipe to his lips and clamped it between his teeth.

"What?" Jacob replied calmly, raising the skillet to his shoulder.

"You good fer nothin' pup. A god-damned worthless pup," Eli hissed as glowing embers of tobacco jumped from the pipe's bowl until the last "pup" erupted in a shower of orange embers.

Jacob stood his ground while Maria stepped closer and stood beside him. Eli glanced from one to the other, his dark eyes searching for a sign of weakness. But both Jacob and Maria held his gaze.

"Ya ain't worth the effort. Neither of ya," Eli said as he spat at Jacob's feet then turned and walked away.

For the remainder of the trip, Eli continued to ride far ahead, pushing the mares along at a pace that kept the distance between him and the wagon gradually growing until the end of the day when he would stop once again to rest and wait and stoke the fires of his anger.

And Jacob's anger and resentment churned in his gut like bitter bile.

Chapter 12

Maria drove the wagon for most of the four hundred miles from the homestead in northeast Kansas to northwestern Arkansas. Sometimes walking beside the team, she would coax the horses along while instructing Evie on handling the reins. Flora remained in the wagon or on the spring seat for most of the journey and for the first week, kept herself occupied with playing nursemaid to Jacob as he slowly healed and regained his strength. She would pat his forehead or hold his hand as she had seen Maria do whenever Jacob would wince with the pain of bound ribs being roughly jostled. As the days wore on, Jacob became more able to help, but with only the one good arm, he was unable to help with the heavy lifting or with driving the team.

A month of travel, of setting up camp at the end of each day's journey, cooking supper and breakfast on the small cast iron camp stove or over an open fire, unpacking every night and repacking each morning, tending to Jacob's healing, Evie's impatience with the long days of sameness, and Flora's too frequent wanderings away from camp had taken its toll on Maria. Their arrival at the rail workers' camp was a welcome relief from the daily drudgery of travel. At least the work camp offered a respite from the packing and unpacking of every day and, while only temporary, the canvas tent provided by the railroad was, by far, more restful than sleeping under the wagon.

During their weeks of travel, Eli and Jacob had avoided any physical nearness to each other, though Eli never ceased his constant criticism of both Jacob and Maria.

"No damn good, either one of you. Just a no damn good mama's boy and a snivelin' squaw that don't know her place," Eli would grumble as he glared through the smoke of the campfire. "No damn good."

They had arrived at the laborers' camp a few miles north of the dying town of Carrollton, where painted survey stakes marked the route of the advancing rails. The camp was, for the time being, a somewhat central location for directing the operations of the workers by the surveyors, engineers, and investors of Missouri and North Arkansas Railroad. Track had already been laid from Joplin down toward Helena and end of track was almost to Harrison, some twenty miles to the east.

Eli had sold the mares that he had brought with him and with the money was able to replenish their supplies and purchase the material for a cabin where Maria, Evie, and Flora would live while Eli and Jacob remained at the camp. Eli had traded one of the mares for a piece of land that straddled Carroll and Boone Counties, a heavily timbered plot of ground on one of the many rocky hillsides in the area. A small but fast-running creek tumbled over moss-covered rocks and meandered along the base of the hills. Eli's plot included the creek's clear, cool water. Eli arranged for the material to be shipped by rail, down from Joplin, and dropped trackside where he and Jacob loaded it on the wagon and hauled it to the homesite. There were other cabins in the area as well, sparsely located among the scattered hills that overlooked a small, neglected graveyard, a reminder of the aftermath of battle some forty years past.

Jacob's cuts and bruises and broken bones had healed and, as Eli had predicted, Jacob had been hired by the railroad as a laborer whose job was building grade with pick and shovel. Eli's predictions were also confirmed when he was given the job of foreman of one of the track laying crews and he quickly earned the reputation of being a hard-nosed taskmaster. Eli gloried in his position of authority, frequently reminding his crew that he was the boss and openly inviting anyone who dared to challenge his command. Mounted on the stallion, Eli carried himself with an exaggerated show of self-importance, rarely dismounting to stand eye-to-eye with the men at work but riding and lording above them.

Work commenced at seven o'clock each morning, Monday through Saturday, with the work train hauling workers from camp to end of track. At six o'clock each afternoon, the engineer sounded the steam whistle causing picks and shovels, sledges and spikes, rails and ties to clatter to the ground in an end-of-the-day avalanche. Sweat-soaked workers hauled their weary frames aboard the flat cars, hunkered down on the plank deck, and collapsed, hunch-backed, over knees drawn to their chests with aching arms. At the end of each day, Jacob would jump off the flat car at the Carroll and Boone County line and walk to the nearby plot of land where the cabin was being built. In two weeks' time, working from quitting time to past dark, the cabin was completed and Maria, Evie, and Flora abandoned the work camp canvas tent and settled into the luxury of a wood plank floor under their feet and a solid roof overhead.

Working together while building the cabin created the appearance of cooperation but the flow of work was stiff and conversation was reduced to Eli's commands and Jacob's necessary responses. With the cabin finally completed and end of track nearing the next whistle stop named Saint Joe, Eli spent most all of his time with his crew at their work camp and Jacob worked further ahead, with his crew, building grade.

As the railroad continued east toward Helena, Eli and Jacob had little opportunity to go back to see Maria and the girls. The work camp near Carrollton had long been abandoned, and the little settlement on the Carroll and Boone County line, where the cabin had been built, had begun to grow. Storefronts were being built on both sides of the steep-sloped main street where horseback men, freight wagons, and family buggies stirred up clouds of red dust. Along with the railroad came progress, and progress had stretched its fingers on roads built around the hills, bridges across the creek, and unpainted raw-wood buildings lined the town square where the graves of fallen soldiers from nearly forty years past, both blue and gray, had been covered over and forgotten. Progress had come to Alpena Pass.

Chapter 13

After the cabin was completed for Maria and the girls and end-of-track stretched farther eastward, neither Eli nor Jacob were able to go back to Alpena Pass with any sort of regularity. Jacob stayed in the laborers' camp where crews were housed in four-man canvas tents arranged in haphazard order with little regard for any semblance of military-style precision. Cook tents provided a common area for meals, and personal hygiene consisted of a common wash pan and a hastily dug trench for standing or squatting.

Eli, as a foreman, enjoyed the additional comfort of a plank floor in a private tent that included a personal wash pan and a small stove, but he also had to share the common trench. The temporary tent cities at end-of-track were as unkempt and boisterous in the Arkansas hills during the early 1900s as they were on the western plains in the 1860s when the Union Pacific pushed its way across the Great Plains where booze, brothels, and brawls were commonplace.

Building rail bed to grade through the heavily timbered and rocky hills of northern Arkansas was slow going and backbreaking work. Where hills had to be cut, valleys had to be filled, and hard-working mules hauled the dirt and rock that hard-working men had to shovel and pick. The sound of axes driven deep into the trunks of oaks and pines and ash and walnuts echoed through the timber. The rattle of chains and harness, the curses of the teamsters above the crack of whips, and the rhythmic thrumming of two-man crosscut saws drove out the chatter of tree-top birds and the timid deer that scurried deeper into the timber. And Jacob, stripped to the waist, sweat streaming down his back, heaved shovel after shovelful of rock and soil into the waiting slip to be hauled away to the nearest fill.

Jacob was tall for his seventeen years and solidly built. The past seven months of manual labor had transformed his boyish frame into hardened muscle. Once slender fingers were now thick with callouses and sinew, formed from long days of gripping the handles of pick and shovel.

"Slow down there, boy," said one of the crew as he pulled a dirty, sweat-soaked bandana from his hip pocket and wiped the sweat from the back of his neck and forehead, "You're makin' the rest of us look bad."

"Then do something with your shovel besides leanin' on it," Jacob said, heaving another shovelful of dirt.

"Hell, boy, we're gittin' paid by the day not the load. Ain't no reason ta git in no kinda hurry. We'll all be gruntin' at the business end of these shovels fer the rest of the day today, tomorrow, an' the day after that."

"I figger I'm gettin' paid to work, not standin' around jawin'," Jacob replied, never looking up or stopping.

"An' I figger you're just a smart-assed little shit that needs to be learnin' some manners."

"An' I suppose you're the dumb-assed hillbilly that can teach 'em, right?" Jacob sneered.

From the corner of his eye, Jacob saw a flash of sunlight off the underside of the shovel when the man raised it overhead and rushed forward. Jacob turned to meet the charge and flung the shovelful of dirt he held into the man's face, dropped his shovel, and rammed himself headfirst into the man's chest.

"Fight!" someone yelled, and the crew swarmed around like flies to a gut pile.

The man fell backward, the breath knocked out of him, and Jacob leaped like a cat onto his chest, grabbed the bib of his overalls in his left hand, and landed a blow to the face of the man beneath him, then raised his fist for another.

"Hold it right there!" The voice boomed above him while a giant hand gripped Jacob's wrist and pulled him to his feet. "Pick up your shovel and get back to work, Collins. An' you, boy, cool down over there," he said, pointing to a huge moss-covered boulder a few yards away.

"I didn't do nothin'," Jacob protested, jerking his wrist out of the foreman's grip.

Collins rolled to his side and wiped the blood from his nose on the sleeve of his shirt, got to his knees, then stood. "You best watch yourself, boy!" Collins growled, pointing a shaking finger toward Jacob, "You'll get yours, that's fer damn sure!"

"Back to work," the voice boomed again.

"I didn't do nothin', boss," Jacob repeated as the foreman approached. "He come at me with a shovel, an' I stopped him, that's all."

"I saw what happened. I know you're a steady worker, Jake, but you've got yourself a smart mouth, a short fuse, and a hell of a temper. And trouble seems to seek you out like deer to a salt lick."

"I come here to work, that's all, an' it weren't my choice, but I'm here just the same," Jacob said.

"Then get back to work and figger out how you're going to get along with other folks," the foreman said, putting a giant hand on Jacob's shoulder.

Jacob looked at the foreman's hand resting on his shoulder, pushed it away, then turned and walked back to the cut. The crew watched as Jacob approached; Collins stared hard, eyes glaring over the bandana he held to his nose. Jacob stooped to pick up his shovel, shoved it into the ground with his foot, and pitched the dirt into the slip.

"Back to work, all of you!" the voice boomed.

"I'll skin you alive, boy," Collins hissed, his threat muffled beneath the sounds of picks and shovels, "'an feed your half-breed hide to the buzzards."

"I hear buzzards prefer white meat," Jacob replied.

"You god damned little breed…" Collins roared, pulling a short-bladed knife from somewhere inside his overalls, and lunged across the half-filled slip that separated them.

Collins gripped the knife like a sword, his arm extending as he thrust the blade toward Jacob's chest. Jacob sprang to the side and grabbed Collins's arm, twisting it back against the forward motion of Collins's body. Jacob felt the sting of the blade as it skimmed across his belly and heard the snap of tendons as Collins's shoulder was jerked from its socket.

Collins fell to the ground, his face contorted with pain, teeth clenched to hold back the urge to scream. He rolled onto his back and pulled himself up, sitting cross-legged, holding his dangling right arm in his lap.

Jacob wiped at the blood that trickled from the gash across his belly. *Not much worse than a barbed wire cut*, he thought and sat down on the pile of dirt in the slip.

"Get back to work! All of you! Get back!" The booming voice of the boss-man cut through the crowd that had gathered around Collins and Jacob. "God-dammit, Collins. You stupid…"

"Oh shit," the boss man muttered, seeing the blood oozing from the gash in Jacob's belly. "Somebody get the wagon! Take these two back to camp. Collins, you're through. Draw your pay and git. Jake, you go see the Doc."

"I'm okay. Don't need to see the Doc," Jacob said, grabbing his shovel and pulling himself up with the handle.

"This ain't over, breed," Collins snarled.

"Shut up, Collins," the boss-man warned.

"It's over, you sorry bastard," Jacob said flatly, tossing a shovelful of dirt into the slip. "It's over."

Chapter 14

For Maria, it seemed as though the dense timber that covered the hills and surrounded the cabin embraced and protected her. During the day, Flora and Evie were off to Alpena Pass, where Miss Pickett was somewhat able to control the energy of the thirty-odd students who attended the one-room school. Evie was working with Miss Pickett and was waiting for her normal school exam results when she would officially become a teacher. With Eli and Jacob away at the rail camps, Maria's chores seemed light, and there was often time for quiet walks in the woods. Days when there was no school, Evie and Flora would walk along, one on either side, holding Maria's hands.

"When's Papa and Jacob comin' home?" Flora would ask whenever the thought would pop into her head.

"Don't know, Sweetheart," Maria would answer, "haven't heard from them for some time now. Maybe soon."

"When's the baby comin'?" would always be the next question.

Jacob's last visit to the cabin had been a little more than four months past, Eli's even longer, and neither had noticed Maria's growing belly, or if they had, they had said nothing. Maria was glad that Eli had not noticed. She was glad to be spared the tongue-lashing she expected when Eli knew another child was on the way.

"Ain't you squaws s'posed to know how to take care of such things?" He would growl.

"Don't need another damned mouth to feed! Can't hardly get by with what we got."

"Hell, we'll all end up in the god-damned poor house!"

Maria lifted the cast iron lid from the stovetop, stuffed in a couple chunks of oak wood, and stoked the fire. Replacing the lid, she slid a kettle of thick broth filled with raw potatoes, sliced carrots, and strips of lean venison over the fire. It was early afternoon, and the stew would be ready when Evie and

Flora returned home. Maria took her jacket from off the peg by the door, pulled it on, and wrapped a light woolen scarf over her ears and around her neck. There were wild onions down by the stream, a short walk from the cabin. The wild onions would add a bit more flavor to the stew.

Maria stepped outside and breathed in the sharp freshness of the trees and the heavy fragrance of the damp earth. An early November breeze blew whispers of winter through the trees where leaves of bright yellow-gold, maple, and brilliant red oak broke free of their branches and fluttered to the ground.

The baby that Flora impatiently waited for would be arriving soon. Maria knew it was close and held her belly with her left hand as she stepped down from the cabin porch. She could feel the baby's head in her cupped hand and knew that the child had positioned itself for birthing. She would take the walk along the stream that meandered through the hills, gather the onions, and be back to keep the cook fire going and finish the stew before the girls were home from school.

Evie and Flora burst through the doorway in their usual after-school exuberance. Coats and scarves were quickly shed and hung on their designated pegs before the door was slammed shut.

"Mother?" Evie's question seemed to float through the empty cabin.

The fire in the cookstove had gone out, and the November chill had crept into the cabin. "Mother?" Evie repeated, lifting the latch of the bedroom door to peek inside.

"Mommy, where are you?" Flora cried. Her voice quivered with uncertainty.

"She's not here," Evie said impatiently.

"But where is she?" Flora whined. Her lower lip quivered and tears puddled in the corners of her eyes.

"I don't know!" Evie scolded. "Now stop crying. Crying don't help anyway, so stop it!"

"But…"

"Just stop it! I don't know." Evie repeated. "Get your coat and scarf; we'll find her."

Evie held Flora's hand as they followed the path from the cabin to the stream. Instinctively, they continued along the path that they had always taken on their walks with Maria as it ran beside the stream leading back into the timber.

"Mother!" Evie shouted through cupped hands. "Mother! Where are you?"

"Mommy! Mommy!" Flora pleaded.

Evie knelt down beside Flora and took hold of both her hands. "Flora," she said with a calm urgency. "Flora, now listen to me. I'll run back to the schoolhouse and have Miss Pickett ring the bell. When people come to see what's happening, I'll tell them our mother is missing and bring them back here. Okay?"

"Okay," Flora nodded vigorously.

"You stay right here until I get back," Evie commanded as she turned and ran back.

Despite Evie's command to stay put until help arrived, Flora turned back and followed the creek further into the timber, calling for Maria as she walked, stopping often to listen for any sounds. She walked as though she were a hunter stalking wary game. In the far distance, she heard the schoolhouse bell ringing.

"Mama!" Flora shouted, then stopped to listen.

"Flora?" Maria called. "Flora girl, over here."

Flora rushed toward the sound of Maria's voice. A few yards off the path, she spotted Maria sitting on a blanket of fallen leaves and leaning heavily against the rough bark of an ancient oak. Her hands were cupped beneath her belly as if she might hold back the inevitable. Flora ran forward and dropped to her knees at Maria's side.

"Are you okay, Mama? What happened? Are you hurt?" Flora gushed.

"It's okay," Maria said softly. "It'll be okay." Maria reached out a hand to touch Flora's thigh. "I stumbled and fell. Must have twisted my ankle pretty bad. Can't stand on it. And the baby's coming. I'll need some help to get back."

"Oh, Mama," Flora sighed, "I don't think I can hold you up."

"That's okay," Maria said, "We'll just give it a try, okay?"

"Okay," Flora said nervously.

Maria pushed herself firmly against the tree trunk and raised herself with her arms, hands pressed against the ground. Then bending her good leg, she dug her boot heel into the ground and pushed herself inch by inch up the side of the tree. Flora straddled Maria's outstretched leg and, with her hands under Maria's arms, helped to lift her. When Maria was standing, Flora supported her with one arm around her waist, and Maria leaned on her shoulder.

"You okay?" Maria asked.

"I think so," said Flora.

A few awkward steps toward the path and Flora's knees began to buckle. "I can't do it!" Flora sobbed, "I can't do it!"

Maria reached out to a nearby tree and steadied herself against it. "It's okay, it's okay," she said softly. "Just rest a bit for now."

"I'm sorry, Mama." Flora slumped to the ground and wiped her nose with the back of her hand.

"Missus Brandt! Missus Brandt!" Several frantic voices cut through the timber.

"Here we are!" Flora cried, then jumped to her feet and ran to meet them.

"Oh, Evie. I just couldn't wait," Flora exclaimed, anticipating a scolding from Evie for not staying where she was told.

When they reached the cabin, the men who had carried Maria laid her carefully on her bed and, tipping their hats respectfully, backed hurriedly out the door. The local veterinarian, who among the others had responded to the schoolhouse bell, rubbed down Maria's ankle with a foul-smelling liniment and wrapped it tightly.

"Best stay off it for a few days," he said. "When you're up and about, you can stop by and we can settle up. Good day, Ma'am. Oh, will you be needing someone to help with your, uh…" he asked as an afterthought, nodding toward Maria's large belly.

"No. I can manage. I've got my girls," Maria replied.

When the bevy of rescuers had seen to it that Maria was safe and the cookstove fire rekindled, they left the girls to their chores and returned to town.

"Evie," Maria called from the bedroom.

"Yes?" Evie replied as she stepped into the room.

"Evie girl, you're old enough now to help me. Put a kettle of water on the stove. We'll need it to be nice and warm to wash the baby when it comes. You'll need some towels and a warm blanket. Bring in a wash pan of water and a couple of wash rags and a pair of scissors."

Evie's eyes widened. "You want me to help with the baby being born?" she asked breathlessly.

"Yes," Maria said, "I want you to help."

Chapter 15

Evie rushed from the bedroom and into the kitchen, where she pumped a wash pan full of water and put it on the stove. She added several sticks of firewood to the cookstove and stirred the flickering embers until the flames danced with a frenzy of heat and light. She quickly gathered clean towels and washcloths from the cupboard and stacked them on the corner of the kitchen table.

"Whatcha doin'?" Flora asked, bewildered by the flurry of activity.

"Mama wants me to help with the birthing," Evie replied. "And I gotta get everything ready."

"You're goin' to help?" Flora exclaimed. "You're going to help the baby be born? What about me? Can I help too? Why can't I help?" Flora whined.

"Oh, hush!" Evie scolded. "Yes, you can help too. Go find Mama's scissors and put them here with these towels. Keep an eye on that pan of water, and let me know when it starts to boil."

Evie returned to Maria's bedroom while Flora jumped to the chores she had been given.

Despite the fall chill, Maria's face was flushed and sweat had beaded across her forehead and dripped along the edges of her jaw. She lay still and rigid on the bed. Her hands tightly gripped the blanket beneath her as she inhaled and exhaled in long and forceful breaths. Her eyes fixed on some imaginary spot on the ceiling above.

"Mama! Are you okay?" Evie said, her voice betraying the fear of what she had to do and the pain she saw in Maria's eyes.

"I'm okay, Evie," Maria said, loosing her grip on the blanket and reaching a hand toward Evie. Evie took her outstretched hand and held it tight. "The pains are getting stronger and coming closer together now. Pretty soon, I'm going to have to push the baby out and you're going to have to help."

"Oh, Mama, I don't think…"

"Yes, you can," Maria interrupted.

"Water's bubbling!" Flora shouted from the kitchen.

Evie rushed to the kitchen and took the wash pan from the stove. "Bring those towels and wash rags and the scissors," she said to Flora, nodding to the stack of cloths on the table.

Flora quickly gathered up the needed supplies and followed Evie into the bedroom. "Put them there on the bed," Evie directed while she sat the wash pan of hot water on the dresser top.

"Can I stay?" Flora asked. Evie looked to Maria for the answer.

"No, Honey," Maria said softly, as she drew a sharp breath against another contraction. "I need you to bundle up and run into town. Find Miss Pickett and ask her to come back with you. She might be needed to help Evie with the baby when it comes. Can you do that?"

"Oh yes, Mama, I can do that!" Flora hurried to the door, grabbed her coat and scarf from the peg, and stuffing her arm into one of the sleeves of her coat, was out the door. "I'll be right back!" She yelled through the door as it slammed shut.

"Evie," Maria said firmly, "scoot one of those towels under my backside and push my dress and slip up around my waist, and you'll have to pull off my underwear."

Maria managed a quick smile in response to Evie's look of shock. "It's okay, Sweetheart," she said, "this is one of a woman's most precious and least dignified moments."

Evie nodded her agreement and proceeded to follow Maria's instructions. "Now," Maria continued, "you should be able to see the top of the baby's head. Can you see it?"

"I think so," Evie said hesitantly, "Oh! Yes! Yes, I do!"

"Okay," Maria replied, "next time there's a contraction, I'm going to push really hard and the baby's head should come out. We'll wait there for a little bit and then the next time I push, you will need to help get the shoulders out. Are you ready?"

"Yes, Mama, I'm ready."

With the next contraction, Evie held the tiny head in her hands and waited. For a moment, mother and daughter held each other's gaze until another contraction forced Maria's eyes closed as she strained to push the baby's shoulders through.

"Oh my!" Evie exclaimed as a rush of fluid washed over the baby, and with a final push, the tiny infant lay exposed between Maria's legs. "It's a boy!"

"Evie, Evie," Maria whispered, "Get a warm rag and wipe his nose and mouth. Hurry up, Honey."

"Okay, Mama."

"Evie, Evie girl, quick now, grab him by the feet and pat him hard across his back. Again. Again!" Evie now understood the panic in Maria's voice.

"Oh Mama, Mama!" Evie cried, "He's not breathing!"

Maria sat up, "Give him to me!" she said urgently.

Maria laid the boy across her lap, face down, and slapped him firmly on the back and waited for a brief moment before repeating the process. Tears streamed down her face and fell upon her hands and on the tiny torso that lay beneath them. Again, again, and again, until it was certain that there was no further need of trying.

Evie fell sobbing against her mother's breast, and Maria wrapped an arm around her daughter's heaving shoulders and held the lifeless infant in her other.

Together, mother and daughter washed the child and wrapped him in the soft folds of cloth that had been prepared for him. They laid him on the bed where he had been born, tucked in the crook of Maria's arm, while Evie lay beside them, her hand resting on his still chest.

"Mama!" Flora called as she burst through the cabin door. "I couldn't find Miss Pic…"

Flora still had on her coat and scarf as she rushed into the bedroom. "Is that the baby?" she whispered, smiling at first then realizing that something strange was happening. The bundle in Maria's arm was strangely still. Evie was crying and Maria's eyes glistened with tears. "Mama?" the question lingered in the darkening room as the late afternoon light faded.

Flora shuffled to the bedside, sat on the edge, and laid her hand on Maria's shoulder. Maria turned and caressed Flora's hand with her cheek.

"Sometimes," Maria said softly, "Sometimes our little ones are too impatient to meet their ancestors. This 'makeeta' was not meant to live with us but his spirit will always live in our hearts."

"What is 'makeeta' Momma?" Flora asked.

"Little Man," Maria said as she softly caressed the baby's cheek.

Chapter 16

"And what is the baby's name?" the coroner asked, making several marks on his index finger with the tip of his pen before holding it suspended over the death certificate that lay on the dresser top.

"Makeeta," Maria replied.

"What kind of a name is that?"

"It is Cheyenne," Maria said proudly.

"I see, Ma'am, but don't you want an American name?"

"I would think that it is very American," Maria said calmly. "Just write it down, M-A-K-E-E-T-A, Makeeta Little Wolf Brandt."

"Yes, Ma'am," the coroner sighed, a bit too loudly, as he pressed the pen tip into the blank space above the line.

When the certificate was completed, the coroner signed his name with a broad stroke of loops and curves befitting his elevated position, then placed the document on his leather briefcase and handed it to Maria.

"Sign here," he said flatly, pointing with his pen at the appropriate line. "I'll make the arrangements for burial. It must be done by sundown tomorrow since you've chosen not to embalm. You understand that, right?"

"Yes, I understand," Maria replied.

Together, Maria, Evie, and Flora washed the baby boy preparing him for burial. Maria held each hand, softly washing each finger, caressing the palms, his wrists, and arms. As they washed, they cried salty tears mingled with warm water until at last the baby-soft skin no longer bore the bloodstains of birthing.

Gently, they wrapped him in the worn remnant of a cotton sheet and draped one corner over his face. Maria picked him up and held him close to her breast, kissed his forehead, and laid him in a tiny coffin. Maria had made the coffin from a wooden shipping crate that had contained half of a set of Encyclopedia Americana, recently purchased by the local school board and given to her by Miss Pickett.

Chapter 17

"And into your hands we commend his spirit, in the name of the Father and of the Son and of the Holy Ghost." Reverend Carson waved the sign of the cross, sweeping the cool evening air with its invisible pattern, and halting briefly at each of its four points.

"And may The Great Spirit guide you on your journey," Maria whispered, too softly for others to hear.

Maria, Evie, and Flora stood beside the open grave, and Reverend Carson stood at its foot. Maria's tears fell unchecked, tumbling from her flushed cheeks to the bare ground at her feet. To Maria's right and left stood Evie and Flora holding tightly to Maria's hands. On the opposite side of the tiny chasm, Miss Pickett and Doctor McClintock, the veterinarian who had helped rescue Maria, stood in quiet solidarity with the grieving family.

As shovelfuls of rocky soil clattered against the top of the wooden crate, Maria sank to her knees and pulled each of the girls close to her. "It'll be okay, Mommy," Flora whispered.

"Oh, Sweetheart," Maria answered, "I wish that were so."

When the grave had been filled, Reverend Carson extended his condolences and turned to leave. Doctor McClintock tipped his hat, shook his head, and mouthed the word "sorry" before he also left. Miss Pickett stepped around the head of the mound of fresh earth and, kneeling in front of Maria and the girls, held the three of them in her arms. Her own tears, mixed with theirs, shared their loss in ways that words could not.

The coroner had sent an urgent telegram to end-of-track, informing Eli and Jacob of the tragic news. By their absence at the graveside, it was obvious that it had not been delivered in time for the two of them to attend the hastily arranged service.

The following day Jacob arrived. Eli did not come.

"I'm so sorry, Ma," Jacob whispered as he embraced Maria. "I should have come back more often, I guess. Didn't even realize you were going to have a baby. What happened?"

"I'm just glad you came," Maria said as she held Jacob at arm's length to look into his eyes. "I didn't say anything to anybody. One never knows. The baby came a little early and never took a first breath. You'd have had a brother. But where's your Pa?"

"He stayed on. He's mad, you know, real mad. Said he never heard nothing about no baby and maybe wasn't even his."

"Serve him right if it wasn't," Maria snapped back. Her dark eyes flashed with anger. "But it was and he'd know that for certain if he'd think on it. Is he coming at all?"

"Don't know, Ma. Way he was when I left, I wouldn't plan on it if I were you."

"Never mind," Maria said flatly. "No matter anyways. You go get yourself cleaned up a bit and get some rest and we'll all go to the cemetery later if you want."

"Sure, Ma, if you feel up to it."

"Of course I do," Maria replied.

Evie and Flora walked ahead, side by side, along the road to town and the cemetery. Maria's hand gripped Jacob's arm as they walked together. She noticed the muscle beneath his shirtsleeve and his work-hardened hands. "Is it hard work?" she asked.

"Oh, I don't mind," Jacob said shyly. "It ain't easy for sure, but pay's good, I s'pose. Course Pa keeps the money. He sends you some regular, don't he?"

"Yes, he sends it."

"Good. I have to go back in the morning, you know."

"You can't stay a while?"

"No, not this time," Jacob replied. "But I'll be back in a couple of weeks."

At the gravesite, Jacob stood awkwardly, shifting his weight from one foot to the other, trying to imagine the brother he had never seen that lay beneath the mound of earth. Maria knelt beside him, reached out her hand, and placed it gently on the cool earth.

"Wha'dja name him?" Jacob asked.

"Makeeta," Maria said quietly.

Jacob looked down at her with a confused frown.

"Little Man," Maria replied.

Jacob smiled and nodded.

"We're going back, Jacob," Maria said.

"Back? Wha'dya mean back?"

"Back to Kansas. We've got a farm there. A place to tend. Not a cabin in the woods where we make do until who knows when. I want you to come with us."

"What about Pa?"

"You can tell him when you see him, or I will if he comes. He can come or stay. That's up to him, but we're going."

"When?"

"You said you could come back in a couple of weeks?" Maria asked.

"Yea, I can settle up and be back in a couple weeks. Are you sure?"

"Yes, I'm sure."

"Okay, I'll be here," Jacob promised.

Chapter 18

It had been nearly eight full months since the Brandts had moved to Arkansas and little more than a week since Maria's baby had been buried when Eli finally came home. Maria was despondent, isolating herself in the bedroom for most of each day. Eli's homecoming did nothing to lighten the heaviness that hung in the cabin and the girls were standoffish to his presence. Evie, for the most part, had picked up the burden of household chores and did her best to comfort Maria and Flora while struggling to choke back her own tears.

Maria and the girls had been sitting at the kitchen table with a meager lunch of soup and bread when Eli walked through the door as if he had just come in from a trip to the outhouse and casually hung his jacket and hat beside the door.

"Enough left for your Pa?" Eli asked, resting his hand on Evie's shoulder. "Fetch me a bowl."

Evie scooted back from the table and stood, then walked to the cupboard while Eli sat in her place.

"Did you cross paths with Jacob?" Maria asked.

"No, didn't. He came?"

"Yes," Maria said, "he was here earlier."

"So, what's this about a dead baby?" Eli said flatly as if he were asking about the weather.

"He came too early," Maria replied. "I fell hard in the timber and that must have started the labor. He never took a breath. Evie helped and Miss Pickett has been very kind."

"How the hell am I supposed to know it was mine?" Eli asked as he reached for the spoon that Evie had put beside his bowl of soup.

Maria simply raised her head and met his eyes with a hateful stare.

"And look at your hair! Looks like you chopped it off with a meat cleaver. Christ, woman, this ain't no god-damned injun camp."

"So," Eli continued, "it never was even alive, eh?"

"Not in this world," Maria said.

"Get a name?"

"Yes," Maria answered. "I named him Makeeta, means 'Little Man'. I'd like it on his tombstone."

"Tombstone!" Eli exclaimed, spewing a mouthful of soup across the table. "You think I'm going to put out good money on a god-damned piece of rock with a silly-assed injun name chiseled in. Makeeta! Jesus, woman! What the hell was you thinkin'?"

"I was thinking that I want people to know who it is that's laying in that tiny grave when the girls and I have gone back to Kansas."

"Back to Kansas!" Eli barked, slamming the spoon down on the table. "What in the hell are you talking about, woman?"

"We're going back to Kansas," Maria said firmly. "The girls and I will be going as soon as I can take care of some things here."

"You listen to me, woman, and listen good," Eli scolded, picking up the spoon and pointing it toward Maria, "If you know what's good for you, you'll be stayin' right here, by God. And I'll make damn sure you'll be goin' nowhere."

"I do know what's good for me," Maria said firmly. "You and Jacob can come when you will, or not, but I'm going, and the girls are coming with me."

"You don't know a god-damned thing, woman! You got no place to go to, and ain't nobody gonna take you in."

"I already wrote to the county attorney. He's told your renter we're coming back. They'll be gone by the time we get there."

"Damn you, woman!" Eli slammed his fists on the table, pulling himself up as he did, and took a single step toward Maria. Before she could react, Eli's fist had plunged into the side of her head and sent her sprawling across the floor.

"Papa! Stop!" Evie cried as she rushed to stand between Eli and Maria, who lay on the floor. Flora sat wide-eyed and shivering with fright as she watched.

Eli lowered his raised fist, his face flushed red, blood pulsing through the veins in his neck and forehead.

"God damn you, woman! Damn you to hell!" Eli bellered as he stormed to the door, jerked his hat to his head, grabbed his coat, opened the door and slammed it shut behind him.

Evie bent to help Maria get to her feet, "You okay, Momma?"

"I'm okay," Maria said, wiping her hand across her face and looking for traces of blood on her fingers. *I am okay. I am Tsitsistas, Cheyenne. I am Little Wolf and my Spirit is stronger than his fists,* Maria thought.

"Papa didn't mean to hurt you," Evie said. "You know how he gets when he's angry."

"Yes, I know," Maria said as she took hold of Evie's arm and pulled herself up from the floor and sat her chair back on its legs. "Sit yourself down now and finish your supper."

"I'm not hungry anymore," Evie said. Her voice trembled with the quivering of her lower lip. "How come you always make Papa so mad?"

"I…" Maria began but did not continue as Evie pushed herself away from the table and stomped across the floor to her room.

"Me either," Flora said and followed behind her sister.

Maria settled heavily onto her chair, elbows on the table, her face in her hands. She ran her fingers through the shortened strands of her hair then pressed her clasped hands to the back of her neck.

"I won't stay here," she said softly, "I just can't."

Eli spent the night at the Alpena Hotel, left the following morning on the crew train headed east, and arrived at end of track later that night.

In the two weeks that followed, Maria spent her time packing the family belongings that she would take with her back to Kansas. Arrangements were made for shipping several crates with housewares by way of the railroad, a benefit of railroad employee's families that also provided passenger tickets for her, Flora, and Evie.

Jacob had arrived late in the afternoon of the day before the family was scheduled to take the train to Kansas City, then north to Atchison, Kansas and west toward home. That evening, Maria, Jacob, Evie, and Flora had taken one last walk to the cemetery. Jacob, Evie, and Flora stood quietly at the foot of the tiny grave while Maria knelt at the side of the mound of bare earth. From inside her coat pocket, Maria took out a small beaded leather pouch stuffed with cedar, stones, and prayers, and laid it at the base of a plain, neatly engraved sandstone marker that simply declared: MAKEETA 1905.

The following morning the family quietly boarded the westbound passenger train to Kansas City. Maria sat next to a window of the coach and watched the buildings and homes of Alpena slowly pass by. As the train reached the outer edge of town, she caught a last glimpse of the cemetery and let the grief she felt spill into the handkerchief that she held to her eyes.

****

"Well, lookey here! What a sorry lookin' bunch of god-damned quitters," Eli growled as he stepped through the doorway from the adjoining coach.

Chapter 19

Back in Kansas, the Brandts settled into the daily routine of stock tending and other regular chores. The livestock had all been well cared for by the tenants, but general upkeep had suffered. Stalls had not been kept up to Eli's rigid standards and Jacob spent days mucking out the manure-laden straw that had been too long neglected. There was fence work needing done and Jacob's orders included the necessary repairs. Eli spent most of his time with the stallion, riding around the country, visiting neighbors, boasting about the money he'd earned with the railroad, and bemoaning the fact that his ever-complaining wife had forced him to return to Kansas. There was little else he could do; after all, his 'crazy squaw' had evicted the tenants and had practically kidnapped the girls and left without so much as a word about it to him.

"What's a fella to do when he's got to deal with a crazy woman?"

Maria had been shocked by the state of the house, where it was obvious that household chores had been mostly neglected. Weeks of cleaning from top to bottom had finally restored the house to its former tidiness. Evie and Flora had eagerly pitched in to help. The three of them had shared the grief of the baby's death, and it had formed a shared closeness among them that helped to ease the pain of loss.

The trip back to Kansas by rail was considerably shorter than the wagon ride from Kansas to Arkansas. Springvale, Arkansas to Topeka was one day, and Topeka to Frankfort was another. Jacob had kept to himself for most of the trip, occasionally joining Maria and the girls for lunch, though his mood was slightly less than sociable. With the awkwardness of the transition from boy to man, Jacob found himself restless and uncomfortable in the confines of the railcar and preferred to be outside. Most often, he was seen on the platform between cars, watching the countryside pass by. Eli made a show of being the comforting husband but Maria, in her black dress and veil of mourning, knew his real feelings and remained stiff and cold when he was near. She had not expected Eli to be along on this return trip and had hoped to have some time to resettle before or if he did return. His unexpected presence made her anxious and unsettled.

For Evie, the trip was the beginning of a dream she had hoped for since she had been a little girl, at least she thought so for a while. At a water and coal stop in Onega, Kansas, a young man boarded the train and caught Evie's eye as soon as he climbed aboard.

Neither tall nor short, Harper Boot was strikingly handsome. Short blonde curls sprang haphazardly from under his hat and brushed his shirt collar. Hazel eyes, framed in a sun-bronzed face, were bright and kindly, and when he passed by Evie's seat, he tipped his hat and smiled an open warm and friendly smile. His rolled-up shirtsleeves fit snugly around muscled biceps, and tanned arms left little doubt that he was not afraid of hard work. Evie guessed him to be not much older than her brother Jacob, maybe in his early twenties. From Onega to Frankfort was only twenty miles away and Evie was not shy.

"My name's Evie, Evie Brandt," she announced as she extended her hand and sat in the seat facing the young man.

Jerking his hat from off his head he smiled and took her outstretched hand.

"Harper, Harper Boot, Ma'am."

"Oh, goodness, don't call me Ma'am. I'm Evie."

"Yes, Ma'am," he said.

In the twenty miles that remained, Evie learned that Harper worked for the Union Pacific, on the Central Branch between Topeka and the Kansas/Nebraska border. He was returning to Marysville after a layover in Onega and was to join the rest of his crew there for track work to be done further north. Evie was pleased to hear that Harper took room and board in Frankfort, and did not hesitate to mention that it was not too far from the Brandt homestead near the forks of the Blue River.

When the train stopped at the Frankfort station, Evie rose from her seat, smiled beautifully, and extended her hand.

"So nice to meet you, Mr. Boot," she said.

"Nice to meet you as well," he replied.

"You may call on me if you like," Evie said, flirting unashamedly.

"Uh, yes, umm, yes, Ma'am. Uh, I mean Evie. Yes, oh, thank you. I, I will," Harper sputtered.

It was two weeks later, on a Saturday morning, when Harper Booth drove a hired horse and buggy up the lane to the Brandt house, tethered the horse to the hitching post, bounded up the front porch steps, and knocked on the door.

"Missus Brandt?" Harper asked as he took off his hat.

"Yes," Maria answered.

"Boot, Ma'am, Harper Boot. I've come to call on miss Evie."

"Yes! Oh yes, Evie has told us about you. Come in, Mr. Boot. I'll get Evie."

Evie had told Maria and Eli about the young man she had met on the train and while Maria was somewhat pleased, she also had asked Evie to be cautious; after all, the two hardly knew each other. Eli had been enraged, scolding Evie for her shameful behavior and threatening to run him off if he ever showed up on the place.

"Railroad scum!" Eli had declared. "I know the likes of men like that. I've had 'em work for me and no daughter of mine is gonna take up with one of them!"

Eli and Jacob had been out fixing fence along the far side of the north pasture when Harper had arrived. Maria invited the young man to sit in the living room with her and Evie and Flora. The four of them visited for some time and the conversation was quite formal. Maria felt comfortable with the young man and did not object when he asked if he could take Evie on a picnic that he had brought along. Although, there was one condition. Flora would have to go along. Despite mild protests from Evie, Harper graciously accepted the conditions, and Flora was thrilled to be appointed the position of chaperone.

The three of them took the buggy to the river and shared the picnic that Harper had brought. It was simple, with fried chicken and apple pie.

"Did you make this yourself?" Evie asked.

"Wish I could say so," Harper admitted. "My landlady did it for me."

"She must be a really nice landlady," Evie replied.

"Yep, she is."

Harper and Evie walked hand in hand along the riverbank sharing the details of their pasts and their hopes for the future. Flora trailed behind. For Harper, the railroad was a good job with chances for better jobs and better pay with the Union Pacific. Evie, inspired by Miss Pickett in Alpena, had hopes of finding a teaching position in either Frankfort or Marysville.

"City living would suit me just fine," Evie declared.

It was late in the afternoon when the three returned to the Brandt home and Eli was standing resolutely on the front porch, Winchester in hand.

"Evie, Flora, you girls get inside now!" Eli barked, "and mister, whoever you are, turn that buggy around and get the hell off my property!"

"Sir?"

"I said get the hell off my land!" Eli repeated, levering a round into the rifle.

"But sir, I..." Eli raised the rifle to his shoulder and aimed it at Harper's chest.

"Now!"

Harper turned the buggy around and slowly drove away.

It was very early on Monday morning when the Brandt family was jolted awake by gunfire. A second shot rang out echoing against the hills behind the house.

"Mister Brandt!" Harper shouted. "I'd like to talk to you."

Eli appeared on the porch stocking footed, his trousers held up with a single suspender strap over his nightshirt, and his rifle in hand. Harper held his rifle at his shoulder, aimed squarely at Eli's chest.

"Mister Brandt," Harper said calmly, "I've come to see Evie and if you think you can draw a bead on me before I put a hole in you, you're welcome to try. Else you best be getting used to me 'cause I plan to marry your daughter."

The day that Evie turned sixteen, Harper and Evie were married by the Justice of the Peace, in a private ceremony, with Maria and Flora as witnesses. Eli did not attend.

Chapter 20

The tension between Jacob and Eli had intensified in the year following their return. On the railroad, they had worked separately and Jacob had enjoyed a freedom that he had not previously experienced. Now, their close proximity to each other and Eli's renewed criticism and demands of Jacob had created smoldering anger that Jacob did not try to conceal. Nevertheless, Eli continued to needle and prod, insult and abuse the boy, although at nineteen, Jacob was no longer the boy that Eli believed he could intimidate and overpower. There would come a reckoning.

The morning's chores had been finished with horses fed and the milk cow milked. Stock tanks were topped off with the rhythmic clanging of sucker rods and the rush of water as windmill blades caught the breeze and a squeaking gearbox signaled the need for an after-breakfast climb to the top with a bucket of grease.

Back at the house, Jacob emptied the bucket of milk into the separator, cleaned up at the washbasin on the porch, and went into the kitchen. Flora was already seated at the table and Maria was taking a pan full of hot biscuits from the oven. Eli washed up and took his place at the head of the table and greeted Flora.

"Mornin', Princess," he said with a wink and a smile.

As was Eli's custom, he brought to the table with him a length of harness leather, a little more than a foot long, which he laid across his lap. Eli forbade frivolity at the table and any unnecessary talking—that is, anything that did not consist of "pass the potatoes" or "please" and "thank you." Any infraction met with a stern warning frown and a threatening display of the strap, although Jacob could never remember it actually being used on anyone but himself.

Flora brought the biscuits to the table, and Maria followed with a large bowl of milk and flour gravy. When everyone was seated, Eli waited until all hands were folded and heads bowed, then began, "Dear God, bless this food…"

When at last came the long-awaited "amen," Jacob snatched up the plate of biscuits in front of Eli and began a litany of forbidden conversation.

"Should'a seen them horses comin' in this mornin'! They come stampedin' in from the pasture like a herd of wild horses. What a sight! An' that new colt, well, he sure is a dandy."

Eli's left hand dropped to his lap while his piercing dark eyes glared a silent warning. But Jacob was heedless. Ignoring the warning and blatantly challenging Eli's rules, Jacob half-stood and reached across, in front of Eli, to the center of the table and grabbed the bowl of gravy as he continued, "That ol' sorrel mare, the mean one with the chewed off ear, I thought sure she was gonna…"

As Jacob sat back down, both hands gripping the heavy ironstone bowl, Eli's hand flashed from beneath the table. Jacob knew it was coming and had planned to be ready to block the blow, or maybe even wrestle the strap away from Eli's grip. But the blur of leather came so quickly that Jacob was still gripping the gravy bowl when he felt the burning sting across his eyes and over his left ear. Too late, he dropped the bowl and, with spread fingers, groped blindly to block the next painful strike.

"Silence, boy!" Eli raged, his face instantly crimson with veins bulging on his forehead and neck. "Shut your god-damned mouth!"

Jacob wrapped his hands and arms around his head as Eli shifted the heavy strap from his left to his right hand and stood. With his right arm cocked high above his head, Eli gathered up the force and momentum of his entire body into the next crashing wave of punishment.

Flora's chair clattered to the floor as she jerked herself away from the table, cupped her hands over her ears, and ran screaming from the kitchen into the front yard. Briefly distracted by Flora's terrified screams, Eli hesitated for one slight instant, and Maria lunged to Jacob's defense. Grabbing Eli's upraised arm with both hands, Maria broke the powerful momentum of his sledgehammer swing. Her ragged fingernails tore thin ribbons of skin from Eli's forearm as she tried to hold his arm in her grip.

"You meddlin' bitch!" Eli howled as he swung around with his left arm. The air from Maria's lungs exploded from her mouth. A hollow thump and the sharp crack of breaking ribs was heard as Eli's fist sank deep into Maria's side. Maria crumpled backward onto the floor; blackness swirled around her head and covered her eyes.

Jacob shook off the stinging pain that throbbed across his eyes and the side of his face. With hands pressed down against the tabletop, he hauled himself up from his chair. Slowly and methodically, he gathered himself together in a visible transformation of defiance. Narrowed eyes glinted with dark anger, tempered muscle flexed across his shoulders and down his powerful arms and into the rigid curl of work-hardened hands. When Eli turned back to face Jacob, he no longer faced a cowering boy, but rather a solid wall of hate and revenge, a wall built from years of ridicule, torment, cruel degradation, and brutal physical punishment.

Eli's eyes widened in astonishment as he realized that his power to dominate Jacob through fear and intimidation had suddenly vanished. With an instinctive reflex of a predatory animal, Eli raised his fists and stepped forward. He did not expect the suddenness or the fury of Jacob's attack.

With all the strength and anger that lay coiled inside him, Jacob plunged his hardened fist squarely into Eli's nose. There was an audible crackling of cartilage and an immediate gush of blood. Staggering backward, Eli stumbled over Maria, who still lay on the floor. When Eli hit the floor, Jacob sprang like a cougar for the kill, landed with a crush on Eli's chest and began to pummel him with both fists.

"You miserable god-forsaken bastard!" Jacob hammered out the words with the same intensity of his blows.

Eli locked his arms over his face to protect himself from the awful blows that rained down on him from Jacob's flailing fists. "Stop!" Eli screamed, "God-damn you boy, stop!"

Jacob wrapped a bloody hand around each of Eli's wrists and pulled his arms away from his face. Eli lay still, blinking away the blood from his eyes. "I've had all of the shit I ever want to take from you!" Jacob began breathlessly. "You are a miserable son-of-a-bitch and I promise you, if you ever again lay a hand on my mother, I'll kill you. You hear me? I'll kill you and pray that your black-hearted soul rots in hell!"

Slowly, Jacob released his grip on Eli's wrists and stood over him. Eli rolled to his side and unsteadily pulled himself to his hands and knees, then bracing himself with one hand against the wall, he slowly stood to face Jacob.

"God damn you, boy!" Eli huffed, "This ain't right. What makes you think you're so damned high and mighty? This ain't over, you good-for-nothin' half-breed pup. I swear by God Almighty, I'll make sure you regret this day! That's my promise."

Eli pulled his handkerchief from his back pocket and held it to his nose, took his hat from the hook beside the door, and stumbled outside. Jacob knelt beside Maria and gently cradled her head in his blood-smeared hand.

Chapter 21

Eli leaned unsteadily against the corner post of the front porch. Blood ran from a deep gash above his left eye while he dabbed at the flow that gushed from his broken nose. Drops of blood dripped from the tip of his nose and splattered in crimson pools between the toes of his dust-covered boots.

"Son-of-a-bitch!" Eli spat out the words as he wagged his head in stunned disbelief. "Who the hell's he think he is? Good for nothin' mama's boy. He'll see, by God, he'll see."

Eli shoved the blood-soaked handkerchief into his back pocket and let the blood flow, unchecked, down his face. Grasping the corner post with both hands, his knuckles whitened as intertwined fingers tightened around the smooth contour of whitewashed pine.

"God-damned cur pup," Eli growled between clenched teeth as he pressed his forehead against his thumbs. "By God, that boy's got a hard lesson comin'."

Eli pushed himself away from the post, pinched his swelling nose between the tips of his thumb and finger and blew the darkening blood from each nostril. After wiping his hand on his pants leg, he reached behind his head and gripped his neck. The vertebrae in his neck cracked as he rotated his head, and Eli winced at the sharp pain it caused.

"Son-of-a-bitch!" Eli repeated as he stepped off the porch and headed toward the barn.

Flora had run from the table to the yard, where she crouched on the ground with her back against the side of the house, chin on her knees and arms wrapped tightly around her legs. When Eli appeared on the porch, she could not comprehend that the unsteady, hunched-over old man with a blood-smeared face was her papa. She had never seen him in any way other than his tall, unbending rigidity, shoulders back, head high with the piercing look of dominance that flashed in his dark eyes. The figure standing on the porch, voice trembling as he muttered unintelligible words, could not possibly be her papa. She watched in silence as the stranger stumbled down the front porch steps and headed down the dirt path to the barn.

As Eli walked toward the barn, Flora sprang to her feet, ran around the corner of the porch and up the steps to the front door. Eli heard the sharp clatter of her hurried footsteps on the stairs and quickly turned to see who it was behind him. Flora gripped the handle of the door and was pulling it open when Eli called to her.

"Come here. Come to Papa." Eli's voice sounded raspy as he spoke in a loud and urgent whisper.

Flora turned to see Eli standing stoop-shouldered in the path as he motioned her to him with a slight wave of his hand.

"Come here, girl," Eli repeated in a harsher and more demanding tone as he pointed to the ground at his feet.

Flora held the handle of the door in an ever-tightening grip as she stared with wide-eyed uncertainty at Eli's horrible and frightening appearance.

"No, Papa, no," Flora's voice faltered as she shook her head and began to cry. Pulling the door open wide, she quickly turned and rushed inside, slamming the door behind her.

"Damn," Eli muttered as he wagged his head and turned slowly back toward the barn, "damn, damn, damn it all!"

Maria sat on the kitchen floor, legs drawn up to her chest as she rested her head on her knees. Jacob's arm supported her back and his large hand held her shoulder as he knelt beside her.

"He won't ever hurt you again, Mom," Jacob said softly. "Never again, I promise. Not as long as I'm around."

Flora leaned heavily against the door at her back, where she stood trembling and crying. Her lower lip quivered involuntarily as she chewed nervously at its plump flesh. She did not understand what had just happened, but she knew that something was different; something had changed.

"What's wrong with Papa?" Flora asked angrily. "What did you do to Papa?" she demanded, scowling at Jacob as he helped Maria to her feet.

"Don't you worry none about your papa," Maria consoled. "He'll be alright. You go on and finish your breakfast now."

"Jacob, you too, sit down and eat," Maria said as she pushed a strand of hair from her face and tucked it behind her ear.

"I ain't hungry," Flora whined as she crossed the kitchen and headed upstairs to her bedroom.

After Jacob helped Maria stand, she moved unsteadily to the window staring absently across the yard, to the barn and beyond, until she heard the slam of Flora's bedroom door. She turned to Jacob who stood near the table, hands in his pockets and a frown of uncertainty on his face.

"Jacob," Maria said as she stepped toward him, "I don't know what your Pa might do, but I'm afraid it will be the worse for you. I'll be okay, but I think you ought not be around here for a while."

"I'm not afraid of him, Mom. Not anymore," Jacob replied with an unfamiliar tone of confidence, "and I'll bet he knows that now. I'm not going to leave and let you here alone. I'm staying right here."

Chapter 22

Eli pulled the heavy, oversized door open and stepped into the quiet seclusion of the barn. As he closed the door behind him, the aging stud, his untamed adversary of more than twenty years, snorted a warning, tossed his head and pawed the ground inside his stall as Eli approached.

"Settle down, you ol' son-of-a-bitch!" Eli snapped as he grabbed the whip beside the stall and laid the sting of leather across the stallion's neck. The stud lowered his head and backed into the stall as he raised a foreleg and struck out, in harmless defense, at the space between him and his tormentor.

"That's right, ol' boy," Eli sneered. "You know, by God, who's boss around here, don't ya? Looks like there's some who just can't seem to learn that lesson. But they'll come to regret it, that's for certain. Stupid sons-a-bitches."

Eli hung the whip on the peg next to the stall and walked to the tack room. Opening the door to the large cabinet that sat in the corner, he reached in and took out a half-full bottle of whiskey, pulled the cork, and took a long, deep pull. The whiskey cut the bitter taste of bile that stung his throat and warmed his belly as it spread its soothing fingers of false courage and poor judgment. He let the warmth fill his torso and felt the tenseness in his neck and across his shoulders dissipate in a reflexive shudder, like a horse shaking off the dust after a good roll. Eli took another long pull through the slender neck of the bottle. With his head held back and eyes closed, he let the whiskey spread its warmth as he savored the sharp, familiar taste of oak and corn. Lowering the bottle from his lips, he slapped the cork back in place and returned the nearly empty bottle to the cabinet.

"Stupid sons-a-bitches," Eli repeated as he lowered himself into the old rocker that he kept in the tack room for his solitary comfort.

As the effects of the whiskey began to stimulate his thinking, Eli began to consider the implications of what had just occurred. His own son had just whipped him in a bare-knuckle fight, overpowered him, and soundly beaten him. No longer did he have the power to intimidate or control either Jacob or Maria. No longer was he the 'boss'; gone was his position of authority. What was he going to do now?

It's all that heathen squaw's fault, Eli thought. *If that bitch wouldn't have coddled him all along and turned him into a mama's boy, he wouldn't have stood up for her. He'd have known his place and would have had some respect for me and my authority.*

Eli's thoughts drifted from anger to rage as he replayed in his head the events of the morning. He thought of the surprising strength that Jacob had and realized he was no physical match for his son's youth, agility, and brute force. He thought long and hard about how he could regain his position as the head of the family and retain the fear and respect he deserved, but no solution presented itself. He thought of the shame, humiliation, and ridicule he would suffer if anyone found out that his nineteen-year-old son had bloodied him and put him out of his own house. His thoughts turned to retribution, but he quickly discarded the notion since murder would not have the prolonged, agonizing guilt that he desired for a traitorous son and a disrespectful wife. And besides, revenge from behind prison bars seemed not quite so sweet.

"By God in heaven," Eli declared as he leaned forward in his rocker and shook his finger menacingly at the saddle on the rack in front of him, "I'm the god-damned master around here. Honor thy father, the good book says, and by God, they'll honor me one way or the other!"

Slapping the arms of the rocker with both hands, Eli heaved himself out of the chair with sudden and forceful resolve. Grabbing a halter and cross-ties from pegs above the row of saddles, he staggered down the alleyway to the stallion's stall. When he flung the gate of the stall open, the stallion lunged forward, but Eli had already collected the whip and drove the stud back with several quick and well-placed stinging blows. When the horse was haltered, Eli led him from the stall and cross-tied him in the alleyway then made his way to the tack room for his saddle and bridle.

As usual, the stallion skittered from side to side, attempting to avoid the rough handling he always received when being saddled. But with the restraints of the ropes and Eli's unrelenting force, the stallion was soon under saddle.

Before untying the stud, Eli went back to the tack room and, going directly to the corner cabinet, reached in and took out another bottle which he slipped into the inside breast pocket of his jacket. Returning to the stud, a smug, half-smile crossed his lips as he raised his hand and patted his chest, reassuring himself that the bottle was still there. He took the quirt from off the saddle horn and stuck his hand through the loop at its base, grabbed the horn in his left hand and hauled himself up into the saddle. With a sharp slap of leather from the quirt and a savage jab of sharp-roweled spurs, the stallion sprang forward.

Flora narrowly escaped the thundering charge of horse and rider as they exploded from the barn. With a sharp scream of sudden terror, Flora froze where she stood and covered her eyes with crossed arms. Eli saw her standing there and jerked the reins back with all the strength he had. The stallion dropped to his haunches and reared upward to avoid the obstacle in front of him. The sliding stop was so sudden and violent that Eli was nearly thrown. Regaining his seat and bringing the stallion under control, Eli quickly dismounted and, holding the reins in one hand, knelt down in front of Flora and grabbed her by the shoulder.

"Dammit, girl! What are you doin' here?" Eli scolded.

"I came to see you," Flora sobbed. "What happened, Papa?"

"Flora girl," Eli began, "Your brother has done a bad thing. I've got to go now, for a little while at least, maybe longer. You may not see me again fer a long time. I'll miss you, but I just can't stay any longer. Just remember, I ain't leavin' 'cause I want to; it's 'cause your brother Jake has made it so's I have to. He's done a bad thing and it'll be a burden he'll have to carry his whole life. Someday you'll understand why it's gotta be this way. Now, don't you cry none. You be a good girl, and don't you be like your mama."

Flora threw her arms around Eli's neck and held him tight. "Don't go, Papa. Please don't go."

Eli pulled her arms from around his neck and quickly remounted the stud.

"Sorry, Flora," Eli said as he checked his coat pocket. "Goodbye."

Eli nudged the stallion forward and trotted away at a much slower pace as Flora stood crying in front of the dark doorway of the barn.

Riding across the pastures to a hill overlooking the farm site, Eli stopped to survey the scene that stretched out below him. Patchwork fields were surrounded by sturdy fences and lush pastures where cattle grazed in rich, green grasses. Horses raced to distant fences, manes and tails flying like silk circus flags at the tips of the big-top tent poles. The house and barn, haystacks

113

and corrals, laid out in rigid alignment, surrounded the small form that was Flora, still standing in front of the barn.

Eli reached inside his jacket and pulled out the bottle. He pulled the cork and tossed it to the ground then raised the bottle overhead. Flora returned his farewell wave.

"Adios, all you stupid sons-a-bitches." Eli pressed the bottle to his lips, threw back his head, and drained the contents of the bottle in one long, bitter, gagging gulp.

The sudden fiery burn sucked the breath from Eli's lungs and though his lips contorted around his gaping mouth in an agonizing scream, no sound escaped through the searing pain in his throat. The dark amber bottle slid from his grasp and clattered to the ground as Eli clawed at his throat with trembling hands.

Eli's body began to twitch in violent, uncontrollable spasms that yanked him from the saddle and threw him to the ground. The stallion whinnied sharply and shied away from the writhing body and thrashing arms and legs that flailed the ground in muffled scratches and thumps. Eli's wide-open eyes were locked in unseeing panic as his head jerked from side to side. The stallion pranced nervously nearby, wary of Eli's strange antics until at last, his body was racked with a final shudder, then jerked to rigid stiffness and lay still, eyes staring blankly at the bright mid-morning sun.

With his muzzle close to the ground, the stallion inched his way cautiously forward until his nostrils touched the unmoving form and drew in the unfamiliar smell of death. A soft whicker fluttered from the stud's throat, the sound of contentment that usually comes from the appreciation of a warm stall and a generous scoopful of oats.

Flora was watching when Eli fell, then lay still.

"Mama, Mama, Mama!" Flora screamed suddenly as she raced to the house. "Papa rode up the hill and has fallen off his horse!"

The stallion raised his head and whinnied, long and loud, which brought a responding call from some of the mares below. Then, with a toss of his head, the stud turned and sauntered down off the hill. Stirrup leathers slapped his sides as he trotted across the fields and into the open barn.

****

The coroner's report stated that Eli Brandt died from ingesting Carbolic acid. There was no sign of foul play, as his injuries were consistent with what would be expected from the violent thrashing and convulsing that would accompany the effects of the poison. It was further reported that Mr. Brandt suffered from a mental disorder.

Chapter 23

September's late summer sun felt as though it would blister the skin on Maria's back as its scorching heat penetrated the heavy mourning dress that she wore. Rivulets of sweat ran freely down her spine and pooled at the small of her back, where the bodice of stiff black cotton stained even darker as the dampness spread. She slid a black-gloved hand beneath her veil and, with the white linen kerchief that she held, dabbed at the perspiration that beaded on her forehead and trickled down her neck. Glancing across the open grave where Eli's casket sat suspended on wooden planks above the gaping hole, she wondered why the small cluster of neighbors who stood there had even bothered to come. She hoped that her veil hid her face as she self-consciously touched the kerchief to each cheek to wipe away the tears that were not there.

Evie's hand rested lightly on Maria's shoulder, more to steady herself than to offer any comfort to her mother. Harper held Evie close to him with his arm around her slender waist and his rough hand pressed firmly to her side. Tears ran freely down her cheeks and she let them fall unchecked as she gripped her kerchief beneath the curled fingers of her clenched fist. Tears rolled along the edge of her sharply defined jawline and dripped from her chin into the folds of the stiffly starched ruffle of her modest blouse. She tried to hold back the sobs that gathered in her tightening throat, but the effort was in vain. Sudden bursts of emotion erupted in choking cries as sharp-edged as the heart she felt breaking inside.

Harper shifted his weight from foot to foot, impatient for the ending of the brief service.

Flora stood bravely beside her mother, gripping her hand so tightly that Maria could feel a tingle of numbness in her fingertips. She released her grip with a violent suddenness that startled Maria, then slowly sank to her knees as if she were being pulled into the ground. Burying her face in her hands, she sobbed pitifully, "Papa, oh Papa." Her shoulders quivered with the ragged breath of her cries as she bent forward under the weight of the cruel burden that Eli had left with her. Punctuating her grief was the sound of Eli's voice as his parting words repeated in her head, *Your brother has done a bad thing ...a bad thing ...don't you be like your mama ...like your mama ...a bad thing.*

The preacher stopped, mid-sentence, in the rote eulogy that he had been reciting as Maria knelt beside Flora and wrapped a comforting arm around her shoulders. Flora shrank away from Maria's touch but pulled herself up, wiped the tears that streaked down her cheeks, and stood coldly and stiffly beside her mother. The preacher resumed his recitation, and the small cluster of townsfolk discreetly nudged one another and nervously glanced across the casket at the curious behavior of Mother and Daughter.

Rumors and speculation had already begun to circulate. Although the coroner's report had stated that foul play was not suspected, there had been an autopsy. According to the local whisperings, that surely meant there must be some suspicion. Adding further to the fuel of speculation was the fact that Jacob Brandt had not been seen since Thursday when he had notified the sheriff of Eli's death.

****

When Flora had run to the house screaming that "Papa rode up the hill and fell off his horse," Jacob walked briskly out to the front porch and looked to the hilltop where Eli lay. He jogged to the barn and without thinking grabbed the reins of Eli's stud, swung himself into the saddle, and urged the horse into a gallop. He had never before ridden the stud, having been forbidden to do so, and was surprised at how responsive the stud was. Leaning over the pommel, he felt the stallion's power beneath him as the stud lurched up the steep hill in long, arching strides. Jacob swung to the ground before the stallion had come to a stop and quickly knelt beside Eli's still form. Grabbing the front of Eli's denim shirt with both hands, Jacob jerked him up into a half-sitting, half-reclining position. Eli's arms drooped lifelessly and his head flopped heavily backward as Jacob lifted him. Eli's blank stare and the dark pink foam bubbling from his lips reminded Jacob of the whitetail buck he had lung-shot last season, and he knew that Eli was dead.

"Dammit Pop, you son-of-a-bitch," Jacob muttered in disbelief, "wha'ja go 'an do this for?"

Gently laying Eli back onto the ground, Jacob placed his fingers on Eli's eyelids, pulled them over the empty orbs that had already begun to cloud, and held them shut until they stayed. The stallion ambled forward and nudged Eli's shoulder and sniffed once more at the unfamiliar smell of death. Jacob pushed himself up off the ground and stood unsteadily as he reached for the cantle. Holding onto the saddle with both hands, he turned and looked down the long slope toward the house and barns. Maria and Flora stood side-by-side at the corner of the porch. Maria's left hand rested on Flora's shoulder and her right gripped the corner post, just beneath Eli's blood-smeared handprint.

Maria watched Jacob swing up into the saddle, gather the reins and nudge the stallion to an easy canter. Jacob sat rigid in the saddle, his legs extended but flexed to absorb the jarring of the downhill ride. The stallion instinctively headed toward the barn but Jacob's firm tug of the reins directed him toward the porch where Maria and Flora waited. Maria expected Jacob to report that Eli was drunk, had passed out, and fallen from his horse.

Jacob pulled up in front of his mother and sister, wrapped the reins loosely around the saddle horn and drew in a long, deep breath. He raised his head to meet Maria's puzzled gaze. Jacob's eyes looked dark and blank under the shadow of his hat brim and Maria noticed an uncharacteristic sluggishness in his movements.

Jacob slowly reached up and pulled his hat from his head and dropped it over the horn. "He's dead."

Flora exploded into a piercing wailing as she broke away from Maria and ran to the barn. Maria stood motionless, her face a blank stare. She reached down and gathered the apron she wore into her hands, wiping as if to dry them.

"I'll ride on into town and get the sheriff. Be back in a bit."

Jacob picked up his hat and set it snuggly on his head, unwrapped the reins from the horn, and jabbed his heels into the stallion's flanks. With an immediate response, the stallion lunged to a full gallop and quickly covered the ground between the house and the end of the lane. With a slight touch of the reins, Jacob directed the stud into a hard right turn, and the stallion's quick obedience ignited a flurry of sparks as shod hooves scrambled for footing on the slick granite stones that littered the dirt road to town. After notifying the sheriff and before returning to the farm, Jacob had stopped to tell Evie and Harper of Eli's death. Evie froze in the doorway, shocked and silent, when Jacob made his stone-faced announcement, "The old man's dead."

Evie stumbled forward, and Jacob caught her by the shoulders, holding her upright until her legs regained the strength for her to stand.

"What happened?" she demanded as her eyes searched for understanding in Jacob's blank stare.

"He just went an' killed himself," Jacob replied flatly.

"He what?" Evie shrieked.

"Killed himself," Jacob repeated.

"Dear God in heaven," Evie gasped as she held firmly onto Jacob's arms and leaned forward, resting her forehead on his chest. "Papa wouldn't do that!"

"Where's Harper?" Jacob asked, peering beyond the open door into the front room.

"Oh yes, Harper. He's out. Where's Mom? Where's Dad?" Evie rattled on, confused and disoriented. "Harper's out with a crew, down track. Could you go get him? What about Flora?"

"I'll go find Harper," Jacob assured Evie. "You go out to the house and help Mom; Flora's pretty shook up."

"Okay, I'll go right now." Evie promised, "What about you? How you doing?"

"Me? Ah hell, Sis, I'm right as rain," Jacob said as he turned to leave.

Jacob led the Sheriff and the Coroner to the top of the hill, where Eli's body still lay. After they completed their investigation and left, Jacob hitched the wagon, loaded Eli into the back, and took him to town for the undertaker. When he returned home, Jacob loaded his gear and a few supplies, put together a bedroll, tied it to the back of Eli's saddle, mounted the stallion, and left.

Maria watched from the kitchen window as Jacob rode from the barn across the pasture and disappeared beyond the crest of the hill where Eli had lain dead just hours before.

****

After the funeral, Maria sent a letter to the Dewey County courthouse in Taloga, Oklahoma. She knew that Eli still had relatives in the area, but since they had not kept in touch over the years, she wasn't sure how to contact them personally. She had finally decided on a short announcement that she hoped would be printed in the Dewey County Ledger. It read:

Eli M.C. Brandt, of Frankfort, Kansas, formerly of Alpena Pass, Arkansas and Dewey County, Oklahoma Territory has passed away on 13 September, Saturday last, in the year of our Lord 1909. Burial followed funeral services on Monday the 15th.

Chapter 24

Jacob sat on his heels as he hunkered down by the fire and poured himself a cup of coffee. The day showed promise of being another hot mid-September day. The skies were clear and the eastern horizon already shimmered with vague mirages in the early morning sunlight. He had made camp yesterday late afternoon on the north bank of the Neosho River near Council Grove. It had been two days since he had ridden across the hill where he had brought the sheriff and coroner to investigate the scene of Eli's death and had then headed south. He had no thoughts of where he was going when he had taken a last, backward look at the home place that lay below. He had seen Maria standing on the porch, her hand raised to her forehead to shield her eyes from the glare of the late day sun, but hadn't had the energy to raise his arm and wave goodbye.

Surrounding the tin cup of coffee with his interlaced fingers, he raised the cup to his lips and took a noisy sip of the too strong, muddy black liquid and shuddered at the bitter taste.

It's peaceful here, Jacob thought as he leaned back against his saddle and stretched his long legs out in front of him. "Maybe I'll just spend the day," he said aloud. It was the first time he had spoken since he had informed Harper of Eli's death, and the sound cracked in his throat like the first words of greeting on a groggy morning after sleeping too hard and a bit too long.

It was a peaceful setting, he observed as he looked around his camp. The Neosho River was lined with dense hardwood timber, and the drying leaves of early autumn hinted at a touch of color. The river flowed smoothly toward the southeast and tiny eddies swirled around rocks and roots that intruded on the river's path. A blue heron stood motionless on a submerged sandbar at the river's southern bank, and a small clutch of mallards paddled silently upstream against the current.

For the first time that Jacob could ever remember, he had no feelings of urgency or fear. He didn't have to be at the barn cleaning stalls, filling feed bunks, or grooming horses that had already been groomed but had to be brushed down again only because Eli could not tolerate idleness or refrain from seizing every opportunity to give orders that must be obeyed. For the first time, Jacob could relax knowing that Eli would not suddenly come up behind him and rap him on the back with a pair of reins or a piece of harness leather. No need to worry about being whacked across the shins with a pitchfork handle for reasons no more consequential than a missed horse apple in a cleaned stall or a clump of horsehair left on a currycomb. No need to worry, ever again, about Mama. For the first time ever, he was free.

Jacob took a long, full sip of coffee then lurched forward off his saddle as he flung the remaining black liquid into the brush and spat out a mouthful of bitter coffee grounds.

"Son-of-a-bitch," Jacob sputtered, wiping his mouth with the back of his hand.

His sudden outburst surprised him, and he looked sheepishly to either side to make sure that no one had heard him. Realizing that there was no one but himself for miles around, he leaned back on the saddle, clasped his hands behind his head and smiled in deep satisfaction.

"I can do or say whatever I want," Jacob said aloud. "Ain't nobody gonna' tell me what and what not to do ever again. Ain't nobody ever again gonna' whale on me just for the hell of it." His voice grew deeper and louder as he proclaimed his newly gained freedom. "Ain't nobody gonna' ever cross Jacob Cain Brandt and get away with it."

Jacob slammed a clenched fist into his open palm and remembered the look of fear in Eli's eyes as he had stumbled out the kitchen door, blood streaming from his nose and down his chin. He remembered the surge of energy, the calming sense of control, and the heady rush of power that he had felt and decided that he liked the feeling. He was now his own master. No one had any hold on him and he was beholden to no one. He thought of turning back. He had been gone two days and knew that his mama would be worried. Also, there were chores likely needing to be done that she couldn't do by herself. He supposed that he was now the so-called man of the house and that he should probably be there to take care of things. He could imagine all the tongue-wagging that was already going on.

He didn't even come to his own Papa's funeral.
Rode off and left his mama and baby sister all by themselves.
Could be it was him who killed his own father.
Hear tell they had a knockdown, drag-out fistfight.
Can't trust a half-breed, even when they're kin.

The imagined gossip began to create questions in his own mind. *Was he responsible for Eli's death?* The question lingered only briefly as Jacob rubbed the palm of his hand across his bruised knuckles.

"Hell no!" Jacob shouted, suddenly pushing himself up from the ground. A pair of Mallards that had been approaching the river's edge squawked an alarm and scurried across the current in a blur of feet and wings until they were safely airborne.

"Hell no!" he repeated, flinging his arm in a sweeping arc out toward the bank on the far side of the river. "He done it to himself," Jacob continued as if addressing a crowd that might have gathered to accuse him. "All I done was whup him. Whupped him like somebody shoulda' done a long time ago. Whupped him like he did me ever since I was little. What he did after was his own doin'. I don't know why, but he done it to himself."

Jacob stood, silent and defiant, as he stared across the river and slowly lowered his arm to his side. He kicked the fine silt at the river's edge, into the small campfire, with the side of his boot. The flames struggled against the barrage of sand and dirt but were quickly subdued into a fleeting spiral of gray smoke that hovered briefly over the ring of river stones, then vanished.

Gathering up his iron skillet, the blue enamel plate and cup, and the old tarnished three-tine fork, Jacob walked to the river's edge, hunkered down onto the heels of his boots, and dipped the grease smeared skillet into the swirling eddy of cold, clear water that filled the space between the bare roots of an ancient cottonwood tree. After his eating utensils were cleaned, he stuffed them into a grimy flour sack, twisted the sack closed, and tied it shut with a short piece of string. He rinsed out the coffee pot, swirling the scorched grounds in the brown liquid, and tossed them into the river. In short order, Jacob had The Jack of Diamonds, Eli's stud, saddled, and gear packed in his bedroll and tied behind the cantle.

Jacob gathered the reins in his hand, stuck his boot in the stirrup, and grabbed hold the horn. After a quick look around the camp, he swung his leg across the saddle and settled himself in. He gazed across the river for some time, watching the current glide past in peaceful ripples that seemed to loosen the knots in his gut. Taking a deep breath, he swung the reins to his left, squeezed the saddle fenders with his knees, and coaxed the stallion forward.

"C'mon, Jack, let's go home," Jacob said softly, thinking of Maria and Flora.

The stallion lined out under Jacob's gentle urging and was soon in an easy-gaited canter as they headed north toward home. They had traveled only a few hundred yards when Jacob suddenly and violently jerked the reins. Jack reared against the pressure of the bit and Jacob jerked the stallion's head to the right. Turning on his hind legs, the stallion spun around then dropped to all four hooves as Jacob loosed the reins.

"Sorry, old fella," Jacob crooned as he patted Jack's neck, "I've got some unfinished business to take care of."

Jack plunged into the river at full gallop, the stallion's broad chest slapped the water with a loud "smack" as sprays of water arched away from the sudden collision and sent a small wake rippling to either side. As the river deepened, Jacob slid from the saddle and held fast to the horn while the stud's powerful strides churned beneath. After they had swum the river, the stallion shook off the wet chill in a spray of sunlit diamonds. Jacob swung back up in the saddle as the water drained from his soaked shirt and trousers and sloshed in his boots. A quick slap of the reins, a nudge in the flanks, and home was forgotten.

The long and powerful strides of the stallion quickly distanced them from the peacefulness of the river, and Jacob's thoughts drifted far ahead to a place where he suddenly felt he had to return, to a place somewhere in Oklahoma.

Chapter 25

Jacob gave the stallion his head and felt the power of the muscular horse's stride between his legs. Until today, this was the only taste of freedom that he had ever experienced. Horseback, he had always felt a fullness inside, a rush of exhilaration that swept away the ugly realities and the cringing fear he felt whenever Eli was around. Horseback, he could be spirited away to a place where earth and sky melted together in the distance and in the space between, there was only himself, the horse, and the cleansing wind that washed over him like a baptism. Being horseback was freedom. Being horseback was wildness. Being horseback was power and dominion and for Jacob that feeling of power was all the more intoxicating astride The Jack of Diamonds, his father's prize stallion, the horse that Jacob had been forbidden to ride. Jacob raked his spurs across the horse's flanks and urged him forward, faster and faster still.

As the stallion swallowed the distance ahead with great, seemingly effortless strides, Jacob leaned against the high-backed cantle and, tilting his head backward, savored the rush of wind across his face and the rhythmic drumming of hooves on earth and stone. Behind the curtain of Jacob's closed eyes, sunlight flickered in random patterns of dark and light as horse and rider passed beneath branches of oak and maple and elm, whose leaves of crimson and gold fluttered in the whirlwind they left behind. The patterns of light and shadow that flashed across his sightless vision became sudden and stark images. He saw Eli standing before him, a massive fist raised high overhead, twisted lips that sneered beneath eyes so dark they seemed to be empty holes. He saw him lying in the dust atop a barren hill, an arm turned awkwardly under his body, his cheek pressed into the fine dust where bloody foam slid from the corner of his mouth. He saw his mother standing at the corner of the porch, one hand shielding her eyes from the glare of sunlight and hiding swollen purple flesh, the other raised in a halting wave of farewell.

The stallion's hooves struck a rhythm that matched Jacob's thoughts and the rush of air as the lathered horse gulped each breath, filled his lungs for the next labored stride, and echoed the words that formed there; *He is dead, he is dead, he is dead.*

Jacob jerked forward, gathered the loosed reins in his hand and pulled them to his chest. The stallion responded quickly and slowed his headlong gallop to an easy lope. His blood bay coat was shining with sweat. A thick white lather covered the cheek straps of the bridle, dripped from the sweat-stained leather breast strap, and oozed from under the saddle blanket. Jacob slowed the horse to a walk. He had pushed the stud a bit too hard and long. The willing horse was winded but he soon recovered, settled into an easy pace, and began to cool down.

"He is dead," Jacob said, leaning forward in the saddle.

"He is dead." He rested his arm across the cantle and spoke to the stallion whose ears had perked and pivoted toward his voice.

"The old son-of-a-bitch is dead!"

Jacob rode the entire day. Most times, he traveled at an easy lope, sometimes settling into a lazy walk, but always kept moving southwest. He crossed a small creek around midday, stopped for a drink, filled his canteen, and let the stallion drink his fill then continued on. The country they traveled through was known as the Flint Hills, the best cattle country in Kansas. The lush prairie grasses on these rugged plains contained nutrients that would put flesh and fat on a cow in the dead of winter. Occasionally Jacob spotted a small cluster of cattle grazing in the distance, then a lone rider who seemed to suddenly appear from beneath the ground. The land looked flat and unbroken but deep-cut arroyos spread across the broad expanse in jagged fingers of sharp, gray rock, unseen until a rider approached the edge. The broken land slowed Jacob's progress, but there was no urgency in this trip, and the lack of any well-marked trail seemed to suit his uncertain destination.

Jacob knew where he wanted to go but wasn't certain of exactly where it was. He did know it was somewhere between the Cimarron and Canadian Rivers in Oklahoma and that he'd know he was there when he saw it. It had been more than ten years since he'd been there, but he knew the place.

Two days after he had crossed the Neosho River, he struck Turkey Creek and dropped straight south, following the Arkansas until it doglegged back toward the east. It was there that he crossed the Arkansas and headed southwest until crossing the Pahabe River. It had been nearly two weeks since he had left the home place and, on this night, he was making camp on the southern bank of the Cimarron. In two days' time, three at the most, he would be where he wanted to be. He knew he was close. He could feel it.

The stallion grazed along the edge of the river, pushing his way through the dense willow saplings as he searched out the most tender grasses. Jacob had gathered several armloads of sticks and twigs and had thrown them in a pile next to the spot where he'd chosen to spread his bedroll. His saddle was propped upside-down in the fork of a double-trunked cottonwood. It would be a perfect backrest once the water from the river crossing had drained from the fleece and the fire he was building had dried it a bit. He had just struck a match, holding it carefully in his tightly cupped hands as he hunched over the pile of brittle kindling when he heard the stallion's sharp whinny. From behind him, he heard the answering whinny of an approaching horse. Jacob dropped the match and quickly scrambled to the scabbard that lay beside his bedroll but before he could pull the Winchester from out of the damp leather sheath, he heard a firm, reassuring voice.

"Easy, son. You won't be needin' that rifle. I don't mean ya any harm."

Jacob turned toward the voice, sat back on his haunches, knees still on the ground, and looked up at the man who sat horseback on the bank above him.

Dammit, Brandt! That was stupid. You're as helpless as a box turtle on his back, Jacob thought to himself. He hadn't even thought of the chance of meeting up with someone and now that he unexpectedly had, he realized just how vulnerable and unprepared he was. He made a mental note to not be caught like this again.

"Saw your horse from over there, nice lookin' piece of horseflesh too," the man said with a sweep of his arm toward the stand of brush behind him. "I was plannin' on makin' camp this side of the river for the night. Just thought I'd make myself known."

Jacob watched the man lean forward and rest his arm, easy, on the saddle horn as he spoke. His voice was soft but firm, and Jacob sensed a certain kindness in his manner as well as more than just a little bit of confidence and authority. He was an older man, and the way he sat his saddle, the tilt of his hat, and the slight stoop of his shoulders, Jacob was pretty sure he was a cowman.

"Shouldn't sneak up on a fella like that," Jacob replied as he stood and slapped the sand off the knees of his pants. He was angry with himself for not paying attention and was gruff in his reply.

"If I'd a mind to sneak up on ya boy, I wouldn't be sittin' here horseback in the wide-open an..."

"I ain't no boy!" Jacob spat out the words as his jaw tightened and his hands curled into tense fists.

"I reckon not," the old cowman said softly, straightening himself in the saddle and raising his hand to touch the brim of his hat. "S'pose I'll just make camp a ways over there," he said as he pulled the reins across his chest, turned his horse, and rode off.

Jacob let out the lungsful of air he had been holding and shifted his weight from one foot to the other. His curled fingers slowly relaxed and, stooping forward, he slid his opened hands down the length of his thighs to his knees. Bracing himself for a moment, he flexed his knees, took a long deep breath and pushed himself up to his full height.

If he'd been up to no good, it'd already been done, Jacob said to himself. *Ain't no need to be so inhospitable.*

"Hey! Mister! Hold up!"

The old cowboy pulled the reins and stopped. For a moment, horse and rider stood without moving, then slowly turned to face Jacob.

"C'mon back," Jacob shouted across the distance. "Reckon I forgot my manners. You're welcome to share a camp if you've a mind to."

Horse and rider sauntered back to the cut-bank clearing where Jacob had begun to make camp. While Jacob fished a match from his shirt pocket and knelt beside the pile of kindling, his guest dismounted and began loosening the saddle cinch.

"Thanks for the invite," he said as he jerked the latigo from the cinch ring and pulled the saddle from his horse's back. He propped the saddle against the trunk of a willow tree that had grown horizontal to the ground for several feet before turning upwards in its reach for sunlight. Loosening the cheek strap, he gently slid the headstall over the horse's ears and let the bit fall easily from its mouth.

Jacob couldn't help but compare the unhurried, deliberate, and fluid motions of the stranger's unsaddling to the rough and careless way that Eli had always handled the same task. Although he admired the ease with which the stranger carried himself and the gentle care he took in handling his horse, Jacob quickly surmised that either way, the same result was achieved, so what did it really matter anyway.

After the horse was unsaddled, it dropped to the ground and rolled playfully in the dirt and sand of the riverbank. The cowman stepped quickly toward Jacob as he stripped the sweat-stained leather glove from his right hand and extended it to Jacob who now stood beside the burning pile of kindling.

"Davies," the cowman said with a broad smile. "Charlie Davies, from Texas by way of Oklahoma and points beyond."

"Brandt, Jacob, uhh, Jake. Jake Brandt. I'm from here in Kansas, up north a way, but I come by way of Oklahoma myself."

"Brandt, huh? You wouldn't by chance be ol' Eli Brandt's boy now, would you?"

"Not anymore," Jacob said spitefully. "He's dead," Jacob continued when he noticed Mr. Davies' questioning look.

"I know," Davies replied. "I'm sorry. Read the notice in the Dewey County paper."

"No need for sorry," Jacob said flatly, then asked, "Should I know you?"

"Prob'ly not, son. Prob'ly not. It was a long time ago."

The two men talked casually as they made camp, and Jacob learned how Mr. Davies had known Eli and the trouble that had caused him to uproot his family, sell the Oklahoma homestead, and head north to Kansas. When Davies told about the incident where Eli had shot Nate, Jacob remembered the terror of that day and how Davies had managed to halt the gun battle and disarm Eli.

Jacob learned that Mr. Davies planned to scout out the country in northern Kansas and up into Nebraska for a piece of ground where he could run a few cows and spend less time in the saddle. "Need a change of scenery," Mr. Davies had said. "What about you?" Davies asked.

"Guess I need a change of scenery too," Jacob answered as he poured himself a cup of coffee then filled the cup that Davies held.

"After I found the ol' man dead, I gathered up my gear an' just started ridin'. No place in particular but now I've got a notion to ride down to the Canadian. 'Spose I should head back home. I reckon Ma's got a heap of chores piled up an' like as not prob'ly a bit worried as well. I kinda just run off, not knowin' just what to do."

"Why's a young fella like you makin' such a long trip horseback, 'stead of drivin' one of them new-fangled automobiles?" Davies asked as he stretched out beside the campfire.

"We don't have one," Jacob replied. "Not many folks do 'round our part of the country. What about you? Why ain't you drivin' one of them clatter traps?"

"I prefer horseback," Davies said emphatically. "It's a whole lot more peaceful; a fellow can enjoy the country and as long as I can get where I need to go without having to go 'round too many fences, I suppose I'll just stick to my ol' pony."

"Yeah," Jacob responded, nodding his agreement.

Conversation ceased as the fire burned down to a small pile of embers that skittered into the evening sky like fireflies when the cool breeze kicked at the ring of stones. Jacob finished his coffee, lay back against the saddle, and pulled his blanket over him. Davies tossed his unfinished coffee into the sand and settled in for the night. The horses, picketed nearby, whickered softly as they nibbled the lush grass that covered the riverbank beneath the willows.

"Jake?"

"Yes, sir?"

"You're welcome to ride along with me, back north, if you'd like."

"Thanks, but I think I'll push on south a ways."

"Suit yourself. Want me to look in on your Ma if I happen to be thereabouts?"

"Reckon so. If you do pass that way, I s'pose you could just tell her you seen me."

"Sure nuff."

"Mister Davies?"

"Yeah."

"Tell her..." Jake stopped and stared into the night.

"Tell her what?" Davies asked, raising his head to catch the words he thought he had missed.

"Nuthin," Jake replied flatly. "Ain't nuthin to tell."

Davies tossed a chunk of wood into the fire then turned his back to the flames and pulled the blanket up and over his shoulder. Out of habit, he reached under the edge of his saddle to make sure that his Colt was handy and was soon breathing the long, deep breaths of relaxed sleep. Jake lay still, looking upward at the star-filled sky but not really seeing the glittering canopy of stars that pointed the way back north, marked the passing of seasons, and measured the steady march of time. The night breeze had a sharper edge to it that he hadn't noticed before, and he realized that fall would pass by all too quickly. A nearby cadre of crickets scratched out their rasping warning that was soon answered by their comrades across the river.

"Six weeks 'til frost," Jake said as he pulled his hat down over his eyes.

Chapter 26

The unmistakable buzz of a prairie rattler brought Jacob to his feet faster than the threatening footsteps of Eli across the kitchen floor had so often jerked him from his sleep. In a flurry of arms and legs, he flung off the woolen blanket that covered him, shook the sleep from his head, and grabbed the Winchester that lay nearby. The rattler had coiled itself on the warm sand near the ring of rocks that surrounded the campfire and had become agitated as Jacob stretched himself awake in the half-sleep of morning. The first shot ricocheted off one of the granite rocks of the fire ring and kicked up a shower of sand that did little more than further agitate the rattler. Springing from its coil, the snake struck out blindly as Jacob chambered a second round. The next shot hit the rattler below the head and also midway through its coiled body. While the serpent was still twisting and thrashing in its final death spasms, Jacob fired a third round just to make sure, and jacked another shell into the chamber.

The sudden blast of gunfire sent nesting birds scattering in all directions, their shrill warnings of danger piercing the quiet of early morning. A small flock of mallards exploded from the smooth flowing surface of the river, squawking angrily as they glided amongst the willows along the river's edge. The stallion squealed in terror at the unexpected blasts, reared upward, pulled the picket pin from the soft ground, and charged headlong through the sparse timber away from the river and out onto the open prairie beyond.

Jacob stood unsteadily in his stocking feet, a white-knuckled grip on the Winchester that silently exhaled a thin spiral of smoke from the muzzle.

"Damn," Jacob whispered in a rush of long-held breath as he gently lowered the hammer of the Winchester and let it hang loosely at his side.

The rush from the morning's unexpected excitement slowly drained from Jacob's body and left him still not quite awake. He propped the rifle against his saddle, picked up his hat by the pinch in the crown, and after scratching out a tangle of thick hair, pushed the battered old hat firmly onto his head. With a careful eye on the mutilated corpse whose multi-buttoned tail continued to involuntarily vibrate, Jacob sat down to pull on his boots. As he slapped the sand from the bottom of his socks, he suddenly realized that he was alone. Davies was gone.

Jacob hurriedly pulled on his boots and walked to the riverbank where fresh tracks showed where Davies had crossed. For a short while, he puzzled on why Davies would leave without a morning cup of coffee or a shared breakfast and not even a cordial "Adios." Maybe it was a trap. Maybe Davies had doubled back and planned an ambush. The stallion would be a tempting prize, and Jacob remembered that Davies had commented on what a fine-looking horse the Jack of Diamonds was.

"Jack!" Jacob spun on his heels as it suddenly registered that the stallion had bolted at the first unexpected crack of gunfire. Jacob raced across the campsite and slogged through the thick stand of willows where the stallion had been picketed. The stallion was nowhere in sight and no amount of whistling brought the spooked horse back to camp.

"You're getting stupider every day," Jacob said out loud. "First, you let a stranger sneak up on you, then you sleep past daylight while he breaks camp and leaves, and now you let your horse run off and leave you scratchin' your ass and shakin' your head. I reckon it's high time to figure out that dumb luck can only last so long."

Jacob walked quickly back to his camp, shoved his rifle into the scabbard, rolled up his blanket, and tied it behind the cantle. Taking his knife from his pocket, he stepped toward the ring of rocks where the now still rattler lay. He squatted beside the mangled coil and cut off the tail.

"Seven buttons," he said as he stood up and stuck the trophy into his shirt pocket, closed the blade of his knife against his thigh, and kicked the carcass into the ashes of last night's fire. He pulled a cold biscuit from a cloth sack in his saddlebags and stuffed the hard chunk of pan-fried bread into his mouth. Grabbing his saddle by the horn, he threw its bulk over his shoulder and headed south.

"Stupid god-damned horse," Jacob muttered around a mouthful of cold biscuit.

The farther Jacob walked, the madder he got as the weight of the saddle dug into his shoulder, and his arm shuddered in spasms against the strain. Despite the cool touch of early fall, sweat dripped from under his hat and ran in steady rivulets down his temples, streaked across his cheeks, and rolled along the line of his jaw until it gathered at the point of his chin and grew too large to hang on. Each drop of sweat marked his trail as clearly as the boot prints he left behind. And each step, each drop of sweat, each muted curse that rattled unchecked inside his head built to anger that would not be contained and once unleashed, would not be controlled.

With his back bowed beneath the burden of the saddle, Jacob walked in silence, eyes scanning the ground ahead for hoof prints. Occasionally he stopped, let the saddle slide down his back to rest on the ground, pulled the dark-stained hat off his head, and wiped the sweat from his face in the crook of his arm. Squinting against the glare of the sun, he searched the horizon ahead for any sign of Jack, then stooping down to grasp the saddle, he raised it to his shoulder and continued on.

It had been several hours since Jacob had left camp that morning. His feet were blistered, his arm and back numb with fatigue, and his empty stomach rumbled with hunger. Absorbed in his anger and oblivious to his surroundings, Jacob literally stumbled into a small spring that bubbled clear and cold from out of the ground. Here he stopped to wash the grime from his face, quench his thirst, find himself something to eat, and cool his burning feet. As he dropped to the ground to pull off his boots, he heard, behind him, the soft, trembling whicker of a horse. Jacob jumped to his feet and spun around to see Jack trotting toward him and the pool of spring water, the picket line still dangling from his halter.

Blinded by his burning anger, Jacob flew into a rage. He jerked his lariat from the leather binding on the saddle, built a loop, and quickly tossed it over the stallion's head. Then drawing up the slack with his left hand, he grasped the rope above the shredded end and began to whip the stallion across the face and neck. Jack reared away from the blows, but Jacob avoided the striking hooves and laid the stinging whip across the stallion's breast. The beating continued until Jacob could no longer raise his arm and the stallion stood trembling in fear, white foaming lather mixed with crimson.

Jacob tied the stallion up short to a nearby tree, away from the water, and fell exhausted beside the spring, soothing his rope burned hands in the cool water.

"That'll teach the son-of-a-bitch not to run away," Jake sneered.

Chapter 27

It was near dusk when Jacob began to wake. The violent outburst of anger and the long, tiresome walk earlier in the day had sapped him of his strength, and he had quickly dozed off beside the spring. Disoriented at first, it took a while for Jacob to realize just where he was and whether the darkening skies were signaling dawn or dusk. He lay still for some time while listening to the quiet murmurings of water lapping around stones as the nearby spring pulsed to the surface from its deep, dark beginnings inside the Earth Mother. A sudden spasm in his back reminded him of the burden of the saddle that he had carried for most of the day, and he rolled onto his back to relieve the cramp.

Jacob's stirring alerted the stallion to his waking, and the tethered horse stomped the ground angrily with his forefoot. Throughout the afternoon and early evening, the stallion had managed to dig a considerable hole as he had pawed helplessly at the base of the tree where he was bound. He had been tied so close and high to the trunk of the tree that he had been unable to lie down or even lower his head. Flies had gathered along the edges of the long strips of raw flesh on his neck and chest, and the stallion could not keep them away with the frequent quivering of muscle and hide. To add to the sting of his wounds and the deep ache in his cramped muscles, the stallion had not had any water since the night before when he had drunk his fill at the spring.

The evening star had burned a hole in the darkening canopy when Jacob finally pushed himself up from the ground and sat cross-legged beside the spring. In the deepening twilight, Jacob groped among the surrounding grass to find his hat, and grasping the brim in both hands, pulled it firmly onto his head. A sharp and pitiful whicker rose up from the stallion's parched throat.

"Shut up, you worthless ol' rip," Jacob growled, picking up a palm-sized stone and hurling it at the stallion.

The rock smacked against the horse's flank, and the stallion jerked back, fighting the confining tether, shaking his head and pulling as he pivoted frantically in a futile attempt to escape.

"Ain't no use in fightin' it," Jacob sneered, approaching the terrified stallion. "I've seen knot-heads like you kill themselves fightin' the snubbin' post. Just flailin' and fightin' 'til they up an' busted their own damn necks. I reckon you best jus' settle down."

Unable to escape, the stallion stood stiff-legged and trembling, his head and thickly muscled neck stretched taut at the end of the ungiving rope. Jacob loosened the knot and slowly unwound the coils that had been wrapped around the tree trunk. As the last coil offered some slack, the stallion attempted to jerk free, but Jacob held the rope firmly, keeping enough tension on it to allow only short bits of slack at any one time. Inch by inch, as more slack was given, the stallion backed away from the tree, but Jacob continued to restrain him. Finally, the wary stallion yielded to the constraint and took a single step forward. When Jacob felt the stallion give, he quickly jerked the rope tight again and held it snug until the stallion took another step forward. When Jacob felt certain that the horse would not bolt, he released the last wrap from around the tree but held the rope tight against the stallion's diminished resistance. The stallion stepped forward, and Jacob responded with one more harsh jerk on the rope, forcing the stallion to follow with halting, unsteady steps. With muscles quivering in nervous fear of the unexpected, the stallion was, at last, led to the spring.

Distrustful of Jacob's intentions, the horse tentatively dipped his muzzle into the shallow pool and drank in short, hurried gulps, noisily sucking the soothing wetness through his lips. After each sip, the stallion jerked his head upward and watched, with wary eyes, the sudden stranger who was now holding him captive.

After Jacob had allowed the stallion to drink his fill, he hobbled and picketed him where he would be able to forage. Taking advantage of his limited freedom, the stallion eagerly tore at the prairie grass, ripping out mouthfuls of needed nourishment.

The last hint of daylight had long since slipped beneath the far horizon, and a sudden evening chill caused an involuntary shudder to pass across Jacob's shoulders. The increasing darkness surrounded the growing numbers of stars, and Jacob tipped back the brim of his hat to search out familiar constellations. The thin crescent of moonlight that hung overhead would not give enough light for night travel, and so Jacob set out to scavenge the area for firewood. A cup of hot coffee would hold off the chill, and a belly full of beans and bread would take the edge off his hunger.

Walking beneath nearby trees, Jacob kicked his way through the grass to locate twigs and branches that he would need to make a fire. A sudden, subtle rustling in the tall grass ahead revealed the presence of some nighttime critter that scurried away, leaving behind its pungent warning. From atop the lofty branches of a nearby cottonwood tree, the soft, clear call of a Great Horned Owl rolled through the darkness while packs of coyotes yipped in shrill chorus from hilltop to coulee.

Despite the darkness, Jacob had soon gathered an armload of firewood. He carried the bundle close to the spring and set himself to the task of building a fire. Snapping twigs from the ends of the smaller branches and scraping together a mound of brittle leaves and grass, he built a small mound of tinder, fished a match from his shirt pocket, and holding the match in the grip of his fingers, struck a flame with the edge of his thumbnail. The carefully constructed pyre of twigs and leaves quickly jumped to life as yellow and orange flames twisted through the crisscrossed jumble of fuel. Jacob broke larger branches across his knee and carefully positioned them like lodge poles above the growing flames. The crack of branches breaking over Jacob's knee penetrated the dark stillness and echoed back like the sound of distant gunfire.

After the fire no longer needed constant vigilance, Jacob ventured into the darkness in search of more firewood. Gathering up the scattered limbs that he stumbled over, he soon had another armload of wood. He turned his back to the night chill that lay beyond the fire's reach and headed back to camp.

Approaching the fire, Jacob sensed a sudden familiarity with his surroundings. Dropping the load of firewood beside his campfire, Jacob stood transfixed, peering into the wavering light just past the edge of his campfire's dim circle.

"This is the place," Jacob said, his voice scarcely more than a whisper. "This is the place where the damned son-of-a-bitch crawled up out of the guts of hell."

The never forgotten scene rose up once more from the depths of his remembering. It was over there, tucked back in that small shelter of trees where his mother had sat beside the wagon, her eyes wide with fear. It was between those two trees where he had been sleeping when he heard the shot that echoed through the trees in an endless, deafening pounding, and the air filled with the sharp, sweet smell of gunpowder. Across the way, in the tall grass that skirted the gently sloping hill, was where he had watched his pony struggling to rise, feet flailing against the sky, his neck twisted upward, panic-filled white orbs unseeing in his terrible agony, his teeth bared, mouth agape in high-pitched screams, screams that matched the awful sound of his mother's own sharp keening.

Jacob sank to his knees, his hands clasped tight against his ears, but the horrible sounds came from inside. Once more, he felt the muzzle of Eli's Winchester pressing into his flesh and heard his father's chilling words, "By damn boy, maybe that'll learn ya!"

"Yes, sir, old man," Jacob said in a venomous hiss, "you damn sure taught me good."

Jacob rocked forward on his knees, his head touching the ground, his fingers tightly gripping the handfuls of grass that he held. He felt that he had to hold on to the earth, perhaps even become a part of it. For a long while, Jacob's grip held the rooted grass firmly in his clenched fists as if he were afraid that if he let go, he might fall off. He felt weak, spent, and empty. His shoulders heaved with the spasms of a man who grieves without crying. And from out of the darkness that crept in around the dying fire came the soft whicker of the stallion.

Jacob unfolded himself from the ground and stood. He pulled a long, deep breath into his lungs and let it out in a rush that shook his tall and muscular frame. Walking to his saddle, he loosened the leather strap that held his canteen and pulled a ragged square of cloth from his saddlebags. The stallion shied away as Jacob approached, then stood nervously at the end of the picket. Though still trembling, the stallion began to relax as he breathed in the smell of Jacob's outstretched hand. Jacob soaked the rag with water from his canteen and began to wash the stallion's wounds.

"It's time to head for home, boy," Jacob said softly as he stroked the flesh that quivered under his hand.

Chapter 28

The stallion pranced impatiently as Jacob reined him into the lane. For the past several miles, the stallion had begun to sense that he was in familiar country and had tried to take the bit and make a headlong sprint to the finish. Flecks of slobber dripped from the corners of the horse's mouth as he fought the bit and tossed his head, but Jacob kept a tight rein, forcing the stallion to hold back.

For a moment, Jacob wondered why there was such a crowd of people gathered around the corrals and clustered near the house and barn but soon recognized the obvious, an auction.

"What the hell..." The words fell from his mouth in a heave of breath. Jacob slumped in the saddle, his shoulders caving forward, his arms limp, fingers loosening their grip on the reins.

With slack in the reins, the stallion thrust his muzzle to the sky and let out a long and loud whinnying that was quickly answered by a number of mares that careened from corner to corner inside the corral where they were being held. An auctioneer stood in a wagon box, shouting out his call for bids in a rapid-fire cadence of dollars and nonsense.

"I've got forty on the buckskin. Forty over here an' I need fifty," the auctioneer announced, words tumbling off his tongue like shelled peas into a saucepan. "Who'll gimme fifty? Gotta forty gimme fifty. Fifty-fifty-fifty. Forty goin' once, twice, thrice, and sold! For a forty-dollar bill." His well-worn gavel crashed against the top of the makeshift podium of wooden boxes and another horse was led out of the corral.

Jacob regained his grip on the reins and forced the stallion toward the house and away from the corral full of mares. As he rode through the crowd heads began to turn, and a muffled rumbling of voices began to spread from one small cluster of people to another.

"Look! Jacob's back!"

"No tellin' what kind of no-good he's been up to."

"Heard tell he might have had a hand in the old man's death."

"Just up an' disappeared. Didn't even show up fer his own daddy's funeral!"

"Oh my!"

"What d'ya think he's going to do?"

"Look at him! Some nerve he's got riding in here like that."

"Worried his mother half to death."

"He should be ashamed."

The auctioneer stood slack-jawed and silent as he watched Jacob ride toward the house. He held the gavel in his right hand and slowly tapped its smooth head into the palm of his left, watching, waiting as if expecting a change in the days' proceedings.

"You gonna sell that horse?" shouted an overall-clad farmer, pointing his battered hat at the haltered sorrel mare that stood beside the wagon.

"We've got an eight-year old broodmare here," the auctioneer began, jarred back to action as Jacob rode past.

A bevy of questions flooded Jacob's thoughts. Why sell off everything? Why didn't she wait for me? What's going to happen now? He looked out across the pastures and up the slope to the hilltop where Eli had left his final and permanent mark on the place, the family, and their future. The cattle were gone, and Jacob realized that he had missed the fall shipping. It looked as though that this year everything had shipped, cows, calves, heifers, the whole lot.

Alongside the barn sat the haying equipment, sickle mower, dump rake and hay rack, side-by-side and carefully aligned. Harness, collars and hames were draped over fence rails along with saddle pads, blankets, and other tack. On the ground beside the display of tack were wooden boxes filled with brushes, currycombs, lead ropes, halters, bits, and cinches, along with tonics and liniments, wraps, and salves.

Maria was on the front porch as Jacob rode toward the house. She had been helping the local ladies of the Methodist church to serve coffee and sweet rolls to those who were attending the auction. She had seen Jacob ride in at the far end of the lane and felt a sudden stab of panic. At first sight, she had thought that it was Eli. The rider who sat the stallion carried himself in the saddle the same way that Eli had, straight-backed and defiant, fighting against the will of the stallion. However, Maria quickly realized that it was not Eli and felt herself

140

foolish for the brief instant of not remembering that Eli had been recently dead. As Jacob rode closer, his face flush with anger, her panic was replaced by a mixture of dread and relief, and the overwhelming emotion caused her knees to buckle, and she crumbled to a sobbing heap on the porch.

Two of the Methodist women who were there with Maria helped her up and assisted her into the house. Jacob saw his mother stumble and coaxed the stallion to a canter. Before reaching the porch, Jacob dropped the reins, swung his leg across the pommel, slid to the ground, and ran to the house. The stallion stood still as if tied to a rail, the reins dangling on the ground.

The ladies on the porch parted in a flutter of aprons and dishcloths, creating a path for Jacob as he rushed across the porch and pushed open the door to the kitchen. Maria sat at the table on the end where Eli had once ruled. When Jacob entered the kitchen, the ladies who had helped Maria to the house quickly left, their hands clutching the folds of their aprons, their eyes focused on the floor. Jacob stood, stiff and awkward, as the ladies passed by, then closed the door behind them. In two short steps, Jacob was at Maria's side when she pushed herself up from her chair and wrapped her arms around his broad shoulders and buried her face against his neck. Jacob held her waist in the grip of his hands and felt her warm tears trickle down his neck and under the collar of his shirt.

"I thought you would never come back; I thought you might be dead," she whispered.

"I'm sorry, Mama. I'm so sorry," Jacob managed to choke out through the lump that threatened to strangle him.

Maria gripped Jacob's shoulders in her hands and pushed him back to where she could look into his eyes. "Tell me where you've been," she said firmly, punctuating each word as if she were scolding.

"That's not important right now, Ma. What's important is what's happenin' here. Why are you sellin' out?" Jacob's voice had an edge of urgency and the rigid chill of controlled anger.

"There weren't any other choices, Jacob," Maria replied as she lowered herself into the chair and placed her hands, palms down, on the table's edge. Jacob took off his hat and tossed it on the table as he pulled a chair out and sat down.

"You've been gone nearly three weeks now, and I've had no word of your whereabouts. I truly did have thoughts that you were gone for good, your chance to break away from all that's gone on in the past, and I even dreamed that you were dead. I saw your eyes, dark and empty like a dead man's eyes." Maria pressed her hands together, her fingertips touching as she raised them to her lips, her chin resting on her thumbs.

"Your pa had debts come due," Maria continued, "and it was time to ship the cattle, so I shipped them all. I didn't know which ones to hold over or which ones to sort off. I just shipped them all. And the horses, aren't none of them broke to ride. The broodmares are bred and the colts and fillies are hardly even halter broke. It was easiest for me to just sell all of them. If you were going to be gone for good, I needed cash money to pay the bills and hang on to this place until I could figure things out. Oh, everybody had opinions, and everybody was willing to tell me what I should do, but I did what I needed to do."

Jacob pushed himself back from the table, slowly shaking his head as he drew in a long and deep breath, then let it out in a gush of exasperation. He could find no words. He had not thought of the consequences of his leaving.

There was a knock on the kitchen door, and one of the ladies on the porch opened it just far enough to poke her head around the edge, "Mr. Chapman, the auctioneer, would like a word with you, Mrs. Brandt."

Maria and Jacob stood and walked to the door, Jacob holding the door open while Maria stepped outside, then Jacob followed.

"Pardon me, Missus Brandt," Mr. Chapman began as he removed his hat in an overly grand display of insincere politeness that ended with a curt bow at the waist. "I see that the stallion standing over yonder bears your late husband's brand. Some buyers have inquired as to whether or not he is to be sold also?"

Before Maria could answer, Jacob rushed forward until there was little distance between Jacob's reddening face and Mr. Chapman's quickly fading smile. "Is the stallion listed on the god-damned sale bill?" Jacob quietly demanded in a voice clear enough for Mr. Chapman to hear yet quiet enough to avoid ruffling the piety of the Methodist ladies.

"Uh, no, sir," Mr. Chapman whispered.

"Then I reckon, sir," Jacob continued, "that you should tell your buyers that the stallion is not for sale."

"Yes, sir," Mr. Chapman meekly replied as he quickly replaced his hat, glanced over Jacob's shoulder toward Maria, then turned and scurried away to the auction wagon.

Jacob turned to find his mother standing directly behind him. She shook her head in mild disapproval but smiled as she took Jacob's arm and led him back to where the stallion stood.

"Take him to the barn," Maria said, "I'll make some coffee."

Chapter 29

The crowd was beginning to clear out as Jacob led the stallion toward the barn. The equipment that had been sold was being loaded on wagons or hitched to teams that would haul them to their new homes. Horses were haltered and tied to the back ends of buckboards and buggies. Two of the best mares on the place were tied to the bumper of a shiny new Ford truck and were trotting along behind as it chugged down the long lane.

Jacob led the stallion into the barn and was struck by the quiet emptiness that stretched before him. Stalls stood empty and wooden pegs that had been driven into hand-hewn beams for hanging tools and tack stuck out like accusing fingers stripped naked of the brass buckled leather straps they once held. In the corner stall, Maria's horse called out with a soft whicker, and the stallion trotted down the alleyway to greet her, their velvet muzzles quivering as they touched. Maria's saddle, the only one left in the barn, hung on the rack nearby. The buggy stood against the far wall, a set of harness draped over the dashboard. Shafts of sunlight spilled down from the cupola and glimmered with hay dust that floated invisibly into the shadows. Jacob smiled, thinking of how quiet and peaceful it seemed, serenity in sharp contrast to the turmoil the old barn was used to.

Jacob walked to the stall and scratched Maria's horse behind the ears, a ritual that was expected, then gathered up the reins as he reached up to unbuckle the stallion's headstall. He pulled the saddle off the stallion's back, hung it on the rack, and went to the tack room for a brush. The tack room was empty, lead ropes, halters, latigo straps, cinches, all gone. A ragged, worthless old saddle blanket lay in a heap in the corner.

"Son of a…!" Jacob swore as he ran outside to see if any of the boxes he had seen beside the barn were still there. They were gone. "Damn!" Jacob yanked off his hat and slapped his thigh in disgust as he watched a bowlegged old man waddle down the lane, a box of tack cradled on his shoulder, the wooden handle of a curry brush peering over the edge.

Back in the tack room, Jacob stood on tiptoe sweeping his hand across the top shelves in hopes of finding a stray brush that had been overlooked; there was nothing. He went to the medicine cabinet, turned the latch, and swung the double doors open.

"Hallelujah!" Jacob shouted and snatched the remaining half of a broken brush from the shelf. "Looks like they left some stuff," he said and began to rearrange the clutter that had been left behind.

There was a jar of coal oil wrapped with an old rag, a hoof pick, a mostly empty can of Watkins salve, and a rusty old currycomb that might still serve its purpose. In the back corner of the top shelf, Jacob could see the top of a bottle. He reached up and grabbed it, shaking it as he brought it down. Although the cork was still in place, the bottle was empty. A handwritten label was taped to the side, "Carbolic Acid." Jacob tossed the empty bottle into the corner, where it landed in the folds of the discarded saddle blanket, picked up the broken curry brush, and went back to take care of the stallion.

After a good brushing the stallion was turned out in the corral, where he promptly lay down and rolled. Jacob hung his elbows over the top rail of the corral and watched the stallion roll from side to side. Heaving himself to his feet, the stallion shook off the dust, then with arched neck and tail held high, he pranced and bucked and careened around the pen. Jacob laughed at the stallion's antics.

By the time Jacob had returned to the house, the auctioneer was gone, the crowds of people had vanished, and the ladies of the Methodist church were dividing up the remainder of the sweet rolls among themselves.

"Thank you, ladies," Jacob said, politely tipping his hat as he walked across the porch.

"You're most welcome," one of the women replied. "Will you take some sweet rolls? There's plenty left over," she continued, walking toward him with a dishcloth-covered pie tin.

"Thank you," Jacob answered, taking the plate and lifting the edge of the cloth to see what was hidden beneath. "I reckon a feller ought not turn down a chance for sweetbreads."

"Good you're back, Jacob," said one of the ladies. "Sorry 'bout your pa."

Jacob nodded his acknowledgment of the condolences, touched his finger to the brim of his hat, and ducked inside the house.

Maria was pouring coffee when Jacob walked in. She put the pot back on the stove and sat at the table while Jacob hung his hat, set the pie tin on the table, pulled up a chair, and sat down.

"Thanks," said Jacob as he raised his cup. The coffee was too hot, and Jacob winced as he took a sip, so he took the cup of coffee and poured a portion into the saucer, then raised the saucer to his lips and noisily sipped. The ill-mannered habit was one he had copied from Eli.

"Do you have to drink your coffee that way?" Maria asked with an unmasked hint of irritation.

Jacob made no reply as he took another noisy sip.

"Why did you go?" Maria asked abruptly.

Jacob paused for a moment, his cup held suspended, ready to pour another portion into the saucer. He set the cup down and ran a finger around the rim several times before he answered, "South, I just took off an'..."

"Not where, Son," Maria interrupted, "Why?"

"I'm not sure I really know, Ma," Jacob said. He sat quietly for some time, sorting his thoughts, gathering words. "I just knew I couldn't stay," Jacob began. "I s'pose it's my fault that he done what he done. I got no regrets, but I s'pose I just pushed him to it."

"You did no such thing, Jacob!" Maria exclaimed. Her dark eyes flashed as she reached across the table and gripped Jacob's hand. "Whatever happened to your pa was of his own makin'. Don't you go blamin' yourself."

"Maybe so," Jacob replied, "but I just had to get away from all the ...all the bullshit. Sorry, Ma, but I did, and the farther away I got the farther I had to go. I almost turned around and came back once. I knew I'd left you and Flora in a bad mess, but I just had to keep goin'. I went all the way to the Cimarron."

"Oklahoma!"

"Yea. I went to the springs where we camped that first night out. I didn't know I was there at first, but then I realized that I was back to where Pa had shot Little Bit. And there, I realized that as much as I've hated the way he treated you and me, I've got that same mean streak myself. "

"Don't say that, Jacob! Don't say that."

"It's true, Ma, I'm sorry to have to say so, but it's true. Sometimes I just can't hold it back, and it comes out like that day." Jacob absently drummed the table with his fist as he spoke. "That day that I just couldn't take it no more. That day that Pa left."

"That's all over with now," Maria said, reaching across the table and laying her hand over Jacob's clenched fist. "For now, we've got to figure out where we go from here."

"Waddya mean, where we go from here?" Jacob asked, jerking his hand away from Maria's grip and leaning hard against the back of his chair.

"I've got a couple of offers on the place," Maria replied somewhat impatiently. "I told you, I didn't know if you were coming back or not. I don't have a lot of choices now, do I?"

Jacob took a deep breath and slumped forward, staring down at his hands folded on his lap. "I s'pose not," he said quietly. "But you don't have to sell out," Jacob began with a tone of urgency. "We can rent out some of the pasture for cash money and maybe go shares on the cropland. I can hire myself out to folks hereabouts and, with the barn set up for horses, I can earn some money breaking and training colts."

"That all takes time," Maria said, shaking her head with obvious doubt. "This auction's not going to put a lot of money in the bank. Most will go to pay off debts and not much left beyond that."

"But we can try, can't we?" Jacob urged. "Just let me try."

Chapter 30

"Easy! Easy! Easy boy!" Jacob drew the words out in a firm but calm voice that did little to settle the two-year-old buckskin gelding that fought against the rope around his neck. Jacob leaned back into the rope that passed behind him, making a deep impression across his buttocks as the horse reared backward.

"Easy now, easy!" Jacob coaxed, pushing downward on the rope with a gloved hand as he shuffled toward the snubbing post that was planted in the center of the pen where he worked. The gelding made a sudden, powerful turn, and the rope sizzled through Jacob's hands and jerked him off his feet.

"Halter broke, my ass!" Jacob groaned as he picked himself up off the ground and grabbed his hat that lay nearby. The gelding crow-hopped around the pen, head tucked between his forelegs, and the rope trailing behind like a ribbon blowing in a stiff wind. Jacob jammed his hat back on as he jogged across the pen to catch up with the trailing end of the rope.

"Ol' man Foley said you was halter broke!" Jacob yelled as if the horse might understand. But the buckskin ignored the obviously false claim, continuing his headlong flight around the pen.

Jogging quickly across the pen, Jacob halted the buckskin's forward charge by stepping into his path. The gelding came to a sudden sliding stop, then wheeled on his haunches and reversed direction. In the brief moment that the horse stopped, turned, and headed off in the opposite direction, the rope that trailed behind lay within Jacob's easy reach. Quickly grabbing the frayed end of the rope, Jacob maneuvered himself toward the snubbing post and was able to get a single wrap around the rope-scarred cedar pillar. As the buckskin continued to circle the pen, the rope wrapped around the post until Jacob and the horse were standing nearly nose-to-nose. Wide-eyed and quivering, the buckskin pulled back until the ungiving rope cut off his breathing. Little by little, the horse began to understand that struggling meant not breathing; yielding to the pressure of the rope meant an easing of the restriction and the ability to breathe freely. During this lesson, Jacob stood still, talking softly, as the buckskin gradually began to relax and finally stood quietly. Jacob slowly reached down and picked up the halter that lay beside the snubbing post and gently slid it over the buckskin's head.

"Nice work," came a vaguely familiar voice from outside the pen.

Jacob looked over the buckskin's neck as he buckled the halter. "Davies?" he asked, shielding his eyes against the low sun that glared over the shoulder of the silhouetted rider.

"Yep," Davies replied, leaning forward as usual to rest his forearm on the saddle horn. "Nice lookin' buckskin ya got there," Davies continued.

Jacob kept a firm grip on the halter's lead and slipped the loop of rope off the buckskin's neck and over his head. "Belongs to a neighbor," Jacob offered. "I'm just trying to work out the stupid."

"Looks like a good start," Davies said, stepping down from the saddle.

Jacob led the buckskin to the pen's gate and whipped a single wrap of the lead rope around the top rail. The gelding had followed without resistance and stood quietly as Jacob opened the gate and stepped out. Jacob pulled off his gloves and extended his right hand to meet Davies' greeting.

"I'd say he's already had a bit of schoolin' by the looks of it," Davies said, nodding toward the buckskin.

"I think so, too," Jacob acknowledged, looking back over his shoulder at the gelding. "I figure it must have been a while back, though, and he's forgotten, or at least being lazy about remembering."

"Might have a bit of a stubborn streak," Davies offered. "But offhand, I'd say he was a keeper. Got that intelligent look in his eyes. Could be a good cowhoss."

"I don't s'pose ol' man Foley cares much about that," Jacob countered. "All he's wantin' is a good lookin' horse for ridin' to town once or twice a week."

"That's a shame," Davies replied, stepping a little closer to the rail for a better look. "Wonder if the ol' feller might have a mind to sell?"

"I s'pose everything's got its price," Jacob said with a sideways nod. "So," Jacob continued, tucking his gloves into his hip pocket, "you been up in this country ever since I seen you last year?"

"Guess you could say so," Davies began. "I was headed north when I crossed the river and it seems I just kept on. Got in on a fall gather round

Wichita and rode the rails with a bunch up to Saint Joe, then figured I might as well see what Omaha looked like. Weren't much to see. Followed the Platte until it started to swing back south, so I turned north again. Wintered on the North Loup, little outfit up there, nice folks, good cow country. When the ice went off the river, I figured it was time to move along. Thought I'd swing down this way, see how you were making out."

"Headed back to Texas?" Jacob queried.

"Not sure."

The corral fence rattled as the buckskin tugged impatiently at the lead rope that held him there. Jacob quickly unwrapped the rope but held firm to let the gelding know he was still tethered and needed to stay still. Opening the gate, Jacob entered the pen and approached the buckskin, talking softly as he reached out to rub the horse's forehead and cheeks under the halter's straps. When the gelding was calm and stood quietly, Jacob unbuckled the halter and let it slowly slip off. For a moment, the gelding didn't realize that he was free and he stood without moving while Jacob continued to rub his forehead.

Jacob stepped back and raised his hand. "Heyeah! Go on boy!" Jacob commanded as he flung the halter over his shoulder. The buckskin bolted through the open gate and into the pasture.

"Stay for supper?" Jacob asked Mr. Davies while watching the gelding paw the ground before lying down to roll.

"No trouble?" Mr. Davies asked.

"Naw, no trouble at all," Jacob assured him. "Put your horse in the barn an' I'll tell Ma we've got company."

"Your Ma still here?" Davies asked casually, "She doin' okay?"

"Yeah, she's fine."

"Glad to hear it."

Davies grabbed the saddle horn and swung astride his horse without a toehold in the stirrup and galloped the short distance to the barn.

Chapter 31

Charlie Davies stood on the porch. His seemingly at ease demeanor belied the nervous flutter that churned inside. While in the barn, unsaddling his horse, Davies had rehearsed the choice of words that he hoped would relate his anticipation and pleasure at seeing Maria after so many years.

"Hello, Maria. No, no, she doesn't even know I know her name. Too forward, ain't it?" Charlie asked his horse while pulling the saddle off.

"Missus Brandt, my pleasure. 'Nah, too stiff."

"Hello, Missus Brandt, nice to see you. Okay, but sure don't sound like me, does it boy?"

"Missus Brandt, good to see you are well. Huh-uh, sounds like she's been sick or somethin'."

"A pleasure to see you again, Missus Brandt. Think that'll work? A pleasure to see you again, Missus Brandt. Yeah, that'll do."

Charlie polished up the toes of his boots by wiping them across the back of his legs, slapped the dust from his hat against his knee, then reshaped the caved-in crown. Gripping the curled brim of the well-worn Stetson in his left hand, Charlie rapped his knuckles against the door twice.

"I'll get it, Ma," Charlie heard the shrill voice of a young girl come from inside the house.

The door swung open, held by the hand of a tall, slender, young lady. Her deep brown eyes sparkled and long dark braids hung down the front of her navy blue dress. Her mixed-blood heritage was evident in her smooth, olive complexion.

"Come on in. My name's Flora," the young lady announced.

"Hello, Miss Flora. Charlie Davies," Charlie said, bending slightly at the waist before stepping inside.

Charlie stood, holding his hat with both hands, wondering where Jacob was and not sure of what he was supposed to do next.

"Come on to the kitchen," Flora said cheerfully; a sideways nod of her head seemed to indicate that Charlie should follow, so he did.

In the kitchen, Maria stood at the stove, stirring a mound of sliced potatoes in a large cast-iron skillet, her back to Mr. Davies. Charlie took notice of her narrow waist, strong back, and the long single braid, now showing strands of silver, hanging below the bow that tied her apron.

"Mister Davies," Maria said brightly as she turned, wiping her hands on the apron that she wore, "It's been a long time." Her onyx eyes sparkled and her warm smile made Charlie's planned words stick in his throat.

"Howdy, Ma'am," Charlie managed to reply. "Guess you never made it down to Texas."

"No, Mister Davies, never did," Maria said as she turned back to stir potatoes. "Go ahead and sit yourself down, coffee's 'bout done an' I'll bring ya a cup. Jacob's out gatherin' up some wood for the cookstove. Should be back in any time now."

Charlie pulled a chair from the table, sat down, and slid his hat under his chair. "Thanks fer havin' me to supper," he said, placing his hands on the table. Turning his hands palms up, Charlie noticed the caked-on horse sweat and dirt and quickly jerked his hands from the table and put them in his lap.

"Reckon I should wash up a bit first," Charlie announced.

"I'm sorry," Maria apologized. "Wash pan's on the porch," she pointed toward the back door with her chin. "Soap's right there an' you can hang yer hat by the door."

"Thanks," Charlie said, leaning down to retrieve his hat from beneath the chair.

Mister Davies had worked up a good lather when Jacob walked through the back door with an armload of wood. The two men nodded a silent greeting and Jacob went on to the kitchen.

"Cream or sugar, Mister Davies?" Maria called from the kitchen while pouring a cup of coffee.

"No, Ma'am," Charlie shouted over his shoulder. "Hot, strong, and black suits me just fine."

Maria continued with the cooking, and Flora placed the dishes, knives, forks, and spoons in all the proper places. Charlie and Jacob drank coffee while Jacob talked at some length about the several horses he was working.

"Sounds like you've got yourself a pretty good business going," Charlie observed.

"Pretty good," Jacob replied. "Took a while to get folks to warm up to the idea of turning their horses over to a kid for training, especially Eli Brandt's kid. But after I turned out a couple of good ones, it kinda picked up. It sure ain't gonna make a feller rich but along with the farm ground and the pasture we're renting out we're doin' okay."

"Just say so if it ain't none of my business, but you gonna just stick with a horse outfit or planning on running some cattle?" Charlie asked cautiously.

"That's alright," Jacob said with a casual wave of his hand, like brushing away a pesky fly. "No harm in asking. We've done some talking, me and mom, and if the market stays down, we're thinking on bringing in a little bunch to build on. I'm liking the Hereford breed myself."

"Pink eye and sunburned teats," Charlie warned, then flinched with embarrassment.

"Sorry, Ma'am, sorry, missy."

"No apology needed, Mr. Davies," Maria laughed, amused by Davies' obvious discomfort.

"True enough," Jacob replied, ignoring the quick exchange between Charlie and Maria, "but they're easy calving and good mamas."

Maria untied her apron, ducked her head through the collar and hung it on a peg near the stove. She quickly smoothed her hair with the palms of both hands, tucked the loose folds of her blouse under the waistband of her skirt, then pulled her chair out from the table. Charlie raised himself from his seat and grabbed for the hat that he had forgotten he was not wearing. Maria acknowledged his act of chivalry with a wave of her hand, and Charlie settled back into his chair.

"Let's eat," she said.

Supper was simple but hearty with fried potatoes, beefsteak and gravy, bread, butter, and wild plum jelly. Fresh baked apple pie drowned in thick cream was an unexpected dessert, and Charlie Davies couldn't seem to find enough words to compliment Maria on the extraordinary pie.

"Best apple pie I believe I've ever had," Mister Davies stated several times, which seemed to please Maria.

"Mister Davies," Maria said suddenly. "Tell me, what brings you to Kansas?"

"Well Ma'am, I suppose it was several things," Charlie began, taking his coffee cup in both hands and leaning back from the table. He had never really thought too much about what he expected to find in Kansas, and he certainly wasn't ready to make it known that his first hope was to find Maria.

"I suppose you could say I'm just driftin'," Charlie continued. "I was born and raised in Texas and danged proud of it, but I got to thinkin' it might not hurt to see some different country for a change. So, one day, I just packed my bedroll, saddled up, and headed north. And then too, there was that bad deal down there in Oklahoma an' I always kinda wondered how you folks made out."

"That was a long time ago," Maria said softly. "I wouldn't have thought that would have made any difference to you."

"It does," Charlie said softly, without thinking, then loudly continued, "Anyway, I ran across young Jacob here when he was headed south. I'd read about Eli, uh, Mister Brandt, in the paper, an' Jacob said maybe I should look you up. I give it some thought but figured it best to just leave it be. So, I ended up goin' further east and then on north a ways."

"Yeah," Jacob interrupted, "you up an' left me there without even a polite adios. Dang near got me snake-bit to boot. I didn't even hear you go."

"Sorry, Jake. Guess I just woke up restless an' it seemed best to just saddle up and go. Didn't see any reason to roust you out in the middle of the night."

"That still doesn't tell me what brings you to Kansas, Mister Davies," Maria said, remembering his reply of, "It does."

"Well, Missus Brandt, I s'pose I'm not dead certain. I reckon I might just wait an' see what Kansas might have to offer."

Charlie raised his cup as if offering up a toast, and Maria nodded her approval.

It had been dark for some time and Jacob had plans for an early morning session with the buckskin. "Reckon it's 'bout time to turn in," Jacob announced. "There's a cot in the tack room, Mister Davies, an' you're welcome to bunk there."

"Suits me fine," Davies replied. "Thank you again, Missus Brandt for the meal. Good pie."

"You're quite welcome, Mister Davies, and good night."

Davies excused himself from the table and crossed the kitchen to the back porch, took his hat from the wall, and placed it firmly on his head then turned to watch Maria gathering dishes from the table. She cradled a stack of dishes in her arm and turned her head to catch a glimpse of Davies before he left. Charlie stood in the doorway and, when he caught her gaze, Maria lowered her eyes though not so much so that Charlie could see the warm smile that crossed her lips. Raising his hand, Charlie touched the brim of his hat with his finger and nodded his head.

"G'night, Ma'am," Charlie said softly.

Charlie Davies pulled the door closed behind him and walked to the edge of the porch, grabbed hold of the crown of his hat, and pushed it back until the brim touched his collar. The night sky was clear with a slivered crescent of a moon that shone like white-hot iron on a smitty's forge. Stars filled the canopy with cold, brilliant light, and the Milky Way cut an overhead swath that glittered like diamond dust on velvet.

Charlie couldn't remember the last time he had actually stopped to look at the night sky but somehow, tonight it just seemed like the thing to do.

"Mighty pretty," Charlie whispered as his gaze swept across the night sky. "Just like I'd remembered."

He pulled his pouch of tobacco from his vest pocket, thumbed a paper from out of the envelope stuck to its side, and pulled the pouch open with his teeth. He curled the brittle paper with his thumb and fingers while tapping a thin furrow of tobacco into the shallow trough, then pulled the pouch closed with its drawstring in his teeth and stuffed the pouch back into his pocket. Moistening the edges of the paper with his tongue, he folded them together and rolled the ends between his thumbs and fingers, licked the edges, then tucked the finished cigarette in the corner of his mouth. Reaching once more into his pocket, his finger swept the bottom seam in search of a match but the pocket was empty.

Charlie turned back toward the kitchen door. He could hear Maria's and Flora's voices, but couldn't hear the words as they chattered back and forth. He intended to rap on the door and ask for a match but decided it might be a bit awkward, so he turned round and stepped down from the porch.

"Yep, still mighty pretty," Charlie said as he gazed skyward, the unlit cigarette still dangling from his lips.

After the dishes were finished and Flora had turned in, Maria took off her apron and hung it on the hook beside the stove. She gave a quick glance around the room and, satisfied that all was in order, retired to her room for the night.

Before changing into her nightgown, she went to her closet and took a small wooden box from off the shelf, sat it on her dresser, and opened the lid. From among the stones and feathers and twist of Sweetgrass, she picked out a large silver concho and, holding it in the palm of her hand, rubbed a finger over the engraved initials, C.D., and smiled.

Chapter 32

Charlie woke early. The fact was he hadn't slept much, restless and anxious, wondering if what he thought Maria was thinking was what she was really thinking. Did that shy smile and quick sideways glance mean what he thought or was she just being cordial? Charlie had been struck with her simple good looks and quiet manner the first time he had met her back in the Territory and had felt helpless when he realized that Eli was mistreating her. He had sometimes wondered if what he felt was pity and a need to rescue Maria or if it was really an honest-to-goodness attraction. After mulling that over for the better part of the night, Charlie had concluded that it wasn't pity and Maria, sure as hell, didn't need rescuing now. He worried that maybe he had said too much, then worried that he hadn't said enough, and then realized that he hadn't really said anything at all that would have let on that he had feelings for her. *Besides*, Charlie thought, *couldn't have said anything anyhow with Jacob and Miss Flora there too.*

The first dim light of morning announced the dawn's advance while the morning star's bright beacon faded from the sky. Charlie was awake and ready to go but wasn't sure where to. As he pondered on what to do next about Maria, he realized that he hadn't been invited to breakfast. Although it was fairly common for an overnight guest to join the family in the morning meal, Charlie convinced himself that the lack of a proper invitation meant he wasn't invited and that meant it was time to go.

Charlie grabbed his hat from the wooden peg beside the bunk, jerked it on and walked briskly through the barn to where his horse was stabled. Stirring himself up to a tolerable state of agitation, he reached for his bridle and was completely off his guard when he heard, "Coffee's ready, Mr. Davies, hot strong and black."

Unaware that Maria had come into the barn, Charlie jumped from her sudden and unexpected presence, and Maria laughed as he clumsily regained his composure.

"Damn! I mean, dang, Missus Brandt, you sure spooked me."

"Sorry, Mister Davies, I suppose I should of just hollered from the porch."

"That's alright. Reckon I just ain't used to hearing a woman's voice first thing in the mornin', and I sure didn't hear ya come in. Kinda caught me by surprise."

"Well, you can turn your horse out to pasture, then come on up to the house. Breakfast will be ready shortly."

Maria turned to leave, and Charlie reached out and put his hand on her shoulder. "If…" Charlie began, but Maria instinctively flinched from his touch and drew a quick, sharp breath as she recoiled from his hand. When she turned to face Charlie, he saw the brief flash of fear that filled her eyes and creased her forehead with deep lines. Charlie stood stock-still, his arm outstretched, his hand held aloft.

Neither Charlie nor Maria spoke. The silence was as awkward and obvious as Charlie's suspended hand, and the two held each other's gaze, unblinking, like cottontails hiding in a thicket. After a seemingly endless moment, the fear melted from Maria's face, and Charlie's puzzled look softened to one of understanding as he realized the depth of her fear and understood her unexpected reaction to the weight of his hand on her shoulder.

"Beg your pardon, Maria," Charlie said as he dropped his hand, took a half step back, and tucked his thumbs into the corners of his pockets. "I was gonna say if you've a mind to hold on a minute, I'd walk to the house with you."

"Of course," Maria said with an apologetic smile, "Thank you, Mister Davies, I will."

Charlie led his horse from the stall and into the pasture beside the barn. Maria followed and waited while Charlie turned him loose and closed the gate. When Charlie reached Maria's side, he stopped, bowed slightly as he touched the crown of his hat, then extended his elbow toward Maria. "Missus Brandt," Charlie said with exaggerated formality.

"Mister Davies," Maria replied as she placed her hand into the crook of his elbow. Her dark eyes sparkled as tears welled and, as they walked together, she gently squeezed Charlie's arm.

Maria and Charlie reached the kitchen door just as Jake was exiting the privy. With obvious surprise at the sight of Maria walking arm-in-arm with Mister Davies, Jake halted mid-stride as he fumbled with fastening the last button of his Levi's. If the couple noticed his slack-jawed countenance, they discreetly ignored his presence as Charlie opened the door with his free hand and escorted Maria inside. When the door closed behind them, Jake finished buttoning his fly and continued up the path to the house. After a couple of hesitant steps, Jake stopped, looked at the kitchen door, then turned to look toward the barn. Mister Davies's horse had just finished a vigorous roll and stood shaking the dust from his coat. Glittering in the glare of the morning sun, the billowing dust settled to the ground like a cloud of gold-flecked fog while the horse bolted from its core and took flight across the pasture. Jake looked back toward the house, shook his head to clear the last groggy remnants of sleep, cleared his throat and spat into the grass beside the path, and spoke his first word of the day, "Shit."

The kitchen door burst open just as Jake reached for the latch.

"Breakfast's ready!" Flora announced as she flew past him on her way down the path.

"I'm here," Jacob shouted back over his shoulder.

"Be there in a minute," Flora hollered.

When everyone had finally gathered around the table, Maria and Flora on one side, Jacob on the other, and Charlie at the end, Flora, resting her forearms on the table's edge, folded her hands, turned toward Mr. Davies, and with a polite nod indicated that he should do the same. Mister Davies, obviously unaccustomed to mealtime prayers, hesitated for a short, awkward moment before quickly folding his hands. Flora glanced around the table at Jacob and Maria and, satisfied that everyone was properly prepared, squeezed her eyes shut tight and began, "Come Lord Jesus…"

Charlie's eyes settled on Maria, her head bowed, eyes closed as Flora continued with grace. Jacob discreetly cleared his throat, and Charlie shifted his gaze from Maria to Jacob, whose furrowed brow and squinting eyes showed certain signs of unanswered questions or perhaps mild displeasure. *Maybe a little bit of both*, Charlie thought and flashed a thin smile then bowed his head.

"…Amen," Flora intoned with punctuated finality.

Breakfast was simple, fried eggs, biscuits and bacon, hot coffee for everyone except Flora, whose glass of fresh milk was soon emptied. The conversation was limited to matters of immediate importance:

"Pass the biscuits, please."

"Thanks."

"More coffee?"

"Yes, please."

"Jelly?"

"Don't mind if I do."

Charlie wiped up the remnants of bacon grease and egg on his plate with biscuit crumbs smashed in the tines of his fork. His last bite was washed down with his last swallow of coffee, then he leaned back in his chair with both hands on the edge of the table.

"Mighty fine breakfast, Missus Brandt," Charlie declared, "My thanks for your fine meals and hospitality."

"You're most welcome," Maria replied with a nod of her head and a warm smile. "So," Maria continued, "where do you plan to go from here, Mister Davies?"

"Well, Ma'am," Charlie mused, scratching the three-day stubble on his chin, "I reckon I've got no fer certain plans at all. Thought I might head into town this mornin', pick up a few things I'm needin'. Figured I might look up that Mr. Foley feller that belongs to that buckskin Jake's been workin'. I like the looks of him and might try to do some horse tradin'."

"He ain't for sale," Jake interrupted. "Besides, I ain't finished with the training he hired me to do."

"If Foley wants to sell, you can finish the buckskin out for me," Charlie offered. "I'll pay your going rate. Wouldn't wanna cut you out of a job."

"Makes no difference to me one way or another," Jake said, his tone a bit sour. He got up from his chair, an empty coffee cup in his hand, and walked to the kitchen stove. As he poured himself a fresh cup, he continued, "I'm just sayin' that ol' man Foley ain't gonna sell you that buckskin."

"Mebby not, mebby so," Charlie speculated, "Just hafta see."

Jake sat back down at the table and poured some of the steaming coffee into his saucer. "Reckon so," he said flatly.

Flora was busy clearing the table and stacking the dirty dishes beside the sink. Maria excused herself from the table, retrieved her apron, and ducked

160

into it, tying the long cotton apron ribbons behind her. "If you're going to be leaving, Mister Davies," Maria said as she fumbled with the bow behind her back, her words sounding more like a question than a casual comment, "and if you've a mind to, stop by before you go. I'll pack you some dried beef, sourdough biscuits, and a few other things that might fit your grub sack. Right now, I've got chores need doing."

"I suppose that depends on my parlay with ol' man Foley," Charlie replied, turning toward Jake to acknowledge his doubts. Jake stared back over the rim of his saucer and sucked up a mouthful of the cooling coffee. "But, either way, I appreciate your invite. I've never turned down good grub."

Maria smiled, pleased that Davies had accepted her invitation. Davies pushed himself away from the table, stood, and turned to leave. He stopped to grab his hat from its peg, held the crown between his thumb and fingers, and set it snugly atop his head. He turned back to see Maria watching him, but she quickly lowered her gaze and then slowly raised up to meet Charlie's eyes.

"Missus Brandt," Charlie said as he touched the brim of his hat.

"Mister Davies," Maria said brightly, her onyx eyes dancing.

Charlie turned and walked out the kitchen door.

Flora giggled at the subtle but unmistakable flirtation between Maria and Charlie. Maria smiled and playfully bumped Flora's shoulder, tipping her slightly off balance. "Mister Davies," Flora swooned.

"Oh, hush!" Maria scolded.

Jake held the empty saucer to his lips, closed his eyes, and shook his head.

Chapter 33

Charlie Davies skipped down the back stairs from the kitchen door and, if anyone had been watching, they would have seen him hook his arm around an imaginary waist, take hold of an imaginary hand, and step out to strains of a fiddle tune that played in his head. Then suddenly aware of his foolish actions, he quickly dropped his invisible dance partner and reached for the Bull Durham tag that hung from his shirt pocket. Pulling the pouch from his pocket, he remembered that he had no matches and shoved the pouch back into place.

"Don't forget matches," Charlie reminded himself and continued on to the barn.

When Charlie reached the gate of the corral that led to the pasture beyond, he gave a loud, shrill whistle that echoed off the barn and silenced the birds that had been chattering away in their own early morning conversations. Another sharp whistle and Charlie's horse came bounding across the pasture, head held high and tail arched. In response to Charlie's summons, the gelding returned the call with a high-pitched whinnying that sent a ripple of excitement through the horses penned nearby. Plumes of dust rose from the horse's hooves as he swung into the corral, leaning into the sharp turn and up to where Charlie stood, elbows draped over the top fence rail.

"Hey, there, old man. Feelin' a bit frisky this mornin', eh?"

Charlie held the gelding's lower jaw in one hand and scratched alongside his cheek and up behind his ear. The gelding stretched out his neck and laid his head on Charlie's shoulder while Charlie rubbed with both hands along the length of the horse's muscled neck.

"That a workin' horse or a pet?" Jake queried, sarcasm thick in the tone, as he walked up behind Charlie.

"Better part of both, I reckon," Charlie replied over his shoulder, "and a pardner to boot," he added.

Jake walked up beside Charlie, laid his arm along the length of the rail, and leaned against the nearby post. He watched as Charlie continued to rub the horse's neck then reach out and pat him on the shoulder. The gelding lifted his head, turned, and ambled away.

"All you need is for them to stand still when you put your foot in the stirrup, move out when you say so, and know what 'whoa' means. The rest is mostly foolishness as far as I'm concerned," Jake said with a cutting edge in his voice.

"Each to his own, I suppose," Charlie responded, ignoring the subtle mocking. "For me, I'd as soon have a horse respond 'cause he wants to rather than thinkin' he has to or else."

"Or else what?" Jake snapped.

"A light rein and a firm hand goes a long way further than a whip or spur," Charlie countered. "A horse that fears you might someday turn on you."

"Most of them will turn on you anyhow, some time or another. Buck you off and leave you afoot or kick you in the head all because something buggered 'em and they all of a sudden turn stupid."

"True enough," Charlie admitted, "but that's less likely if they trust you instead of fear you."

"Either way, it's all the same," Jake said matter of factly. "In the end, all you need 'em to do is the work you expect from 'em. Beyond that they're nothing but hay burners."

"Mebby so, mebby not," Charlie said as he pushed himself away from the corral and headed for the barn.

Jake followed Charlie into the barn, where Charlie gathered up his tack from the saddle rack where he had hung it earlier that morning, and Jake retrieved his catch rope and a halter.

"Workin' the buckskin this mornin'?" Charlie asked on his way out the door.

"Later. You?"

"I'll be ridin' into town," Charlie answered as he turned and stood in the doorway, his saddle slung over his shoulder. "Need a few supplies, plan on lookin' up Mr. Foley, inquire about the buckskin. I'll swing back by here to let you know if we've made a deal or not."

"I think you're wasting your time with Foley," Jake warned.

Charlie saddled his horse while Jacob caught up a blaze-faced sorrel mare and wrestled her to the working pen. Once inside the pen, Jacob took a dally around the snubbing post at the center, tied it off, and approached the mare hand-over-hand up the rope. Fighting the tightening loop around her neck, the panicked horse reared, striking out with her forefeet while Jacob, gripping the rope with both hands, continued his advance. The mare jerked back, pulling the slack that had gathered behind Jake, and sent it sizzling through his gloved grip. Unable to restrain the horse with brute force, Jacob gave up the battle and retreated to the outside rails of the pen, stripped the gloves from his hands, and spit on his palms to cool the rope burn.

Charlie had saddled up and mounted while Jacob attempted to bring the untrained mare under control. Sitting outside the working pen, Charlie leaned forward in the saddle, forearm resting on the horn, and watched. When Jacob had given up the fight and leaned against the rails, Charlie spoke. "I'd say she's got a good bit of Mustang blood. High spirited and a bit ornery to boot, not mean, just feisty and more than a little scared. You need to back off, let her come to you. She don't trust you."

"I don't need her to trust me; I need her to give up and quit fighting," Jacob snapped.

"You won't get one without the other," Charlie advised, "not with that horse."

"She'll come around soon enough," Jacob threatened, "and she can just stand there, tied to that post until she does."

"I won't try to tell you what you won't listen to," Charlie said with a hint of warning, "but I won't abide cruelty. There's more than one way to get what you're after. Just think on it some. You'll figure it out."

Jacob kept his back turned to Charlie and had nothing more to say. Charlie reined his horse around and headed out in an unhurried, easy trot.

"Think on it some, my ass!" Jacob growled, mocking Charlie's advice. "You, you knot-headed sack of bone and hide, you think on it some. Go ahead and choke your damn-fool self; you'll figure it out."

Jacob tucked his gloves into his back pocket, walked out of the pen and into the barn. The mare stood stiff-legged, straining against the rope, neck stretched, ears back, panic showing in the red-veined whites of her eyes.

Chapter 34

Charlie Davies rode out from the Brandt place heading northwest toward the town of Frankfort. Jacob had reluctantly given directions to the Foley farm located a few miles south of the town and had again stated his strong opinion that Foley wouldn't sell. Charlie had already decided to go a long way toward making a deal, mostly because he was really impressed with the buckskin, and the "old man" as Charlie called his bay had a full twenty-five hard seasons on him and deserved to take life easy for a spell. And then there was the notion of proving Jacob wrong. No particular reason, but Jacob's insistence that Mister Foley wouldn't sell seemed more like a challenge than a statement of fact. Charlie liked the boy well enough and figured he deserved a bit of slack. After all, the last couple of years had to have been a little hard on the kid, but he appeared to have handled it all fairly well and seemed to be on a good track even though he was carrying a mighty big chip. Charlie hoped he could make a deal with Mr. Foley on the buckskin before he went on to Frankfort, where he planned to pick up the supplies he needed, get a bath, shave, and a haircut before heading back to the Brandt's.

It was an uncommonly pleasant mid-summer day as far as Kansas summers went. The ever-constant breeze carried the smell of fresh-cut hay as it cured under a white-hot sun. Not a scorcher like it could have been, but the sky was cloudless and, despite the close proximity of the nearby Big Blue River, the air was dry. The rolling sameness of the land felt familiar to Charlie and the long, gentle rise of Capital Bluff, to the west, put him in mind of the range country of Texas.

"Well, Ol' Man," Charlie said as he leaned forward and patted his horse's neck, "I reckon there's worse places for a body to settle in. That is, if it works out that way. Just hafta wait an' see what comes up."

Charlie scratched the length of his horse's neck then leaned back in the saddle, left hand holding the reins and resting on the saddle horn, right hand dangling at his side, "Just hafta wait an' see."

Charlie's horse followed the two-track road toward Frankfort without need of guidance. The dusty ruts showed the sharp cut track of iron-rimmed wheels as well as the increasingly familiar markings of rubber-tired automobiles.

"We're both gonna be obsolete," Charlie grumbled, lifting the reins and turning off the two-track onto the lane that, according to Jacob's directions, belonged to Mister Foley.

The lane followed the curve of a grass-covered hill and continued toward the base of another small hill that partially hid the house on the other side. The ridgeline of a roof, with a brick chimney at the far end, showed above the crest of the second hill and came into full view when Charlie rounded the corner. The house was a well-built two-story frame house, probably a mail order from Sears or Montgomery Wards, Charlie guessed. The outbuildings and corrals were all sturdy and immaculately maintained. In fact, Charlie was pretty certain that the oversized barn, built for hay storage above and livestock below, had just recently been painted. Perfect post and rail fencing boxed in three sizable paddocks, each paddock holding a well-groomed horse, part Thoroughbred, part old Spanish Barb, or so Charlie's trained eye for horseflesh affirmed. Another larger paddock, apparently a holding pen for a sizable number of cattle, stood empty at the opposite end of the barn. Charlie also noticed a small shed, built close to the house, with a pair of large hinged doors. The doors were closed and rubber-tired automobile tracks trailed back and forth from inside and continued along both sides of where Charlie sat astride his horse and out to the road. Beyond the house and barnyard, the land sloped gently toward the southwest, and a three-strand, barbed wire fence confined a cattle herd of moderate size, all she stock with heavy udders but no calves in sight, Charlie observed. The cattle, with their varied patterns of white and brown, reminded Charlie of the Longhorns he had gathered on the Texas plains years ago, but these weren't Longhorns.

"Ayrshire's!" Charlie exclaimed, recognizing a breed he had heard of but never seen until now. "I declare, them are milk cows! This here's a dairy farm, Ol' Man!"

A windmill near the barn and another at the far end of the pasture whirred quietly in the breeze. Hayfields bordered the perimeter of the fence line and

166

several farmhands were busy with teams of horses gathering up the cured hay and stacking it in high domed piles.

"My, oh my!" Charlie whispered.

The house was surrounded by a white picket fence whose purpose, it seemed to Charlie, served to protect the lush green grass that blanketed the other side all the way up to the steps of the front porch. Further proof of its purpose was the white picket gate that blocked what appeared to be the only entrance that led to the house. Charlie shifted himself forward in the saddle, slackened the reins, and his horse moved forward toward the gate and stopped when he reached it.

"Hello, the house!" Charlie shouted toward the porch, "Hello!"

"Hello!" came a reply from behind.

Charlie reined his horse around and saw a man standing in the doorway of the barn and, in the next instance, two large animals came bounding out the open door past the man and came at full gallop toward Charlie. Their deep-throated baying indicated that they were dogs, but Charlie had never seen the likes before. The dogs were almost as big as a month old colt and hairier than a Welsh pony. Charlie's horse shied at the onrushing charge of the two hounds, but Charlie held him steady with a firm rein as the dogs halted a few feet away, stiff-legged, back hairs bristling, barking in defiance of the intrusion.

"Back, boys, back!" shouted the man who was now walking toward Charlie in long, hurried strides. "Pitka! Shiel! Down, down, boys!" The two dogs stopped their barking and lay down side-by-side, quiet but still alert and trembling in anticipation of a possible command.

Charlie stayed in the saddle as the man approached. When the man reached the place where the dogs lay, he reached down, scratched the massive head of each animal, and spoke, "Good boys." The dogs relaxed, opened their mouths, and began to pant, saliva dripping from their long, pink tongues.

The man stood and looked up at Charlie. "Wat's your business, lad?" he asked, his left hand cupped above the brim of his slouch hat to shield the sun that glared just over Charlie's shoulder. It struck Charlie as being a bit amusing that he should be called "lad." The man who stood there looking up was likely not too many years older than himself. Broad-shouldered and stout, with an expanding girth that comes with the slower pace of aging, the man carried the marks of a life of hard and heavy work. His thick fingers, calloused hands, and hard-muscled arms would be a match for men of far fewer years. The man wore a blue cotton work shirt with woolen vest, denim trousers held in place with a brass-buckled leather belt a full three inches wide, and pants legs tucked into the tops of calf-high riding boots. The flush of crimson that spread from beneath the kerchief tied around his neck and upward to his fleshy cheeks was likely the result of hard work in the heat of the barn or perhaps from a fondness for good whiskey. The man's outfit convinced Charlie that this must be a hired hand.

"Well, sir," Charlie began, "I've come to do some business with Mister Foley. Is he hereabouts?"

"Yes 'e is lad, I'm Foley. Just wat is this business you 'ave?"

"Well sir, yes sir, uh," Charlie stammered, "I didn't, uh, 'scuse me, sir, I…" Charlie began to dismount, and the two hounds began a low, deep growl, hair rising along their shoulders and down their spines. Charlie stopped, his right leg suspended over the cantle, waiting for some word from Foley.

"Easy now, boys, it's okay," Foley spoke, holding his hand out toward the two dogs, palm down.

"You sure it's okay?" Charlie asked as his right boot touched the ground, his left still in the stirrup.

"Aye, sure, lad." Mister Foley said, then with a hint of warning continued, "If anythin' should go amiss, I'll be certain to gather up all the pieces fer yer next of kin."

Charlie stepped to the ground and turned toward Mister Foley and with a sideways glance at the dogs, cautiously extended his hand, "Davies, sir, Charlie Davies."

Mister Foley took Charlie's hand in a firm grip, shook it once, and released his grip. "Pleased to make your acquaintance, Mister Davies. Now tell me, lad, wat business might ye 'ave wi' me?"

"Well, Sir, I've come to ask about a horse."

"Ahhhh, horse business it is, is it? Well, we best be gittin' in outta the sun if it's horses we'll be talkin' about, eh?"

"I reckon so," Charlie replied.

With a broad sweep of his hand, Mister Foley directed Charlie toward the house, and the two walked side-by-side to the white picket fence. The two dogs trailed behind, and Charlie held on to his horse's reins. When they reached the fence, Charlie dropped the reins between pickets, and Mister Foley unlatched the short gate and held it open. The two dogs rushed in, and Charlie followed.

The dogs bound up the stairs to the porch and promptly lay down in what was obviously their accustomed spot, each on either side of a large wooden chair that Mister Foley walked to and sat down.

"Sit. Sit," Mister Foley commanded, directing Charlie toward an empty chair that sat opposite him and the two dogs.

Must be more used to talking to dogs instead of humans, Charlie thought as he lowered himself into the chair.

Mister Foley reached into his vest pocket and retrieved a short-stemmed pipe, blackened with age and hot ash. From his shirt pocket, he pulled a soft leather pouch of tobacco and began stuffing the cut leaves into the bowl.

"So, Laddie, wat is this horse business you've come to talk to me about?" Foley asked, studying the pipe he cradled in his hand while packing the bowl with his thumb.

"Beg your pardon, Mister Foley," Charlie said, leaning forward and shifting himself toward the edge of his chair, "but right now, I'm wondering if you've got an extra match."

Mister Foley looked up from his pipe packing ritual and stared at Charlie with an arched eyebrow that implied a question but came with no words.

"I ain't had a cigarette since yesterday afternoon, all for want of a match, an' I've got one powerful hankerin' for a smoke, an' I'd sure be obliged if you could spare me a match."

"Of course!" Mister Foley exclaimed then laughed heartily as he reached inside his vest pocket and withdrew a match. He tossed the sulfur-headed stick to Charlie who caught it and promptly placed it in the corner of his mouth while pulling the cloth pouch of tobacco from his shirt pocket.

"Thank you, Sir!"

The two men sat quietly on the porch, each enjoying their respective choice of tobacco. Foley puffed deliberately on the stem of his pipe held firmly between his teeth. Charlie took long, deep draws on his cigarette and had soon reached the point where the butt was too hot and too close to his fingertips to hold any longer. Charlie smothered out the last embers of tobacco on the heel of his boot and stuffed the remains of unburned tobacco and paper into the cuff of his jeans.

"Yes Sir," Charlie began, leaning forward with one hand on each knee, "about that horse business. I'm an acquaintance of the Brandts over by Vliets, and young Jacob Brandt is doing some work with a fine-looking buckskin that I understand belongs to you, that right?"

"Why yes, Mister Davies, that is a fact, truly is. I reckon there's nary a problem wi' that, eh? The boy's doin' a fair job of it I s'pose?"

"Oh no, Sir, no problem at all. Appears to me he's makin' good progress with the buckskin. Maybe a little impatient at times and a bit too aggressive in some ways, but that's just my opinion. Time and experience will be a good teacher if he pays attention and learns to work with the horse." Charlie emphasized the word *with*. "It can sometimes be a short step between controlled force and unnecessary cruelty."

"Aye," Mister Foley said in agreement, "I myself 'ave always been of the opinion that one can take a fair measure of men, by the way they treat their horses."

"No argument there," Charlie replied.

"Anyhow," Charlie continued, "like I said, your buckskin is a good-lookin' horse. In fact, Mister Foley, I took a shine to that little buckskin first time I saw him. That's why I'm here, askin' if you might have a mind to sell him."

"Ah, Laddie," Mister Foley said with a long airy sigh, "that's a question that demands a great deal of thought for me. I myself am rather fond of the little fellow and have a mind to keep 'im for myself. I like his color and his build and the tiger stripes on his legs really sets him apart from most buckskins."

"He is all that," Charlie agreed, "an' he's got that intelligent look about him, willing and savvy. I'm bettin' he'd make a fine cow pony."

"You wantin' him fer yourself, Mister Davies? Appears to me like you've already got yourself a good-lookin' animal."

"That I do, Mister Foley, and a good workin' pardner as well. But the ol' man has got a passle of years an' a whole lotta miles on him, an' I've been thinkin' it's time he spent his days pasturin' somewhere's the grass is thick, and there's shade trees aplenty."

"Well, Mister Davies, I can't give you an answer yes or no right now. Like I said, I hadn't ever thought of selling, just always figured I'd keep him for myself."

"I understand," Charlie said, leaning back in his chair.

"Tell you what, Mister Davies. You give me some time to ponder on it. I'll be plannin' on driving down that way in a week or so. Check on the progress the lad would be havin', and 'ave myself a nice visit with Missus Brandt. Ah, and a fine-lookin' woman she is, eh?" Foley said as he nodded his head and winked. "I'll let you know my decision then."

"Fair enough," Charlie said as he rose from his chair and extended a hand to Foley. "I should be there. At present, I'm bunkin' at the Brandt place. Reckon my welcome won't be wore out fer a while yet."

A low growl began from the dogs, and Mr. Foley calmed them with a subtle gesture as he stood. "Fair enough," he answered and shook Charlie's hand.

Charlie turned to leave and started down the porch stairs then, hesitating for a moment, turned back toward Mister Foley. The dogs sprang to their feet and stood on each side of their master. "What the devil kinda dogs are they?" Charlie asked.

"Wolfhounds, my boy, Irish Wolf Hounds," Mister Foley said with a broad smile. "They be hell on coy-o-tees around here."

Chapter 35

Charlie Davies rode into the town of Frankfort as the sun reached its mid-day peak. Shod hooves clattered on the paved brick street as the "old man" shied from the patter of gasoline-powered automobiles. Along each side of the two-block long main street, several shiny black vehicles were wedged, nose first, against the curbed sidewalk. Charlie spotted a lone hitching rail in an alleyway between the barbershop and the hotel and was making his way out of traffic and toward the rail when the twelve o'clock whistle split the air like a sudden thunderclap. The "old man," already skittish from the unfamiliar bustle of the town, exploded in response to the wailing siren. Charlie leaned forward over the pommel as his horse stood upright on his hind legs then back against the cantle as he slammed stiff-legged on the pavement. Sparks flew as iron skittered across stone while the horse scrambled to keep his footing while trying to escape from the blare of the siren. Charlie sat firm in the saddle and shifted his weight as needed to help the horse keep his feet. As the siren slowly faded and the shrill scream died to a long, low growl, the "old man" settled a bit, and Charlie leaned forward to pat the horse's neck, "Easy, boy, easy now."

Charlie felt the horse shudder beneath him and continued to stroke the horse's neck while the "old man," with nostrils flared and ears laid back, trembled in anticipation of the next unknown.

"Get a Ford!" someone shouted from among a small group of pedestrians who had interrupted their sidewalk stroll to watch the impromptu, one-man rodeo.

"Go to hell," Charlie said quietly, between his teeth, as he politely tipped his hat to his rude but amused audience and nudged the "old man" toward the nearby hitching rail.

At the hitch, Charlie dismounted, looped the reins over the rail, and loosened the saddle cinch. The "old man" hunched his back and shook out the kinks of a long ride, and Charlie headed toward the nearby red and white striped barber pole.

A brass bell above the barbershop door announced Charlie's arrival. As he stepped inside, another customer was on his way out, and Charlie held the door open.

"Needin' a shave a haircut, an' a hot bath," Charlie said as he closed the door, took off his hat, and hung it on one of several wooden pegs along the wall by the door.

"Lucky thing you caught me, mister. I was just fixin' to head out for lunch, but I don't suppose I'd have much of a business if it weren't for the customer, so I reckon I'm at your service."

The barber finished sweeping up the hair around the chair and motioned Charlie to sit down. Charlie settled back into the chair while the barber shook out the white cotton drape and fastened it around Charlie's neck.

"Can't do a bath though," the talkative barber continued with barely a breath in between, "City won't allow it, against an ordinance they got, so you'll have to go across the alley behind the hotel, gotta bathhouse back there. Cost you a dollar, plus ten cents for your personal bar of soap and another two bits if you call for more hot water. That's a little steep to my mind, but I suppose if folks are willing to pay."

Charlie nodded in agreement, but his verbal comment was cut off.

"Six bits for a haircut, four bits for a shave in my shop. I know, used to be a fellow could get all three, a haircut, shave, and a bath all for a buck but those days are gone. Progress, you know."

"Yep," Charlie acknowledged.

"Close your mouth while I lather up your face," said the barber. "Just passin' through?"

"Mmmmhuh," Charlie hummed.

With a fresh shave, haircut, a high-dollar bath, and supplies gathered, Charlie stood on the concrete sidewalk outside the Frankfort Mercantile, leaned against the wall, and pulled the makings from his shirt pocket, built a smoke, and struck a match with the edge of his thumbnail. The match head blazed in the cup of his hands, and a dense cloud of smoke rose upward and swirled around the brim of his hat. With a flick of his finger, the still-burning matchstick sailed into the street and landed with a scattering of wood ash.

His craving for a smoke satisfied, Charlie gathered up the packages of supplies that he had laid on a nearby wooden bench and crossed the street to the alley where the "old man" stood, patiently waiting. As he approached, the horse lifted his head and nickered a familiar welcome.

"Surprised you recognized me, Ol' Man," Charlie spoke to the horse, "me being all slicked up and smellin' of bay rum."

The "old man" nickered again and turned his head to nuzzle against Charlie's shoulder. Charlie stuffed some of his packages in his saddlebags and tied the larger parcels on top of his bedroll behind the cantle. After tightening the saddle cinch and loosening the reins from the hitch rail, Charlie stepped into the stirrup, swung into the saddle, and with a subtle prodding of spurs, coaxed the "old man" to a leisurely walk.

The clip-clop of hooves mixed with the thrumming of gas-powered progress as Charlie rode out of town. As traffic skirted around him, horns honking and fists waving, Charlie noticed a man bent over at the front of his automobile, vigorously cranking away at its unresponsive engine.

"Get a horse!" Charlie called out and tipped his hat to the red-faced gentleman, then lifted the reins and gave the "old man" his head.

It was already late afternoon when Charlie left Frankfort, and the lingering heat of the summer sun, lying low on the horizon, drew the sweat from Charlie's back and stained his shirt with a damp 'V' from his collar down to his belt.

"Won't make it back to the Brandt place 'fore dark," Charlie said. The "old man" swiveled his ears backward in recognition of Charlie's voice. "We'll just make camp somewhere's out here. No need to hurry."

Horse and rider ambled past the two-track road that curved behind the hill to the Foley place and continued on. Charlie had briefly considered turning off and imposing himself on a meal and a bunk but quickly decided against it. A couple of hours further on, Charlie pulled up near a small cluster of cedar trees growing at the mouth of a shallow gully that cut deeper as it followed the slope of the land westward toward the Blue. The stand of cedars was well watered by a seeping spring that would suit Charlie's needs as well as water for his horse. He dismounted, unbuckled the bridle strap, and dropped the bit from the bay's mouth, then loosened the latigo and pulled the saddle from the horse's back. The bay braced himself on his four stiffened legs, shaking vigorously

174

from mane to tail, then bounded off to roll in a nearby patch of stiff, dry prairie grass.

Charlie propped his saddle against the bare dirt wall of the gully, untied his bedroll, and tossed it on the ground nearby, followed by his saddlebags. A short walk down the gully soon produced an ample supply of dry wood, and Charlie returned to his campsite and built a small fire. With a big meal in town and a lazy afternoon in the saddle, Charlie wasn't really hungry, so a chunk of beef jerky and a sourdough biscuit was plenty enough to satisfy his hunger, and the cold, clear water from the spring washed it all down.

As the sun dropped below the horizon, a quicksilver, three-quarter moon bright enough to cast a shadow, had already risen and hung just above the eastern horizon. Charlie leaned back into the curve of his saddle, cushioned by the sheepskin, warm and damp and strong with the smell of horse. He pulled pouch and papers from his shirt pocket and tapped a furrow of tobacco into the trough of yellow paper, wrapped it tight between deft fingers, and sealed it with the tip of his tongue. Glowing embers on the end of a smoldering stick saved the use of a match, and Charlie settled back to contemplate the diamond-dust trail of the Milky Way while a spiral of smoke curled upward from under the brim of his hat.

"Just a speck," Charlie said to himself, shaking his head as he gazed at the blanket of stars. "Just a little ol' speck."

Charlie flicked the stub of his cigarette into the fire, unrolled his bed, and repositioned his saddle to serve as a pillow. His sharp whistle carried through the still night, and the bay answered with his own high-pitched reply as he trotted into camp. Charlie slipped a halter over the horse's head, buckled the cheek strap, and held the end of the attached rope in his hand as he lay down and pulled a blanket over his chest. The bay nickered softly, sauntered over toward Charlie's feet, and nuzzled the soles of his boots.

"Cut it out, Ol' Man," Charlie mumbled and rolled onto his side.

Chapter 36

Charlie Davies had just reached the edge of deep slumber when he felt the bay's tether being jerked from his grip as the horse whirled and galloped out of camp. The rustling of grass among the nearby cedars betrayed the presence of some critter that had no doubt spooked the horse. Charlie reached under the saddle to retrieve his Colt and sat upright, waiting. Presently the masked face of a mama raccoon, followed by three clumsy cubs, emerged from the shadows of the cedar grove and into the soft light of the moon. Charlie eased the hammer down on his Colt and watched, unmoving, while the ring-tailed parade, unconcerned with the presence of a human intruder, ambled past the smoldering campfire and on down the draw.

The moon had not yet reached the peak of its arch in the overhead path from east to west and still hung high above the eastern horizon. In the bright moonlight, Charlie could see the bay a couple hundred feet from camp, calmly grazing through a patch of good grass. He whistled for his horse, and the bay responded with a soft whicker, lifted his head, and came trotting back toward camp, the long tether trailing between his legs.

"Okay, Ol' Man. Let's just settle down now and get some shut-eye," Charlie said as he pulled the length of rope from under the bay and took hold of the end.

Charlie led the bay over to his bedroll and lay down once again, pulling the blanket over his shoulders as he rolled onto his side. The bay relaxed with a shudder of flesh and a rattling of halter leather as he shook out the last remnants of built-up tension, then lifted his right-hind and stood hipshot on three legs. Charlie looped the rope around his palm, took a full, deep breath, and let the night air rush from his lungs in a long sigh.

The sudden frantic shrieks of nesting birds and the rustle of flapping wings among the cedars told of a silent hunter in the night, a great horned owl, raiding a nest of sleeping doves. The bay shied from the ruckus and scrambled to get away while Charlie was jerked from his bedroll, though he was able to quickly gain his footing and hauled back on the rope.

"Whoa, boy, whoa!" Charlie shouted as the bay pulled against the restraint of halter and rope. "Whoa, there, boy. Settle down."

Charlie worked his way up the rope, hand over hand, calming the bay with a steady patter of words. When his hands reached the halter, Charlie stroked the horse's cheek and scratched behind his perked ears. "S'okay, big fella, easy does it."

"Don't know 'bout you, Ol' Man," Charlie mused, "but I'm gettin' the feelin' we picked the wrong place to camp. How 'bout we just saddle up an' head on out? Seems the notion of sleeping has gone plumb away."

The bay nickered in response. "Thought so," Charlie said, bending down to pick up the saddle blanket and toss it over the ol' man's back.

Charlie saddled the bay, packed his gear, and swung into the saddle. It was a perfect night for riding. The moon was bright enough to light the trail and offered a cooling relief from the glaring daytime sun. Charlie figured it to be about midnight and only another three, maybe four hours ride at a long trot to the Brandt place. Time enough for a couple hours of sleep before breakfast.

****

Charlie reined the 'old man' off the road and onto the Brandts' lane. Just a short quarter-mile to go, and the imagining of a soft bunk with a real pillow would be a reality. It had been some time since Charlie had ridden a full day and most of a night and, although he had enjoyed this moonlight ride, he was keenly aware of some bothersome discomfort that he wouldn't have noticed a few years back. The 'old man' had kept up a steady, ground covering, long trot between short stints of walking to cool down, and Charlie knew that he was ready for a rest as well.

When the pair reached the barn, Charlie slid from the saddle, loosened the latigo, and pulled saddle and blanket from the bay's back and laid them over the top rail of the corral fence. He unfastened the bridle and let the bit drop from the 'old man's' mouth, then opened the corral gate and let him into the pasture. He'd let the bay roll in the dirt and grass for now and brush him down good in the morning while he munched on a scoopful of oats.

Charlie was headed into the barn when he heard the uneasy breathing of a horse in one of the working pens. He turned and walked toward the pen. In his gut, he somehow knew what he was about to find but hoped that his gut was wrong. It wasn't. There, in the middle of the pen, tied to the snubbing post, stood the sorrel mare that Jacob had been trying to subdue earlier that morning. The mare stood trembling, weakly straining against the rope that held her to the post. Running sweat mixed with the dried lather that covered her sides and chest. The rope around her neck had been refashioned into a halter that ran along her cheeks, behind her ears, and around her nose so that too much resistance would stifle her breathing and giving to the pressure of the rope would allow for easy breathing. In and of itself, it was not a cruel training device at all but an effective way to teach a horse to stand without fighting being tied. The cruelty was in the likelihood that she had been left there alone for most of the day and night. And there was no water.

"Son of a..." the words trailed off as Charlie climbed the fence rail and jumped inside the pen.

The mare responded with fear when Charlie approached her, pulling back on the rope until her inability to breathe forced her to step forward. Charlie stopped his advance and stood still.

"Easy there, little lady," Charlie whispered. "Easy, easy now. You'll be all right. Just take 'er easy. Easy, easy does it. You're gonna be just fine."

The mare's ears turned to listen to Charlie's soft crooning, but her eyes showed the fear and distrust that was well deserved. Charlie took a small step forward as he continued to talk to the mare. The mare stepped forward and turned her head just a bit toward Charlie.

For more than an hour, Charlie talked to the mare, soft and slow, extending a hand then dropping it to his side when she shied away. With nearly imperceptible half-steps, Charlie advanced toward the mare, always talking in soft, soothing tones until he was able to reach out and touch her. The mare reacted to his touch with a sudden sideways recoil and stumbled on her unsteady legs, landing on her hindquarters while her stiffened front legs held her chest and head up, neck straining against the rope. Charlie took a step back and let the mare regain her feet. Again, Charlie began his one-sided conversation and for most of another hour, began to gain the mare's trust until at last, he was able to reach out his hand and rub the mare's neck.

The mare shivered under his touch but didn't retreat. Charlie let his hand move up the side of the mare's neck and around behind her ears, scratching lightly under the rope that had chaffed her hide. Charlie stepped back and the mare took a single step toward him, and Charlie untied the rope from the snubbing post.

It was a short while later that the mare was following Charlie around the pen, and so he opened the gate and led her to water. She drank long and deep but Charlie stopped her from overdoing it with a slight tug on the rope. Still a bit wary and uncertain, the mare was cautious but responsive to Charlie's suggestions. He led her into the barn and switched out the rope for a soft leather halter. Back in the pen, Charlie tied the mare to the snubbing post, and she stood there quietly while he walked around her, rubbing her neck and sides and hindquarters as he went.

"There you go, little lady. That's not so bad, is it?" Charlie kept up the quiet encouragement as the mare gradually began to relax under his touch.

The moon had dimmed to a silver shadow, low on the western horizon, while the pink light of dawn spread across the eastern sky. Charlie untied the rope from the snubbing post, unbuckled the halter, lifted it over the mare's ears and draped the halter and rope over his shoulder. He was pretty sure the mare would follow him out of the pen, but after he had taken a few steps away, she still stood, unmoving. Charlie stopped and looked over his shoulder.

"Come on, little lady," Charlie coaxed.

The mare cocked her ears toward Charlie's voice and took a half step forward.

"That's it. C'mon."

Charlie turned and walked toward the gate. The mare followed, and when they reached the gate, Charlie stepped aside and let the mare pass through. Outside the pen, the mare raised her tail and flew into the open space of the pasture, bucking and kicking as she went. Charlie shook his head and smiled as he ambled to the barn.

"What the hell do you think you're doing, Davies?" Jacob shouted as he ran from the house toward Charlie.

Charlie stopped and waited for Jacob, who came barreling down the path to the barn. Explosive rage flashed in Jacob's eyes, and hot blood flushed his neck and face. Charlie braced himself for what he saw coming and quickly sidestepped as Jacob's fist flashed past his face. Jacob staggered, off-balance from the missed blow, and Charlie grabbed him by the collar. Jacob turned and threw another punch, but Charlie caught his fist in his hand and held it.

"You son-of-a-bitch! What gives you the right to interfere with my work?" Jacob sputtered.

Charlie's grip tightened, and Jacob's arm trembled as he tried to break loose. Each man stared into the eyes of the other, Charlie calm and controlled, Jacob seething with rage.

"I told you I won't abide cruelty," Charlie said, speaking each word with calm force. "You have no right to treat an animal like you've treated that mare."

"That's none of your damn business!" Jacob growled.

"It is as long as I'm here to see it."

"Then you best saddle up and get the hell off my place!"

"This is my place," Maria shouted, "and I'll be the one to say if anyone needs to get the hell off it."

Neither Charlie nor Jacob had seen Maria as she ran down the path toward the two men. Her sudden appearance caught both Charlie and Jacob off guard.

"You taking his side?" Jacob sneered.

Charlie loosened his grip on Jacob's still raised fist and pushed it away.

"I'm taking the mare's side," Maria snapped. "I told you last night at supper that you should turn her loose for the night."

"I don't need you or nobody else telling me how to handle horses," Jacob growled between clenched teeth, his face still flushed with anger as he pointed an accusing finger at Maria then turned toward Charlie. "The how don't matter none, it's results that counts!"

"Don't you go waving your finger in my face!" Maria shouted, her cheeks flushed and dark eyes flashing. "You're getting mighty careless with your manners, young man, and Mr. Davies is here at my invitation, and you'll show him some respect as well, ya hear?"

"Respect!" Jacob spat, "For him? For you? I seen the two of you come sneaking up from the barn the other morning."

Charlie Davies' spine stiffened, jaw and fist clenched instinctively as he started to lunge forward, but Maria's reflex was quicker. In a single long stride, she stood toe to toe with Jacob; her hand flashed across his face and snapped his head sideways. Jacob slowly turned his head back until he again faced

Maria and stared blankly at the sudden tear that rolled down her cheek, then turned and walked away.

"Apologize," Maria called after him, "apologize!"

Jacob went to the barn without so much as a backward glance, yanked a halter and saddle from the tack room, and walked angrily to the stallion's stall.

Maria stood trembling, trying in vain to hold back the tears of anger and hurt that coursed down her cheeks. Charlie closed the short distance between them in a few short steps and put his hand on her shoulder. Maria reached across her chest and placed her hand on Charlie's.

"He just needs some time to think things over," Charlie said, more hopeful than confident that he was right.

Jacob and the stallion burst out of the darkened doorway of the barn and into the barnyard. The stallion's eyes showed white with fear as Jacob laid heavy blows with his quirt across the stallion's shoulders. Jacob's cold, hardened look startled Maria, who with a sudden involuntary gasp, clasped both hands over her mouth.

"Dear God," Maria whispered, "He looks like Eli."

The stallion raced down the lane, Jacob laying on the quirt with each long stride. At the end of the lane, the stallion scrambled to keep his footing as Jacob jerked heavily on the reins into a tight turn, then spurred and whipped the stallion as if in the final stretch toward a finish line. For the better part of a mile, Jacob spurred the stallion forward at a punishing pace, and not until he felt the horse falter beneath him, did he pull the reins. Foaming sweat rolled down the stallion's neck, tumbled over the breast collar and down his chest, ribs heaving as he gulped lungsful of air. Jacob, too, was drenched in sweat, dark stains soaking through his shirt, down the middle of his back, and under his arms. Jacob leaned forward and stroked the stallion's neck, then flicked the sweat off his hand, patted the slick, soaked hide, and began to laugh.

And he laughed, long and hard. He laughed from the exhilaration of the ride. He laughed to loosen the knot of anger that twisted in his belly, and he laughed because it was the only way he knew to keep from crying.

Chapter 37

The sun had crested the eastern horizon barely an hour earlier, but it was already promising to be another typical Kansas late summer day, hot and humid. Charlie had quit the bunk just before the first faint light of dawn and had brought the buckskin in for a few basic reigning lessons intending to be finished before it got to the point where not even a shade tree could bring relief from the sweltering heat. The air was already thick and hot, and both Charlie and the buckskin were drenched with sweat. The young gelding had made considerable progress in the past few weeks since Charlie had taken over the training after Jacob had left, following the clash of opinions between the two of them.

Evie had come to visit Maria a few days after Jacob's explosive departure and announced that Jacob had been hired on at the railroad and was working on a section crew with her husband, Harper. She had gathered up a few of Jacob's belongings that he had asked for and told Maria that he would stop by, when he could, for the rest.

"Is he okay?" Maria had asked.

"Well enough, I suppose," Evie snipped, "for being run off the place and all."

"Run off!"

"That's what he says. Said you and your friend Davies," Evie spat the words "your friend Davies" as if they had left a sour taste in her mouth, "said you pretty much told him he wasn't welcome here."

"We did no such thing, Evie!"

"I reckon it makes no never mind now anyway, said there's no room for both him and Davies, and you made it pretty clear who you favored. Said there's something unseemly going on with the two of you."

"Evie Boot," Maria gasped, "you mind your tongue, young lady! There's nothing unseemly going on here. Mister Davies is, first off, a gentleman, and secondly, he has always been kind to us. If your brother has decided to make his way with the railroad, that's his doing; nobody ran him off. He left of his own accord, and it seems pretty clear that he has decided not to come back."

"I'm just saying what he told me," Evie whined. "But don't you care what folks might be saying, what with you and Flora here alone with a stranger?"

"Charlie Davies is no stranger, young lady; he's a friend. And as long as he's willing to stay and help us out, he's welcome, and I don't give a hoot in hell what folks might be saying."

Evie had left after their short visit, declining an invitation to stay for lunch and thinly masking her dislike for Davies. She had not come back to visit since, and Jacob had not yet come to collect the rest of his things. Maria had agonized over the events that had caused Jacob to leave and the spiteful accusations that had led Evie to lay the blame on her. She fretted over her indecision: should she go and try to make amends, or should she wait out Jacob's stubborn anger in hopes that he would come to talk things over and reach some measure of agreement. But the days had stretched into weeks, and nothing had been settled and perhaps never would.

Charlie held the reins lightly as he worked the buckskin, the cues nearly invisible as the horse responded, left then right, stop and back. After each series of maneuvers, Charlie would lean forward and pat the horse's neck, then rub briskly while praising the animal with a softly spoken, "atta boy, nice work," then urge him forward with a nearly imperceptible shift in the saddle and slackening of the reins.

The kitchen door slammed shut behind Maria as she stepped carefully down the stairs with a laundry basket full of heavy, wet bedding. She held the basket with both hands while balancing its weight against her right hip, descending the three stairs one at a time, left foot first, then right. When she stepped off the last stair and onto the lawn, she looked toward the corrals where Charlie worked the buckskin. Holding the basket on her hip, she shielded her eyes from the glare of the sun with her thumb and finger pressed against her forehead. Charlie had heard the screen door snap shut and had stopped to watch Maria. When he saw her looking his way, he gave a nod of greeting and touched his fingers to the brim of his hat. Maria answered with a smile, then turned and walked toward the clothesline of number nine wire stretched between the green-leaved canopy of two mature elms.

While Maria hung the bedding, Charlie dismounted the buckskin, pulled the saddle from its back, and set it over the top rail of the corral. The buckskin stood, ground tied, with the reins hanging loose from the bit while Charlie gave him a vigorous rubdown with a dry gunnysack. After the rubdown, Charlie unfastened the bridle, gathered up the dangling reins, and let the bit drop from the buckskin's mouth, then lifted the saddle from the railing and headed toward the barn. The buckskin lowered his head, pushing the dirt of the corral with his nose as he turned in a tight circle, pawing at the ground. After several turns, the horse dropped to his knees, then lay down on the sun-warmed dust and rolled to his back. Writhing like a broken-backed snake, the buckskin pressed himself into the warm earth, rolled from side to side, then gathered his legs under him, pushed up with his forelegs then his hind and vigorously shook the dust from his hide.

Charlie never tired of watching horses, the graceful yet powerful displays of strength and agility like the buckskin's roll in the dust or the delicate scratching behind an ear with a hind hoof. But this morning, Charlie wasn't watching the gelding as he carried the saddle to the barn but kept his eyes on Maria instead. The sky-blue cotton dress that she wore seemed to draw the light of the sun and deepen the silver-streaked, raven black braid that hung over her shoulder as she bent to pull the folds of linen from the basket. He watched the curve of her back and the roundness of her hips as she stretched on tiptoe to toss the wet cloth over the wire, then tug at its wrinkles as she pulled it across the line and fastened it with wooden pins.

Maria sensed that she was being watched, as she had hoped, and turned to acknowledge Charlie's admiration. Embarrassed at being caught, Charlie hefted the saddle a little higher and lengthened his stride as he hurried toward the barn. Maria smiled to herself and turned back to her chore.

The unfamiliar pop and sputter of a gasoline engine grew louder as the dusty, black Ford automobile bounced in and out of the wagon-rutted lane and came closer to where Maria stood beside the basket of laundry. Charlie had heard the chug chug of the engine and stepped out of the tack room doorway as it passed by the barn and turned toward the house. The automobile lurched to a stop as the driver gripped the steering wheel and reared back to slam the brake pedal to the floor. The vehicle, still in gear, lugged down under the mechanical restraint and died with a blast of exhaust that split the air like a gunshot and sent the horses to the far side of the pasture.

"Top of the mornin', Missus Brandt!" the driver shouted his greeting, a broad, bright-toothed smile crossing his face as he lifted the goggles from his eyes and let them snap back on the crown of his flat-brimmed driver's cap. Bounding out of the automobile, he walked briskly toward Maria, stripping the leather gauntlets from his hands, finger by finger, and stuffing them in the pockets of his bleached linen duster as he advanced.

"Mister Foley," Maria replied, greeting him with a smile then dropping her eyes in a polite bow. "It's been some time since we last saw you."

"Aye, that it has, mi' lady, that it has. And how might you be this fine day?" Mister Foley asked.

"Very well, thank you."

"And young Jacob? And the little one, Flora, isn't it?"

"Yes, Flora. She's fine," Maria replied as she searched for a simple answer that would explain Jacob's absence and was relieved to see Charlie approaching.

"Mister Foley," Charlie said as he stepped past him and stood beside Maria.

"Mister Davies," Foley replied as the two men greeted each other with a strong but brief handshake. Foley took a step back and looked from Charlie to Maria and back. The unspoken question was plain in the slight furrow of his brow.

"Jacob's gone to work for the railroad," Charlie announced. "I suppose the pay's a bit better than breakin' horses and likely a mite safer to boot."

"Aye, the adventurous nature of youth," Mister Foley suggested, then continued, "I'd 'ave come by a wee bit sooner, but I 'ad a bit of business to see about down to Topeka. I reckon the boy finished with the buckskin before he left?" Foley asked.

"Pretty much so," Charlie replied. "I did put a little bit of time on him myself, and he's come along right well. He'll make a fine saddle horse for ya, that is if you've a mind to keep him."

"Well, Mister Davies, I reckon that depends," Foley answered, rocking back on his heels and crossing his arms over his chest.

"Depends on what?" Charlie asked.

"If you gentlemen are set on horse tradin', I'm going to finish hangin' my wash," Maria interrupted. "But if you like, I've got some fresh lemonade in the icebox, might as well cool off a bit on the porch."

"Splendid!" exclaimed Mister Foley, "I reckon I could stand to wash down the road dust."

Maria turned toward the back door to the kitchen while Davies and Foley ambled toward the porch. When they passed by the automobile, Mister Foley took off his duster and tossed it over the door and into the front seat.

"Tis a tad warmer when a body's not catchin' a breeze on the road," Foley remarked.

At the porch, Charlie sat on the porch floor, leaning against the post beside the stairs. With a wave of his hand, Charlie directed Mister Foley to the bent-willow chair nearby, which Foley dragged a bit closer to the edge of the porch and sat down. Relaxed in the shade of the porch, both men instinctively reached for a smoke. Mister Foley filled the bowl of his stubby pipe while Charlie rolled a cigarette.

"So, depends on what?" Charlie asked again, flicking the end of his charred matchstick into the dust.

"In your opinion, Mister Davies, how'd that little buckskin finish out?" Mister Foley countered with a question of his own.

"I've handled better, but not many," Davies replied a bit cautiously. "I just turned him out after a bit of practice before you showed up. He's smooth, responsive, and good-natured."

"Um, huh," Mister Foley acknowledged as a thick stream of smoke tumbled from his nostrils.

"You wantin' to sell?" Charlie asked.

"Lemonade, gentlemen," Maria announced, pushing the porch door open with her hip as she backed out of the house with a tall glass of lemonade in each hand. She offered a glass first to Mister Foley and then to Charlie, and each of them smiled at her and nodded their thanks.

"You're welcome," Maria replied with a slight curtsy of mock formality. "Now, if you all will excuse me," she said as she opened the door and disappeared inside.

"Not really," Mister Foley said, then took a long drink of cold, pulpy lemonade. "But things have changed just a wee bit since we last met, Mister Davies. I mentioned earlier that I'd 'ad some business down to Topeka. Well, turns out there's a sizable commercial dairy down there that's come up for sale."

"You figurin' on moving to Topeka?" Charlie inquired.

"Mebby so, mebby not. I've made an offer, and if they take it, I'll be obliged to follow through. Won't know till early next week."

"What about the buckskin?"

"You still interested?"

"Yep."

"What's your offer, Lad?"

"Whatcha askin'?"

Mr. Foley took another long sip of lemonade then set the glass on the floor beside his chair. His pipe had gone out, so he fished a match from his pocket and struck it to flame along the side of his boot. Holding fire above the pipe bowl, Foley drew the flame in until a great cloud of smoke escaped from his mouth.

"Five hundred," he said as the smoke drifted down across his chest.

"Five hundred!" Charlie exclaimed, sloshing a bit of lemonade onto his jeans as he jerked the glass away from his mouth. "Five hundred could buy a well-matched team!"

"True enough," Foley admitted, "but if he's as good as you say…"

"I'll go you two hundred, tops," Charlie countered.

"Two hundred!" Mister Foley sputtered, sending hot ashes flying from the bowl of his pipe. "Bloody 'ell, you get a hundred back for the training. That's only a hundred for the horse."

"That hundred belongs to Jacob if that was your deal. I'm just barterin' for the horse."

"Three fifty," Foley countered.

"Two hundred."

"Okay, Laddie, three hundred it is."

"Two hundred," Charlie insisted, holding up two fingers for clarification.

"Now look here, Sonny," Mister Foley said firmly, poking the air with the stem of his pipe, "appears to me that I'm the only one negotiating here. You haven't moved a penny."

"True enough," Charlie said with a good-natured smile. "So, what's your bottom dollar?"

Foley leaned back against the woven willow branches, lifted his hat, and scratched his head. "Two seventy-five," he said with an air of finality.

"Two fifty," Charlie countered.

"Jesus, Mary, and Joseph!" Mister Foley exclaimed, "You'd put every Scotsman I've ever known to shame. Two fifty it is then, and let's be done with it."

"Done," Charlie said and reached across the porch to reach the hand extended by Foley, and the two shook.

"Done," Foley echoed.

"Mister Foley, would you care to join us for lunch?" Maria asked from behind the porch door.

"It would be my pleasure, Ma'am. Thank you."

After lunch, Mister Foley made out a bill of sale, then he and Charlie, Maria, and Flora walked to the barn. Charlie whistled for the horses, and the small herd came bounding in from the far corner of the pasture, the buckskin in the lead. Tossing his head and kicking up his heels, the buckskin seemed to be showing off his strength and agility, and Mister Foley shook his head in silent admiration.

"He is a fine-looking fellow, isn't he?" Mister Foley said with a hint of remorse.

"Yep," Charlie replied.

Charlie went to the bunkhouse to retrieve the two hundred and fifty dollars from his saddlebags while Maria, Flora, and Mister Foley admired the horses and watched their rambunctious antics as they nipped and kicked and squealed in playful combat.

As they walked back to the house, Flora skipped ahead, scattering the chickens that scratched and fluttered in the fine dust. Maria walked beside Charlie, her hand holding on to the crook of Charlie's arm. Mister Foley walked alongside as the three chatted in friendly conversation. They gathered beside Mister Foley's automobile while he retrieved his duster from the seat and pulled it on. Foley reached in and switched on the ignition, adjusted the throttle, walked to the front and, with a quick, deft twist of the crank, the engine sputtered to life. Charlie held the door open and Mister Foley slid in under the steering wheel, eased back, on the throttle and let the engine settle into a smooth patter.

Charlie handed a roll of bills to Mister Foley. He took the roll of tens and twenties and peeled off two twenties and a ten and handed it back to Charlie.

"Give this to Jacob and tell him thanks from me."

"I thought you said the training was a hundred?" Charlie questioned.

"Nah, mi' boy, just the fifty," Mister Foley said as he grinned and waved goodbye.

After Mister Foley had disappeared from view, Flora and Maria went on to the house, and Charlie ambled back to the corral where the buckskin still waited. As Charlie approached, the buckskin tossed his head and nickered and stretched across the fence rails to receive the customary scratch behind his ear.

"Yeah, spoiled already, huh?" Charlie said gruffly, "So, little fella, what am I gonna call you?"

"How about Scotty?" Maria asked.

Charlie hadn't seen Maria approaching and, startled to hear her voice, turned quickly around to face her.

"Scotty?" Charlie repeated.

"Yeah, for the Scotchman, Mister Foley."

"Sounds good to me," Charlie replied.

Charlie turned back to the buckskin, and Maria stepped forward and stood beside him.

"I know an old cowboy down in New Mexico," Charlie said quietly. "Has a spread he calls the Escondido. He was an old trail driver for a lot of years, knows his cattle and loves his horses. Jack Potter's his name. Told me a story once 'bout a horse he had an' how he'd met his future wife, Cordelia, an' courted her. Said he wanted the horse to be a sort of engagement present. An' well, it's got me to thinkin'."

"'Bout what?" Maria asked.

"'Bout this here buckskin," Charlie said, leaning closer to Maria to touch shoulders. "Should I call him mine or should I call him ours?"

Printed in the USA
CPSIA information can be obtained
at www.ICGtesting.com
LVHW060833080823
754340LV00006B/79